BROOKE

THE METCALFES || BOOK 4

RONIE KENDIG

DEAR READER ...

The contents of this book will not be easy to read.
Readily I admit—this story was hard to write, finding that
delicate balance of sharing the brutal truths behind human
trafficking and respecting the survivors. Between helping people
understand the depths of depravity, yet not glorifying the
shadows.

You may find this story *too* hard to read, but I hope you will
brave the journey and allow your heart to be moved by the
plight of so many. If you need a breather in the midst of the
trials happening for the characters, take it—and in the pause, I
beg you to remember those trapped in this nightmare and *pray
for them*!

Ronie

Rescue the weak and the needy;
deliver them from the hand of the wicked.
Psalm 82:4

CHAPTER ONE

DEATH HAD NOT BEEN KIND—IT'D rushed in with more agony and torment than the brutality life had handed out. Darkness swirled and blurred in a haze of red and white. Distant screams fought through the chaos, demanding her attention.

A voice warbled, its tone urgent and … strange.

Feeling something digging into her shoulder, Brooke Metcalfe Mulroney groaned and shifted. Where was she? What was happening? She blinked. Searing light stabbed her corneas. With another groan, she tried to look around, but her vision was grainy, blurry.

A shape appeared over her.

Brooke yelped—and daggers sliced through her corneas. She shifted and realized she was restrained. Heart hammering, she cried out. Breath trapped in her throat, she felt the familiar dread of the last few weeks rising again.

"*Nǚshì?*"

At the Mandarin "ma'am," Brooke twitched and glanced at the dark blur beside her. "Wh-what … what happened?

Where—" Memory and agony stole over her. She recalled running from … men—

The men! Chasing her. Trying to kill her. When she'd broken out of the alley, she'd seen the car too late. It'd struck—

"*Nǐ jiào shénme míngzì?*" Navy vest over a light blue shirt. His dark ballcap. EMT.

Her name? "I …" If she gave her name, *they* could find her. No. No no no. She had to get out of here before it was too late. Scrambling, she tried to free herself of the straps. Pain erupted through her side. "Augh!" She dropped back against the mattress, felt her head spinning again. It must've hit the street when the car hit her because it hurt like crazy.

"*Bǎochí jìngzhǐ.*"

His instruction to keep still made her panic more. "I need to get out of—"

"*Nǐ yǒu nǎo zhèndàng.*"

A concussion would explain why the spinning lights of the emergency vehicle made her head pound and vault the contents of her stomach up her throat. Heels of her hands to her eyes, she groaned through the pain consuming her torso, then felt the EMT probing her side. Searing pain stabbed her, making her cry out again.

"Your ribs are likely broken," he said in Mandarin. "We need to take you to the hospital."

Brooke moaned and her vision slowly focused. She took in the growing crowd along the edge. Was the man here? Among those watching …?

Merciful heavens, her head hurt! But she had to get moving before she was caught. "I'm okay," she said in Mandarin. Even as the words escaped her lips, she saw a broad-shouldered figure shift between two onlookers. *Him!*

"No. Stay." The EMT gave her a curt nod. "I cannot let you leave."

"I have to go." Holy fire, it hurt to breathe! "I have to go. I can't ..." Gaze locked on the man, she shook her head. Fought tears. "I can't—no. I have to—"

"You're going to hurt yourself more. Your broken rib could puncture your liver."

"I don't care. I have to—" *Wait. That works.* "O-okay." No way she could run. Could possibly walk—limp—but never fast enough to get away from Mr. Dark. But if the EMTs took her to the hospital ... She eased back against the gurney's mattress, scanning the people as the techs loaded her into the ambulance. In a blink, she lost sight of the man.

The first tech climbed in and perched next to her, threading an IV into her arm. Brooke focused on searching for the man. What if he appeared there with a gun and shot her?

If he wanted to shoot you, he could've done that at the hotel. Or restaurant. Or on the bridge when she'd tossed the phone.

The second EMT joined them, drawing the door closed behind himself as the first called in to the hospital. When the vehicle pulled into traffic, Brooke slumped against the vinyl mattress. Let herself relax ...

A breath tremored through her chest, and she then felt the full brunt of the adrenaline dump. The shake of her limbs, the scream of pain through her torso. Whimpering and fighting tears again, she cursed herself for being so weak. She'd just wanted to find Jihan and Caliyah. Do something for Mazin.

In minutes as they arrived at the hospital, the EMTs transferred her into the care of the staff and to a bed, which pitched her pain through the roof. Biting back the tears as the EMTs exited, Brooke started planning her escape. Having them bring her here wasn't a solution but a means to buy time. And maybe get some morphine or something to take the edge off the agony ripping through her side.

"Ma'am?"

Brooke only then realized someone was talking to her. "Sorry, what?"

"Your name," the nurse said curtly.

"O-oh." She'd managed to avoid giving a name to the EMTs because she couldn't think around the pain then. Giving her real name was impossible, since the man chasing her would be searching for that—assuming he hadn't just followed the ambulance. And using Jane Doe would be a dead giveaway. "Ariane," she said quietly, tingeing her words with a French accent. "Ariane Chavasse."

"And do you know what happened, how you were injured?" the nurse asked.

"I …" She swallowed, remembering how close she'd come to getting caught. "A-a car. I was hit by a car. There …" Telling them she was being chased would only draw authorities, and she'd already tried that once. "I guess … I just wasn't paying attention."

"We will get X-rays." The nurse tapped into a device as she noted the vitals—and that's when Brooke noticed her name badge read Min in Mandarin.

To thwart the pain in her back, Brooke shifted—pain exploded through her side. Crying out, she stiffened.

"But first something for the pain," the nurse said in faltering English. "Is there someone you want us to contact?"

"I—" Cradling her side and screwing up her face bought her a moment to think. Mark and the girls weren't talking to her. Her brothers …

"You absolutely cannot tell them." Mazin's voice reverberated across her conscience.

"No …" She had no one to help her. Not anymore. Yet a pair of steel gray eyes argued with that. Pleaded with her to call him, much like the dozen voicemails. "No. I'm alone." She had endangered the kids and her relationship with Mazin, so bringing Cord Taggart into it would only make things worse.

She'd figure this out; she always did. Resting back, she shuddered a breath, feeling the sting and pinch of the broken ribs. As she closed her eyes, she saw a blur. A shape moved past the semiprivate room. Breath backed into her throat. "I have to go." Anxious to get out, she jerked up—and screamed with the pain ripping through her side.

The nurse was there, telling her to calm down. Stay in the bed. But Brooke wasn't going to stay here to end up dead or caught by—something pinched her hip. She glanced down, seeing Nurse Min removing a needle. Felt the strength drain from her body. She slumped into a heap, her fear chasing her into the hollow, cold darkness.

"Eh, sorry."

She turned and found Mazin there.

A sheepish grin slid across his handsome face. "This … is too much."

Brooke noticed his gaze linger on her wine and dumped it down the drain so she did not offend his Muslim beliefs. "I am sure it is overwhelming here," she said, setting the glass in the dishwasher. "I see you managed to extricate yourself from the little mouse …"

"She found the dollhouse in her room." He inclined his head. "That is too much."

"Probably," Brooke admitted, "but I thought that maybe, eventually, she would like it here." Like me.

"I will warn you," he said, his gaze roving the penthouse, "the kids will never want to leave here." No doubt his life in Afghanistan had been simple, despite his brilliant mind and work in cybersecurity. "This home is too much, and I am sure the cost of this place could fund our lives for decades."

Never before had she felt ashamed about her home, but that feeling rose strong and virulent as he strolled through her living room and took in her home. "I … understand." She didn't really. "It is my only home, so I hope you will feel comfortable here in time."

Hands hooked in his back pockets, he wandered to the living room. Eyed the fireplace, the narrow pool that separated the gym from her office. "I should have become a lawyer …"

Brooked crossed her arms and smiled. It was an oversimplification, assuming that simply being a lawyer was how she afforded this. With most men, she would be miffed at their assumption, at the way they wrote off how hard she'd worked.

He whistled at the arches that lined the portico leading to the open-air patio. "How much did this place cost?"

"Enough." She moved to the sectional and hiked her leg up, perching on the corner. "What happened, Mazin? Can you talk about it?"

His expression tightened as he drifted back toward her and sighed. "They—" His gaze darted to the side even as a blur of pink whipped across the kitchen and into his arms. He caught his daughter up and held her tight, laughing. "I thought you were enjoying the dolls."

Caliyah shifted in his arms, leaning against him as she produced a dark-haired Barbie. "She's like me," she muttered, then huffed.

"Is it time to eat yet?" Jihan asked, walking into the kitchen with his gaze stuck on the handheld device, playing a game.

"Where did you get that?" Mazin frowned.

"Oh, the games are all non-violent," Brooke said. "I hope it's okay."

The man hesitated, glancing at his son with a hefty dose of reticence. "I had hoped to avoid having his nose stuck in a device for as long as possible."

"I'm ten," Jihan said. "That's a whole decade, Dad." He moved to the kitchen table that lined the wall of windows and sat, still playing the game.

"And yes!" Brooke moved to the counter and lifted the prepared food, relocating it to the table. "The pizza should be here any—" The elevator dinged, and she smiled. "Ah." She made quick work of receiving the pizza and delivering it to the table as well.

Though awkward at first, they sat and ate together, Caliyah staying close to her father, and Jihan frustrated at having to set aside the game device.

"You must have a lot of money," Jihan said and took another chomp into his second slice of pizza.

"Jihan! Guard your tongue," his father said.

"I have enough to enjoy this home and share with those who are important to me."

"Do you love my dad?" Jihan held nothing back.

"Jihan! Leave the table at once," Mazin barked.

Manhattan, New York

"You're sure?" Hand fisted on his thigh, Cord Taggart leaned forward—and was sure he felt the entire world shift on the fifty-third floor of the Manhattan high-rise that housed the Loritz, Bettencourt, Fiske, and Mulroney law firm. LBFM sounded too close to a sex crime for his taste. "You're sure she took a sabbatical?"

Partner Prentice Fiske stared at him from behind those invisible wire glasses for a half second before his thin brow—had he used brow liner?—rippled. "Yes," he said, drawing it out as if Cord had a few braincells missing.

"And how long ago did she file that sabbatical request?"

Fiske tossed down a pen, canted forward in his office chair that probably cost more than Cord's car, and leaned on the desk. "Look, I'm not sure who you think—"

"So, you're not worried about her safety in light of the—"

"No." Fiske's pasty face seemed to take on the appearance of a dumpling. "There is no evidence that anything is wrong, and we've indulged your visits and borderline interrogations each time you've come, Mr. Taggart. If she wants a six-month sabbatical, then she has done more than enough for this firm to deserve that." He sniffed and shook that slicked head of his. "I think we've been more than accommodating, but to be frank—Ms. Mulroney's business is none of yours."

Cord grunted. "And it's not weird to you that she told her family she was on a business trip?"

"Mr. Taggart—c'mon. Do you tell your family everything you're doing?" He came to his feet. "Now, if you'll excuse me, I do have another meeting."

"Right. Sure." Cord learned long ago to never burn bridges. He shook the man's hand and thanked him for his time.

Ten minutes later, he was on the ground floor, still rankled. His intermittent search for Brooke wasn't working. He couldn't exactly take weeks off from MiLE to search for her, especially when there was no proof that Brooke had disappeared. Just his laser-honed intuition and the way that woman drove him crazy. Not in *that* way, though she had done that, but her incessant questions over the last six months about trafficking, questions that grew more specific and showed a level of experience and education he did not like. It was one thing for *him* to know those things—he waged war against human trafficking on a daily basis—but for a beautiful, high-powered New York attorney to know … That dug under his skin and burned.

He exited the elevator and strode toward the revolving doors. Sensing the attention of the armed guard, he nodded to the guy. It was a habit, drawing their attention. Just like in airports and banks. He "randomly" got the pat-down every time he traveled commercial. Had nothing to do with the bald head, sleeve of military-related tattoos. Or the raw intensity that rolled off him.

Her words, not his.

Man, he liked her. And was worried. Something wasn't right. Her brothers blew off her MIA status as "just Brooke." But none of them knew she'd taken a sabbatical. And Slick up there had given two different timeframes—first three months, now six months.

Cord pushed into the morning sunlight that fought its way

past the high-rises and potted trees that lined the small courtyard in front of the LBFM building.

He eased to the side and swiveled around to look up at the façade that bore her last name. Standing here, this fifty-two story Manhattan high-rise towering over him … Dang if it wasn't just like every time he stood talking with Brooke Metcalfe Mulroney. She was larger than life, a conqueror, a take-the-bull-by-the-horns lawyer … and had his willpower in a chokehold. Which explained why he was yet again trying to find her. Everyone had said he just didn't know how to take a hint, but this wasn't adding up. And he didn't like where his thoughts were leading.

Where are you, Bombshell?

Ya know what? Might as well give her condo one more try. Cord hiked the three blocks to her penthouse. Stepped into the building and was met with the same impenetrable, unyielding door guard.

"Again?" The suited guy glowered at him. "Man, give up! Answer hasn't chan—"

"Just … tell me this: has she been here in the last two weeks?" Cord rapped on the quartz counter as he glanced around the foyer, wishing someone would come out of that elevator, give him a chance to sprint into it.

"I told you." Guard tapped a monitor in front of him. "Not. On. The. List."

With a growl, Cord roughed his hands over his shaved head.

"Dude. Is that the Marine logo?"

Cord slapped his palms on the counter. "Tell me to take a hike—fine—but you don't have to insult me."

"Insult?"

"Special Forces, Mall-cop. Special Forces."

"*Mall*—" The guard's eyes bulged in outrage and challenge. "Oh—you … You ain't never going up now."

"Mr. Cord?"

The quiet voice cracked like a whip that yanked him around. Took his thick skull a second to connect the face with— "Ishwin ..." For the life of him, he could not conjure her last name.

"Thank you for coming." She pointed toward the elevator. "Ready?"

Cord stood there stupefied as she flashed a polished smile at the guard. "Thank you, Bertram. I'll see him up to the penthouse."

What just happened?

Roll with it, idiot.

He did his best to not throw a cocky grin at the guard—and failed. A lot. Maybe even waved at the guy. Once in the box, he thrust his chin at the guard as the elevator set off a tone and the doors started to close. "Thanks, Mall-cop."

"You have to come back down, Marine," the guy said in warning.

Sniggering as the elevator lifted, Cord swiped a hand over his beard.

"You don't actually."

He glanced at Ishwin and wondered at her conspiratorial grin.

"You can use Ms. Mulroney's private elevator."

Now he grinned. "Guess that's why you're Brooke's assistant." He shifted to face her. "Want to explain why you just got me past the mall cop?"

"First—you should be nice. Bertram is really good at what he does."

Duly chastised, he watched the numbers climb on the digital display. "Noted."

"And I did that because I'm worried about my employer."

Sobered, he bobbed his head. "Same." The elevator was still climbing.

"I thought if I let you look around the house, perhaps you might see something that could help find her."

"So, you think she's missing?" Was he going to end up with a nosebleed?

"No." Ishwin took a step forward a second before the doors slid open. "I *know* she is." The petite Indian woman moved into the small hall that had five doors banking off it. Two had locks, one was marked *Stairs*, another *Maintenance*, and the last *Garage*.

"Garage?" he asked, scowling. "Is there an invisible highway in the sky?"

Ishwin smirked as she unlocked the left door. "The penthouses have their own private access and garage."

"That's not normal is it?"

"No," Ishwin said with a sniff, "most condos in the City charge just as much for their parking garage as they do for rent."

Cord followed her into the condo … and was struck stupid. Discovered an inability to voice his thoughts. Probably because he couldn't think past what he saw—the place was like the Taj Mahal. A series of arches rushed down a long marble hall. To the left, another hall cleared ten feet before it banked to the right. How the heck was it so freakin' big?

"Have you had dinner?"

Brain lagging by about fifteen facts and tripping over the luxury of this penthouse, Cord looked through the series of arches to where the voice was echoing from but didn't see the woman. "I, uh … No, I haven't." He trolled ten yards, passing through an impressive library with floor-to-ceiling bookshelves, a leather chaise, fireplace boasting a white canvas with the black outline of a woman wearing a large hat. Put him in mind of that old-timey chick from the movies. Wasn't she a call-girl in that movie?

A picture on the mantel drew him over. He lifted the framed selfie and considered the faces. Two kids, a handsome man who looked Middle Eastern, and Brooke. All laughing. Comfortable in each other's arms.

What ...?

He returned the picture to the mantle, rolled his shoulders, and kept moving. Slid his gaze to the right and—

"Holy Mother ..." He stopped short. Stared in that direction, eyeballing the wall of windows that opened out onto a terrace with a table that easily sat fifteen and a stone wall at least six meters tall anchored by a fireplace. Plants and lights strung from side to side gave the place the feel of a lavish English garden ... a mile up in the air. Crazy.

He angled to the side and—again. Froze at the sight of the pool that stretched to his left. "You *gotta* be kidding me." Long and narrow, flanked by walls of glass, it seemed to fall right off the edge and down the hundred or whatever floors into Central Park. Over it, Roman columns and arches were all bathed in an ethereal blue glow. A jacuzzi hugged the farthest corner that had a clear view—through one of the glass walls—into an office. "Rapunzel, Rapunzel ... come down from your lair ..."

This place blew away any notion of "penthouse" he could've dreamed up if he'd had ten years. As for the cost—he was pretty sure he couldn't count that high. He let out a low whistle, his gaze settling on a massive art piece of a woman's eyes in that office.

"Mr. Cord?"

He pivoted. Saw Ishwin standing there, head cocked in amusement. "I, uh ... got lost. A few more minutes and you would've needed to send in SAR."

With a smile, she motioned him to follow. "Come on." She headed down the hall, her rubber-soled shoes padding on the marble floor.

He hustled his way after her. Had every intention of planting his butt at the kitchen island, then saw the glittering lights of the city through the entire wall of windows that lined the far side of the kitchen. Good thing he wasn't afraid of heights.

But his attention swung back to the more important topic—Brooke. "So, uh ..." He tucked his hands on his belt as he took in the view. "You *know* she's missing ...?"

"I do." Ishwin moved around the kitchen, pulling vegetables and meat from the fridge—where there was a child's drawing of two adults, two children. All holding hands.

His heart squeezed, suddenly feeling like he was intruding. Like he didn't belong here.

"How?" He made his way to the island and slid onto a barstool. "I was at her office—they said she took a sabbatical ..."

"She did." While sautéing some vegetables on the cooktop, she sighed. Then leaned on the counter and gave him a mournful look. "If I say these things, you must swear not to tell her brothers. Ms. Mulroney did not want her family knowing about Mazin."

"Mazin," he repeated, testing the name, his thoughts bouncing back to the picture on the mantel.

"Yes, he was very special to her. I think she loved him, but she was not one for emotions, so she never say that. She took the sabbatical when Mazin and the children came."

Mazin.

"But when the children go missing, she look for them. Now, she—poof!"

Cord felt his heart jam. "What children went missing?"

CHAPTER
TWO

"*Everyone ready?*" *Brooke shouldered her purse, grabbed her attaché case, then lifted the iridescent backpack and helped Caliyah slide it on.*

"We need to hurry," Jihan said, running toward the elevator. "I want to get there before they stop serving the French toast."

"I told you I could make—"

"It's not the same," Jihan said.

"It's literally the same," Brooke said, only then realizing she was arguing with a ten-year-old. A fact that reopened the wound that was Kaleigh. "C'mon." She ushered them into the elevator, and they rode it down in silence.

"Dad said after school, we could get some Sprinkles," Caliyah said, lifting her hands, insisting on being picked up. "Will you come, too?"

Brooke hoisted the little one into her arms and perched the precocious child on her hip. "Not this time. I have a big meeting this afternoon." It had worked out well with Mazin's new job—she took the kids to school each morning and he picked them up. "In fact, I might miss dinner."

"Again?" Jihan whined as they crossed the foyer and headed into their day.

"I hope you can make it home," Caliyah said, arms hooked around Brooke's shoulders. "I like you. I'm glad we live with you now."

"Yeah, but I hate these clothes." Jihan tugged at the button-down shirt of his school uniform. Then he shrugged. "At least we have other clothes."

"We didn't before," Caliyah said. "Not really. Not pretty ones like you got us. Can we go shopping again? I like when you take me shopping." She kissed Brooke on the cheek. "I'm so glad you're our mommy."

"She's not our mom!"

The world shifted and tilted.

BROOKE SNAPPED AWAKE. Pain stabbed like daggers. "Augh!" Crying, she slumped back down, only then feeling herself moving. Cold air rushing over her. "Wha … what's going on?" She blinked and saw Nurse Min at the side as they moved down a hall.

"Miss Chavasse, we are putting you in a private room."

"What? Why? I was just—"

"There is blood in your urine which gives us concern that the lower broken ribs may have impacted surrounding organs. It could simply be a kidney contusion, but to know that, we need to do additional imaging—"

"Okay, then let's do that. But I don't need a room."

"Unfortunately, we are a small hospital and"—the nurse paused as they angled her rolling bed into a room that had one other bed—"and we need the bays in the ER. We're also short-staffed, so once the techs are here on Monday, we can check—"

"Monday?" Brooke balked, then regretted it, feeling as if she were breathing fire. "That's two days." But she'd seen the German in the hall just before they'd sedated her.

Yet, he hadn't done anything while she was out … so, maybe he hadn't seen her? Had her luck finally changed?

Stone would berate her for even hoping for luck. Their family had been raised on biblical values ... and though she hadn't done the same with her girls ...

My girls ...

Heel of her hand to her forehead, she focused on calming herself. Couldn't change the past. *So don't dwell on it. Move on. Make better choices.*

She snorted at the irony—that advice had come from her dad, the one man who knew how to make solid choices while in uniform. Beyond it ... Colonel Metcalfe became Major Failure. Reason number 515 she'd have nothing do with the military. Including a certain bald operator with more tattoos than brain cells.

I should've called—

She sucked in a breath. Grabbed her throbbing ribs. "What time is it?" The room had no clock and the nurse wasn't here. But merciful heavens, she was in trouble if—

"Almost eight o'clock, thankfully," a tech said in Mandarin as he came in with a tray of food. "Counting the minutes—I get off soon."

"Do you have a laptop I can borrow?" Brooke's heart drummed, its cadence beeping on the nearby machine.

The tech looked at her with a scowl. "No, sorry—"

"I really—"

"You can use mine."

Brooke glanced to the side and spotted a petite teen, who held out a tablet.

"It's an iPad—it'll work."

The tech hesitated, then retrieved the device and handed it to Brooke.

"Thank you. Do you mind if I download a free app? I'll delete it as soon as I'm done." Brooke opened the app store and downloaded the digital diary app and watched it downloading ... Eyed the time in the upper left-hand corner. Shoot. Shoot-shoot-shoot. Two minutes!

"Wi-Fi not good here," the tech said with a lazy shrug.

No kidding! It was still downloading … downloading … *What was this, the Stone Age?* "Come onnn," she groaned. Glanced at the time stamp. One minute! Her heart jolted.

The app finished downloading. She tapped it and logged in, fingers tapping over the keyboard as fast as she could make them go. She hit enter, eyed the time—still had time. "Yes!"

The iPad's haptics vibrated. Red lettering declared, INVALID LOGIN OR PASSWORD.

With a growl, she hurriedly tapped login and tried again. It autocorrected what she typed and again gave her the failed login notice. "Stop." Again, she attempted the login and hit enter— just as she noticed the password had a wrong number. Shriek-growling, she flew through login. Heart thumping, she watched it cycle through the login. "Please please please."

She eyed the timestamp.

Blinked. Breath held, Brooke glanced at the time.

0800 appeared at the same time the login screen surrendered to her digital diary. She tapped on the Make An Entry and the screen went black. "Oh."

"Did it work?" the girl asked.

"I … I don't know." She angled the device sideways and held down the power button. "I … It died."

"Oh," the teen said, "maybe battery was low. Sorry."

The tech returned the iPad, and Brooke relaxed against the bed, no clue if she'd managed to beat the timer on her diary. The last thing she needed … Ugh. Her head really hurt. If she were one to pray, she'd beg God to make sure her digital diary hadn't just been sent to Cord Taggart. She did not need him in her business.

"I don't need you up in my business, Mom!"

"Kaleigh, listen—"

"Why? You don't ever listen to me."

"I'm just trying—"

"Ha! That'd be a first."

The line went dead, and Brooke sagged as she rounded the corner, firmly gripping Caliyah's hand as they wound their way to the restaurant.

"Why are you sad?" the insightful kindergartener asked.

"She's always sad when she talks to Kaleigh," Jihan said.

"That's not true," Brooke countered as they entered the Italian eatery.

"Daddy!" Caliyah darted through the tangle of tables toward the back office. The door stood open, and the handsome Afghan native looked up from his work. Smiling, he caught his daughter up in his arms as he moved into the open. "How is my angel?"

"Great. Ms. Messer said she's watching to see who will get to take Hermes home for the holidays to watch him."

"Hermes?"

"The class hamster," Brooke said with a laugh. "And I wouldn't be mad if Caliyah acted up a little more between now and then."

"A little more?"

Brooke shrugged and arched an eyebrow. "Okay ... ever ..." There was a reason he called the girl "angel." She excelled at being sweet. "So—all good?" She thumbed over her shoulder toward the door. "I need to head back to the office for a couple of hours, then I'll be home for dinner."

"Sure, yes. Thank you for picking them up for me. It was totally last-minute and—"

"Mazin." She touched his shoulder. Smoothed Caliyah's dark braid. "It's okay. We're in this together, remember?"

With a relieved smile, he pulled her into a hug, surprising both of them. Mostly because neither of them were touchy-feely people, but their lives had been upended, and in each other, they found solace. Comfort. Maybe a new beginning. She planted a kiss on Caliyah's cheek. "See you all back at the house."

As Brooke headed back toward the front of the restaurant, she felt a warmth spreading through her. Family was a tricky road to navigate and had always left her feeling less than inadequate. She was glad for this second chance.

MANHATTAN, NEW YORK

"And you're sure ..." Cord held his hands out, almost steepling them as he pointed his fingertips across the desk at the agent. "Brooke Metcal—Mulroney. Partner at—"

"Dark hair, blue eyes. Attitude of fire."

"Definitely her."

FBI Assistant Special Agent in Charge Abe Cantor chuckled. "She was breathing down our necks daily when the kids went missing, asking what we knew. What we were doing. Nothing was good enough as far as she was concerned."

Processing the guy's words, Cord nodded though his gut was hating this. "And these kids and their dad vanished six months ago."

"Just over five," Cantor confirmed.

"Did she ..." What the blazes was going on? "Uh, she say why she was so interested in them?"

"Said they were family. All but threatened a lawsuit if we didn't find or do something."

"Family. Kids are his." Glancing at the photo on the iPad Cantor handed him, Cord struggled to understand. He knew all Brooke's brothers. Could be a cousin, but the whole Middle Eastern thing of one Mazin Daghestani ruled out blood relative. Yet she considered this guy ... *family?* "This doesn't make sense."

Cantor shrugged. "Employment, phone, and insurance records—all list his place of residence the same as hers." He glanced at the paperwork littering his desk. "Guess he was living with her. Guy really stepped up in life, hooking up with her. Can't blame him—I mean, have you seen that place? Or her?"

Have you seen my fist? "Were they … married?"

"No record of that." Cantor narrowed his eyes.

"What'd her ex-husband say?"

The special agent frowned. "We don't have that contact information or knowledge. Besides, with no legal connection between Daghestani and Mulroney, we were limited on what we could discuss with whom regarding the case."

Cord lifted the iPad again and watched the video taken from the Italian restaurant where Daghestani had worked. Saw him leaving around dusk with the kids. A van pulling up. When it left, the guy and kids were gone. "You ran the plates."

Cantor nodded. "Stolen. Traced the van to the tunnel, where it vanished. Kids have been vanishing around the city, but we can't get a bead on where they're taking them."

This reeked of trafficking. And Brooke had been asking all those questions when he first met her while delivering Brighton for safekeeping to Stone's lodge … then she'd shown up in Nigeria, frantic, skittish … months of touch-and-go conversations. Never willing to tell him squat about what haunted her. All that time, she'd been searching for these missing kids. And the dad. In general, when you told someone kids were being trafficked, they'd show disgust, be sad, donate to a cause … and move on with their lives. But Brooke … she'd given up her life to search for these kids and Daghestani.

His gut churned. She must really love him, them.

And I never saw it. The attraction. He'd noticed her unusual curiosity and knowledge about trafficking. Her showing up in Nigeria should've tipped him off. He should've pushed, taken his usual uber-direct route of getting in her face … but he'd let his attraction to her get in the way. Ignored his own instincts.

"So, we've done some work with you," Cantor began, "and if

you're here, asking about the Daghestani case—is this trafficking?"

Groaning, Cord tossed the iPad on the desk and slumped back. Roughed his hands over his face. He'd been in this gig long enough to know that when it smelled like trafficking, looked like trafficking … "I want to say no, but she's been asking me about trafficking and showed up in Nigeria after her sister had been involved in an operation there … and now she's gone dark. But do I have definitive proof? No. Are my instincts buzzing?" He grunted. "Yeah—*lit*."

"Hold up," Cantor said, leaning forward. "Ms. Mulroney is missing?"

"Her assistant believes so, and since I haven't been able to reach her in a while, I'm … concerned."

"What does her family say?"

Cord huffed. "They …" It felt wrong to say the Metcalfes weren't close or weren't talking. It was Brooke who had put space between them. "From what I can tell, haven't heard from her in a while either."

"So, they're not close."

"Not a word I'd use to describe them." He'd leave out that non-communication was SOP for Brooke. "Her assistant said she took a flight about six weeks ago and hasn't returned. I've got a team looking into her last-knowns. But it isn't normal for her to not communicate with her assistant." At least, Ishwin said it wasn't.

With a grunt, Cantor dragged a notepad across the papers littering his desk. "I can open a missing person's case, since she was connected to Daghestani and is now apparently missing as well, but it's been six weeks …"

"In other words, don't get my hopes up."

Cantor looked chagrined. "We've worked enough cases together that you know what we're up against, the number of cases, how many get solved." He tucked his chin and exhaled heavily. "How many don't."

"Yeah." Scratching the back of his bald head, Cord was painfully aware that last year, after Texas, New York had the highest rate of missing persons cases in the U.S. with over 1,500 still unsolved. "Appreciate it." He rose and nodded. "You have my number. If you need anything—"

Cantor shook his hand. "You mentioned her family. Happen to have their contact info?"

"Sure." After listing out on the legal pad Stone and Canyon—a good starting point—he extracted a promise from the agent to keep him posted and left.

Thoughts heavy with concern over the dark-haired beauty and the convos that were going nowhere, he felt an obligation to update Stone Metcalfe. Heading to the subway, he spent three of the five blocks arguing with himself before he tugged out his phone and called.

"Hey," came Stone Metcalfe's baritone voice, "still trudging up trouble?"

"Life is dull without it."

"Man, you're addicted to stress."

Cord winced. That was a little too close to home. "Look, I … Have you heard from Brooke?"

Stone grunted. "So, Canyon was right—you're hot for my sister."

More than I'd like to admit. "That's not why I'm calling." What did he have to lose this time? "I know you blew me off last time I tried to suggest this, but I've done some hunting around and I'm convinced Brooke is missing."

Hesitation strangled the line. "I'm listening."

"I don't have much, but the basics are this: a couple of kids"—leave out the dad? Ishwin made him swear … but was that the right thing to do?—"went missing, apparently upset her. So she started looking for them."

"Who were these kids to her?"

"No idea." That was the truth. "Her assistant-slash-housekeeper told me she took a flight and hasn't returned. No calls, no updates. You're going to be hearing from Assistant Special Agent Cantor, who's trying to help me with this. I already briefed him that y'all weren't in communication much."

"Not since she moved Mom here. And you verified the flight?"

"I did." Cord made his way to his hotel. "She flew from Newark to Nigeria."

"And you saw her?" Stone asked, reviewing the convo, likely to make sure he had heard the details correctly.

"Yeah—and each time I've seen her since bringing Brighton to you, Brooke asked about trafficking."

"Huh." Stone sighed. "Willow said she didn't see her."

Running a hand down the back of his neck, Cord struggled to process that. Really, any of it. He hadn't been able to stop thinking about how frantic she'd seemed in that narrow alley of the village.

"Why would she be in Nigeria and not talk to Willow?" Stone asked. "When she was right there? Was it a cry for help? Why didn't you—"

Cord hesitated. Thought back to that moment. The way she tangled up his brain and ticked him off with her divertive efforts. "I tried, but she shut me down."

"She shut you down."

"Ran off. I've tried to reach her since, but nothing."

"You think she was in danger?"

"I didn't get that sense at the time, and I've got a pretty solid radar for trouble like that." Had he been wrong? Was he to blame …? "She was upset, but … not scared. Frantic, but it was more about trying to do something than getting away from someone. Like she was afraid I'd stop her."

"Why didn't you?"

He appreciated why her older brother would ask that. "I've asked myself that a dozen times since her assistant talked to me, but honestly, have you ever tried to tell your sister to do something she didn't want to do?"

Stone grunted. "Fair enough."

He entered the lobby and aimed for the elevator.

"But you think it's connected to that now?"

In the steel box, he punched the floor and leaned back, pinching the bridge of his nose. "I do. Which annoys me that I didn't pick up on it sooner."

"I think you did. But you got distracted."

In the room, Cord tossed the keycard on the table. He dragged a hand over his face and dropped onto the edge of the mattress. Knew he had to own it. "Yeah, I did."

"You're not the first sap to fall under her spell. Obviously."

"Maybe, but I'm the first to fall under it and fail her completely."

Stone didn't respond, a judgment in and of itself.

Cord went to the window that paled compared to her penthouse view. "Stone, her questions went on for months. So long that I started thinking she was just looking for an excuse to see me." His phone buzzed against his ear, indicating he had a message, but it could wait. Nothing was more important right now. "But ..." He exhaled heavily, hating himself for the mistakes. "Then again—now that I think about it, her questions seemed too ... specific. Knowledgeable."

"You said it was two kids from the city."

Cord hedged, feeling his phone buzz and ignoring it again. "Yeah ..."

"I don't get that—why would she take a sabbatical for two city kids when she didn't give a squat about her own daughters?"

"I think that's unfair," he said, deliberately focusing on the kids and avoiding names or connections. Or the fact they and their father were living with Brooke. He'd tried not to dwell on that much himself. It stung like a bugger.

"You don't know Brooke or her history. How she left her husband for her career. Abandoned her kids."

Cord swallowed. It was true—he didn't know that. Adding to his irritation, his phone buzzed again. "No matter what she did then, she's trying to help these kids. She's your sister, and now she's missing."

"Why do I feel like you're not telling me everything?"

"Because you're a suspicious politician."

"Low, Taggart. That was low," Stone said. "Okay. Let me get my brothers up to speed. Keep me updated."

"Will do." Cord slumped into the nearby chair, flipped the phone on the desk and buried his head in his hands. He'd been so hung on the blue eyes and killer smile. Was that why he'd hadn't seen this coming? What had he missed? Of course, she hadn't been exactly forthcoming, so while he did bear some responsibility for missing ... whatever it was he'd missed, she had withheld stuff. A lot of stuff. Like that she was sitting at the airport restaurant laughing and flirting with him while she was living with a guy and playing mom to his kids.

Dial it back, Taggart.

He dragged his hands over his bearded face and growled.

What were you doing with that guy, Brooke? Where are you? The one that drove the knife deeper ... *What did he have that I didn't?*

His phone buzzed again. Then ... again.

"For the love of ..." He snagged the phone from the bed and gaped at the notifications. Thirty-two texts. "What the ...?"

He swiped and entered his passcode. Opened the texts. Not a number he recognized. Every one of them with a link. Some spammer was trying to takeover his phone. Not the first time. "Nice tr—" He noticed the very first text wasn't a link. His gut dropped when he saw the words.

BROOKE

Cord, if my digital diary has sent this text and its subsequent entries, something has happened to me. Hopefully there's something in here that will help you save the children. My life is of no consequence if anything happens to them. If anyone can find them, it's you. Please, do this for me—no, for them. They're worth it.

Cord, if my digital diary has sent this text and its subsequent entries, something has happened to me. Hopefully there's something in here that will help you save the children. My life is of no consequence if anything happens to them. If anyone can find them, it's you. Please, do this for me—no, for them. They're worth it.

CHAPTER
THREE

Munich, Germany

"Herr Sauer?"

At the pitched tone of his secretary, Gunnar Sauer slowed in his approach toward the chancellor's office and skated a glance around to verify they were alone. He did not know what was so urgent, but Sylvie was not prone to hysterics. And she knew better than to waste his time. Then again, a beauty like her could not be considered a waste of any kind. Still, he leveled a glower at her for interrupting his pace. A good measure to insure she understood her place and the value of his time.

"My apologies, sir," she said, sidling up to him. Tucked her chin, those large blue eyes striking against her platinum hair.

Gunnar let his gaze slide over her five-nine frame with an appreciative glance. "What is it?"

"Her phone—there's been activity, sir."

He frowned, remembering what Anton had said. "The phone was destroyed."

"Yes, sir, but her account and number are still active. I've kept tabs on it—thinking if she was in Taiwan alone, without a phone or identification, she could get a phone and have it set to the original number."

"So this means Anton hasn't found her."

"Not yet, sir. He's been checking hospitals, but there aren't any Americans or Jane Does."

"Maybe she was released."

"Possible, but he doubts it. She was hit by a car and unconscious at first. He tried to follow the ambulance—drew attention of authorities. Had to outrun them." She lifted her chin and exhaled, as if she were about to burst.

"You seem very happy for a person delivering absolute failure."

She held up her palms at him. "This morning I discovered that an app tied to Ms. Mulroney's number sent messages to Taggart."

That piece of work. He'd stuck his nose in their business too many times. What he wouldn't give to bury that guy. "What messages?"

Her assured persona faltered. "The messages were sent from that app, which"—she cocked her head—"had next-level encryption. Odd to be sure. I have our team working on it."

"In other words, you don't know." Every time he turned around, one Metcalfe or another was interfering with the network—or Taggart. He'd been trying to take down the guy's organization since they stole Horvath's pet out from under their noses. Then also nearly destroyed the Trench.

"We'll find her—"

Gunnar grabbed her by the ponytail and yanked her against himself. "You had better or you are useless." He sneered down at her. "And you know what happens to useless women, do you not, Fraulein Sylvie?"

The marginal widening of her eyes confirmed his words.

He thrust her away.

"No." An idea stole into his thoughts, one that gave him sick pleasure. "Tell Anton I want her found. She's caused enough trouble. But put everyone on Taggart. If she reached out to him, he'll hunt her down."

KAOHSIUNG, TAIWAN

"Hey. What did you do to my iPad?"

Yawning, Brooke glanced across the room to the teen girl. "Sorry?"

"My iPad." The girl waved it in the air. "It's dead. Charged all night—and nothing."

Brooke's heart skipped a beat. "Is the charger working? Sometimes—"

"Charger's fine. It charged my phone."

"I—that's strange." Only if strange was common. That was exactly the type of thing that started happening. "I … It was fine when I was using it." Until the end. When it *died*. She'd never had a device actually die while they were tracking her, but there had been a lot of hiccups. Surely …

"You owe me a new one!"

"I …" What if they somehow were tracking the app? Was that even possible? Her phone was in the river. Could they monitor the app? She had no idea. With her logging in, did it somehow connect to her phone? She'd started noticing strange things with her phone. When the guy showed up in three different places, she grew convinced they were tracking her and dumped it. If it was connected to her phone, maybe they could make the link between it … which would lead them straight to her. Here. In the hospital.

I have to get out of here.

But if one of her broken ribs had punctured an organ, she

couldn't afford to leave. She'd need medical care. Antibiotics. Painkillers. Ever since Canyon's addiction, her brothers had sworn off painkillers. Besides being incredibly addictive, they impaired judgment. So forget the painkillers.

"Hey! What are you going to do about my iPad?"

Though Brooke did feel bad about whatever happened to the girl's device, there was no way she could pay for it. She had no cash, no way to get money from her bank, and no credit card. Even if she had her purse with her, she couldn't use them— they'd be another trail for the traffickers to find her.

"Hey! I want a new iPad!" the girl yelled.

"You have no proof that anything I did compromised your tablet," Brooke said in Mandarin. "For all I know you did something to it before you gave it to me, just so you could trick me."

Nurse Min came in and shook her head. "What is all this noise?"

"She ruined my tablet and needs to buy me a new one."

"You cannot prove it is her fault," the nurse said clicking her tongue as she came toward Brooke's bedside. "How are you feeling today, Ms. Chavasse?"

The pain seemed to have reach new heights, but it was time to vacate the premises. "Better." The lie seemed to have elicited more than she remembered having. She angled to the side to relieve the pressure. "I would like another test to check for blood again."

With an amused smile, Nurse Min produced a lidded plastic cup and set it on the food arm table. "You read my mind, Ariane."

Gritting through the pain, Brooke made her way to the restroom with the cup. Did the deed amid excruciating pain, then handed off the sample. Back in the room, she saw the girl digging through the pile of Brooke's things. "What are you doing?"

"Looking for a credit card."

Brooke shuffled over. "Get away—"

The girl whirled, shoving Brooke backward. Her back and side struck the table. Blinding agony hollowed her hearing. Her vision grayed. Nausea swirled and roiled.

"What is this?" Nurse Min cried. "Security!"

Brooke felt herself falling. Heard a scuffle as she plummeted into unconsciousness.

Boom! Crack!

Jolted awake by the thunderstorm, Brooke glanced to the window. Lightning splintered across the sky just as she heard a yelp.

Caliyah!

She sat up in the bed and looked to the door even as a blur of pink pajamas swirled in and hovered at the other side of the bed. The intermittent flashes of lightning illuminated the small, oval face and dark eyes staring at her. "Afraid of storms?"

Three fingers stuffed in her mouth, Caliyah nodded as she hugged the little gray stuffed elephant. She removed her hand. "Daddy usually lets me sleep with him."

"No, he doesn't," Jihan muttered from where he now also stood at the threshold. "She always wants to stay with Dad."

Reminded so much of the nights she'd let Kaleigh climb in bed with her, Brooke patted the king mattress and tugged back the comforter. "C'mon. We can keep each other safe."

"I don't need to be protected," Jihan argued even as his feet moved him further into the room. "But I always watch over Cali, so I should probably stay."

The pre-teen was every bit his father with his strength and even this touch of pride. "Of course. I'm glad for your help, Jihan."

Adjusting to the side of the bed, Brooke checked her phone and time. Just a few hours before dawn. Not that she would have to get up that early today—with Mazin working an overnighter at the restaurant for inventory, Brooke had offered to handle the children and get them to school on time.

She relaxed against the headboard as Caliyah clambered over the taupe duvet and slid between the sheets. With a coy but delighted grin, she dropped back against the extra pillows and pulled the comforter up to her chest, resting her arms over the top. "Your bed smells like you."

Surprise lit through Brooke amid a peal of thunder. "Does it? I didn't realize ..." Was that a bad thing? She hadn't really thought of her bed as having any scent other than fabric detergent.

"It smells like your perfume. It's nice," Jihan said, his mannerisms so grown up and mature for a kid who had just hit double digits.

Brooke felt sad for a second that she hadn't been able to throw him a big party for that birthday. For Kaleigh, it'd been a big celebration.

"Did your daughter sleep with you during storms?"

Settling back against the pillows, Brooke stared up at the ceiling. "She did, yes. Not very often and she outgrew it very quickly, because by the time she was te"—she dared not say ten and make Jihan feel embarrassed—"older, she grew to love storms."

Caliyah shifted onto her side and tucked her hands under her olive cheek. "I don't love storms. They're scary." She suddenly sat up, splaying her arms wide. "Whoa. Did you feel that?" The tremor in her lip sifted down into her chest. "I thought the building was falling down!"

Brooke brushed the little one's hair back from her face. "We're very high up, so when it's windy, you can feel the building sway. But they made the building to do that so it wouldn't fall."

"It's scary," Caliyah said with wide eyes.

"I like to think of it as being in a rocking chair." Brooke nestled into to the bed beside the six-year-old. "If you let it, the motion can be very relaxing. I often fall asleep to it." Though she wasn't getting up at dawn, she did have a full day of work and needed some rest. Maybe this would work and get the children to sleep. "Let's try it."

"I want Daddy," Caliyah said, dropping against the bed with a pout-filled emphasis.

Hooking an arm around the little one, Brooke wished just once that someone wanted her. Even her girls had preferred Mark. Then again, he had been the better parent. She'd exceeded the requisite 1.75 children, but that maternal gene was one her mother had definitely not passed down to her.

Caliyah curled onto her side and eased toward Brooke.

A moment later, Brooke felt Jihan slide in next to her, perched on the very edge of the bed. When he nearly fell off and grabbed her arm to keep his balance, she laughed and scooted over, which forced a now-grumpy Caliyah to move as well.

The little girl whined and plastered herself into Brooke's side, arm wrapped around her waist. "I was here first, Jihan."

"You don't own the bed, Cali," he said as he propped himself up. "Tomorrow, can we leave early like we did when we first got here and go to the bakery."

Though Brooke thought to chastise him for stealing the moment from his sister, she couldn't help but laugh. And chose, instead, to enjoy this moment. She could not remember the last time anyone fought to be near her. "The bakery," she crooned. "You are a boy after my heart. What do you want to get?"

"I like the ones with cream in the middle," he said.

"Boston crème—or raspberry?"

"Lemon!"

"Those are gross," Caliyah huffed, her cheek now on Brooke's ribs. "I like the ones with chocolate sprinkles."

"Chocolate is always a winner."

Moments later, as if fairy dust had been sprinkled on her, Caliyah was fast asleep and tucked into Brooke's side.

On her left, Jihan hugged her arm and lay there quietly. For a moment. "Did Dad tell you about my mom?"

Angling her head to the side, she met the boy's hazel gaze. "A little."

"She's dead."

Brooke nodded. "Does it make you sad? Do you miss her?"

The sway of the building and the quiet drumming of rain against the windows settled between them for a long moment. "Yeah, I am sad. But I don't miss her. I don't remember her, really. She left shortly after Cali was born."

"That makes me sad, too." She never had sons, but with four brothers, the male psyche was one with which she was well acquainted. *"Your mom missed out on learning what a wonderful young man you are. The way you take care of Cali, and even the way you take care of your dad."*

His eyes brightened. "I think it makes him mad."

"About your mom?"

"Well, yeah, but I meant that I try to take care of him. He told me once I shouldn't have to do that. But I like to do it. He doesn't smile much."

"It's nice to see him smile, isn't it?"

"He always works so hard to take care of us. And he was worried we wouldn't like it here."

Her heart skipped a beat as she drew her fingers over his dark hair. "Do you?"

The year old nodded. "I don't like the big city—there are too many people and they're not very nice. But I like being with you, and this beautiful house. But mostly, I like how happy Dad is here. Because of you."

"Well," she said, pressing a kiss to his temple, *"I am happy with you here, too."*

Newark International Airport, New Jersey

"You still in good with the Agency?"

"So far," Canyon Metcalfe said warily.

"Good, because I need some major string pulling. There's an Agency safehouse in the Philippines—recruit as many operators as you can and rendezvous with me there. Immediately."

Hesitation seemed a well-timed ally as Cord strode up to the self check-in terminal and tapped the screen to get his boarding pass.

"Brooke." The way Canyon said his big sister's name was loaded with concern, protection, and a deadly warning. "You thought she'd gone missing. Guessing you now have proof."

"Long story, but yes. I got a quasi-coded message from her with way more intel than I can process right now."

"That's sending you to the Philippines."

"Indirectly."

"If you're asking for operators and heading there yourself, then you think …"

He knew how hard it was to say that word when it came to family. "Afraid so." He got a sticker for his suitcase and slid the thing around the handle, then rolled it up to the counter, where the attendant weighed it, checked his ID and boarding pass, then told him how to get to the TSA Pre-Check line for security. "Look, when we're on the ground there, I'll give you all the details. But let the Agency know that I think this situation could snip the head off the dragon we've been hunting."

"Serious?"

"As a heart attack." Cord banked around the corner and aimed for the security lines. "I'm on the next flight out."

A clutter of noise rattled through the line. "Understood. Someone will be waiting for you there."

"Appreciated, brother. See you there." In the security line and with roughly twenty people in line ahead of him, he called his admin. "Jess, hey. Thanks for getting me on this flight. Now, I'm going to need you to run down some things for me. Got a pen?"

"No, but I have my keyboard. Ready when you are."

He smirked and appreciated his cousin's wife more than he could ever express. "Hike onto Brooke's line—tell me if there's been any activity on it in the last twenty-four."

The clicking of keys carried him through two people processing with the TSA agent.

"Nothing."

Just like before. "Okay, I expected that." He ran a hand over his bald head. "Those texts that hit my phone about an hour ago? I need to know where they originated from and how they were sent, since her phone isn't active. Whatever you can find out."

"Okay."

"Second, do some searching on all of Brooke's vitals and credit cards, bank account. Find me a trail."

"I'll do my best."

"I know you will. Especially with a life on the line. And last, get hold of Low and put him in contact with Canyon Metcalfe. I want him out there, too."

"I'll call him as soon as we hang up."

"Thanks." He ran a hand over his beard. "Actually—one last thing. Find what you can on Mazin Daghestani. He and his kids went missing in the City about five months ago. Dig around. I want to know who he is."

"Is he connected to Ms. Mulroney?"

Cord frowned, hating the question. "Don't know." But they were living together …

"Sir," the TSA agent commanded. "Next."

Cord twitched. "Gotta go," he said as he stepped forward and handed the agent his passport and boarding pass. Pocketing his phone, he shifted his ruck onto his shoulder.

The agent scowled at him, gave him a once-over, then another.

Not again.

"Special Forces?"

He started. Blinked. "Uh, yeah …"

"My brother was 5th Group."

Cord managed a grunt. "Not you, though?"

The agent tapped his chest. "Bad ticker. Got medically discharged right after Basic."

"That's tough."

"Sucked. I was going career." With a nod, the agent waved him through.

Grabbing a bottled water, Cord planted himself at a café table across from the gate and dug out his laptop. With forty minutes before boarding, he wouldn't waste any time. Called Jess again. "Hey, another thing. Those messages that hit my phone—can you put them into text format and send that to me?"

"Sure. Hey—already found out some things on Daghestani."

In less than ten minutes? Why was he impressed? "If it weren't for you—"

"Yeah, yeah. I know—you wouldn't be able to find your shampoo."

It was an old, lame joke, since he'd been shaving his head for over ten years.

"Scant information on Dhagestani from the media reports when they went missing. He worked at an Italian restaurant, had two kids—a boy, Jihan, aged ten, and a girl, Caliyah, age six—and supposedly had only been in the city for the last six months. His employer said he was diligent. Had worked himself up from waiter to host and had started taking courses to become the next assistant manager."

"Impressive. Anything else?"

"Not yet. No driver's license, but he did have a New York ID with a ..." Jess grunted. "His address is the same as—"

"Yeah."

"They were living together?"

Cord slapped his laptop shut. Glanced up at the bar in the middle of the concourse. Thought to grab something to help him stomach where this story was going. But what else could it mean for them to have the same address? "Apparently."

"Was he a pro bono case or something? Lawyers do that—"

"They work cases free. They don't bring clients into their home and live with them." Man, this was putting him in a foul mood.

"Huh," Jess said. "I guess I just didn't see that coming. She seemed so straitlaced."

"I gotta go. Stay on those things."

"Yep, sure—"

He ended the call. Cupped his hand over his mouth. Raked his hand over his beard slow and hard. Was that why she kept putting him off?

Though … that time they'd run into each other in this very airport—

Ruck in hand, he strode up the umbilical into the airport and thumbed his passcode into the phone. "Hey. Yeah, landed. Be there in about an hour." The MiLE team was meeting up with LEOs in New York on trafficking. Sometimes it felt a lot like beating a dead horse, trying to get things to change, to break the cycle here in the City. But he'd never give up. As long as victims were fighting for their next breath, he'd fight to bring down those responsible and stop others from being caught up in the nightmarish existence.

"Cord?"

His gaze flicked to the side where the voice had come from and settled nicely on a dark-haired beauty. "See? I knew God loved me."

Brooke Metcalfe Mulroney rolled her eyes. "I think you're mentioning the wrong deity."

"You calling me the spawn of Satan?"

"Your words, not mine."

He grinned as he stepped out of the stream of traffic heading to baggage claim. "You coming or going?" he asked, noticing the shadows under her eyes.

"Going. Though"—she gave a cockeyed nod—"not soon. They just delayed the flight three more hours."

"That right?" He had an hour to waste, though that's not what he'd call any time with her. "Wanna grab a bite?"

She straightened. "To eat?"

"Well, I don't know what you do with a bite, but that's the general idea." He indicated to an American grill gaping at them. "Their burgers are killer."

She wrinkled her nose. "I don't eat red meat."

"Pretty sure they have rabbit food, too. Maybe even some of that toe food."

"You mean tofu."

"You sure?"

She shook her head, but there was no hiding the smile. Though it did little to cast off that weariness that clung to her like predawn mist.

"And as much as it will kill me," he said, "I won't offer to pay for your meal, you being one of those independent types."

The smile this time was softer, more … inviting. "How about I pay for your meal?"

Dang, if his heart didn't just do a jig—not over her paying, but that she was accepting the invite to grab some grub. "Just don't tell the guys. I got my pride, you know."

Twenty minutes later, he gulped a glass of water as she nursed a glass of wine. "So," he said, chomping into a fry, "you going to tell me?"

"That you're a thick-skulled oaf."

"Aw, baby. Keep sweet-talking me like that, and I'll skip my meeting."

Her gaze sharpened as she set down the stemless glass and came forward a bit. "Your meeting—it's about trafficking."

Chewing the fry, he considered her. What the heck was going on in that beautiful head of hers? "I'll tell you mine if you tell me yours."

She scrunched that pert nose. "Mine?"

He nodded. "Why you were asking about trafficking, why you were in Nigeria …" Cord watched her lift her chin, realize her mistake, and draw in on herself again.

"Curiosity."

Cord had seen too much to believe that or to be put off by her attempt to distract. Yet he also knew she was a woman used to getting her way and controlling the narrative. Push too hard and she'd bail. Then again, he wasn't going to just let her jiggle the wires on a brick of C4. "Bullspit."

That gaze now hardened. She really knew how to work those blue eyes, didn't she?

When she didn't shut him down, Cord sensed a hesitation. An opening. "Brooke, whatever it is, I'm the guy to talk to about it."

"Why? Because you're—"

"Because I'm Cord Taggart, CEO of MiLE," he said, intercepting her at the pass. "I've been working this gig for the last decade, and there's not a tactic out there that I haven't had to intercept in trafficking."

When she sat back, he wasn't sure if she was about to rail at him, leave, or what. And he somehow felt like he was supposed to keep his trap shut this time.

"What do you do when someone you ... love is caught up in something very ... bad?"

"Trafficking."

She held his gaze, neither affirming nor denying.

This wasn't the time to back down. "I get that you want to protect someone, but not talking doesn't do that. Silence is the grave in which trafficking buries its victims. Keeping quiet will only jeopardize this person."

Her blue eyes turned into sapphire pools. "I can't ..."

Cord frowned. "Brooke, I'm not going to tell—"

"It's not that."

"Then what? Your brothers—"

"No!" She was on her feet.

"They can help."

"Did you not hear me? I said no. They can't ..." She slung her purse over her shoulder and brushed her hair from her face. "They can't know. It's not my secret to tell and I promised."

"That's not a promise worth keeping, Brooke—"

"Maybe you compromise your word, but I don't."

It'd gone downhill from there. Two minutes later, they were leaving, a stiff awkwardness trailing him as he headed to baggage claim with only a marginal agreement from her that they'd talk later.

Only, he'd gone to help Range, and she ... well, she'd vanished.

With a groan, Cord ran both hands up his face and cradled his head in his hands, elbows on the table. She'd promised someone ... this guy, obviously—Mazin—that she wouldn't tell his secrets. He hadn't seen it—what she'd meant then. He'd thought she meant one of her kids or a friend. Not a boyfriend. Lover? They *were* living together.

He was going to be sick.

And ticked. Very ticked.

CHAPTER
FOUR

"Never thought I'd see a man like you watching movies like that."

Glancing at the gray-haired woman beside him, Cord retrieved his phone from the brace attached to the seat in front of him. "You and me both. A girl I know has posters from them on her walls. Thought I'd check them out."

"Watch out," teased the older woman next. "Start watching movies like that, and next thing you know—you're married with four kids."

"A guy can hope."

That earned him a broad smile. As the plane taxied to the gate, Cord checked his phone. Saw a half dozen messages but none were the one he wanted. He rubbed his eyes and sighed, trying to shake the last umpteen hours trapped in this tin can that left him with nothing but time to think the worst.

Though frustrated that she hadn't read her brothers in on what was happening—men who were special operators who would've dealt with the danger she toyed with—Cord couldn't blame anyone but himself that she was now missing. Caught up in a dark world he knew all too well. She'd been reaching out for months asking questions. He had known things were off. And what was the one thing he'd always told everyone?

Silence enables.

And how had he responded?

By doing nothing.

Now she was MIA.

God forgive me … help me. Please.

He wouldn't forgive himself if Brooke ended up in a ditch or worse—never found. Pinching the bridge of his nose, he warded off the overwhelming sense that things were very bad. That she had gotten way in over her head. What had possessed her to chase after kids that weren't her own. Where was the dad? Was he with them, too?

They had to be serious to live together, right? Personally, it wasn't a thing he'd ever do, but he knew a lot of couples did it nowadays. Had to admit he felt a little disappointed in Brooke. And hurt. She could've just told him she was dating someone. Or were they engaged?

He was going to be sick. Or was that angry? Both, probably.

His phone buzzed in his hand, and he glanced at the screen, then answered it. "Jess. Talk to me."

"A driver is waiting at baggage claim, and he'll ferry you to the base, where Omen is waiting."

"So, you found her." Pulse amped at her words, he dragged his ruck from beneath the seat in front of him, accidentally bumping the woman in the seat next to him. "Sorry." But airplane seats nowadays were sized for children, not adults. He switched his phone to the other ear, elbow hitting the bulkhead. Maybe it was not the size of the seats but the size of the operator …

"Indirectly," Jess said. "We've been working those messages like you asked. Pulled in a friend of mine, Mercy, who was able to backtrace them. They were sent from an app tied to Brooke's phone account. The app sent those messages via an IP address that belongs to a hospital in Lingya District in Kaohsiung City."

Hospital. Lingya. Kaohsiung. "Did you—"

"Immediately called them," Jess said with a heavy sigh. "But it looks like we were too late. She's not there."

He bit back a curse. Eyeballed the front of the plane as passengers started disembarking. "Okay, stay on it. I'm deplaning now."

"Will do. Stay safe, boss."

"Never." Cord smirked at his old joke—staying safe didn't get the job done. Staying smart and alert did. Deplaned, he stopped in the restroom to relieve himself, then hoofed it to baggage claim. Even as he strode toward the right carousel, he picked up on potential trouble spots. Cues. His gaze hit a particularly large black man fighting with a soda machine, his attention skating to Cord. Then there was the guy at the unmanned information booth. The dude striding toward him.

He sniffed. "Not very subtle," he said as he gripped the hand of the five-nine mountain of muscle that slammed into his right shoulder.

"Subtle is boring." Pike Auberon slapped his back. The guy wasn't tall but he more than made up for that in his ability to operate and address threats. "Good to see you, man."

"Same." Cord nodded, spotted his ruck on the carousel and snagged it.

They headed out, and he might be able to breathe now that he'd connected with Omen Tactical Group on the job. OTG had connections Cord only wished he could cobble together. Even after all these years, all his cooperative efforts with local authorities around the globe, he still felt like his hands were tied half the time.

The big black guy took the ruck and flung into the back as if it were a pebble. "Good to see your slow butt, Tag."

"Landry." Cord sniffed a laugh, both at the derisive comment and the nickname, and climbed into the SUV. He was half surprised the wheels would turn with what had to easily be an added half ton of weight with these operators. His buddy Lowell butted shoulders and patted his back. "Glad you made it."

"Wouldn't miss this party for the world."

"You remember Tycho," Pike said, his well-muscled arm dangling over the steering wheel as he signaled to the guy who climbed in with them.

Cord nodded. "Appreciate the help on this."

"Think we owe it to Range." Pike raced toward Subic Bay.

"How's that?"

"Whole lotta messed-up happened in Afghanistan," Landry's deep voice rattled from the middle row.

"We left him high and dry," Tycho said.

Cord eyeballed the guy, then Landry and Pike. "Think I missed that part of the AAR."

"Things went south fast—corrupt Brass tried to set up Pretty Boy to come home feet first." Pike shook his head and scratched a beard sprinkled through with a little silver. "Showed me how deep and high the Trench went."

"And that's just one arm of the network," Cord muttered, turning his gaze out the window as they headed to the base. "Taweel Abdul-Ghulam was only one of a half dozen lieutenants answering to the big dog, who is still an unknown." He eyed the buildings and greenery whizzing by.

Pike absorbed the information for a few klicks. "So this whatever-it-is with Metcalfe's sister might be connected to that?"

"No proof, but my gut says yes."

With a cockeyed nod, Pike swiped a hand over his beard. "Read us in."

From start to finish—that being today—Cord spelled out everything that had happened. There wasn't any way to avoid mentioning Daghestani, and it ticked him off. Again. By the time he'd relayed all he knew, they were pulling up to the base security checkpoint. After clearing it, they made their way to a large crossbred building that was part warehouse, part barracks. There they connected with the remainder of Auberon's team: Tariq Wadi and red-headed and -bearded Brick Archer.

Tycho snorted and thumped Cord's shoulder from the rear passenger seat. "So, you're putting life and limb on the line for a chick who's doing the dude whose kids went missing?"

Anger shot through Cord. He glowered at the guy.

"Go ahead," Landry rumbled. "Punch him. I'll hold him for you."

Cord had considered it, but he tucked the anger aside. "Doesn't matter who Daghestani is—what matters is that he and his kids were taken from the streets. Brooke tried to find them and now she's missing, too."

"Except maybe she's not," Brick Archer said, jutted his red-bearded chin to his Iraqi counterpart.

Wadi inclined his head solemnly. "I have narrowed it down to two patients in the hospital."

"Narrowed down—wait, so you *know* she's there? In a hospital."

"Hold up," Auberon said shifting in between Cord and Wadi. "Sorry. Wadi likes to get to the point."

"It is usually most efficient."

"We don't *know* she's there," Auberon countered. "What he has is a theory drawn from a series of facts."

"True," Wadi conceded with another nod. "The messages you received were sent via an app—"

"I know where—"

"—that was on a tablet registered to a teen girl named Wu Ming. Said female was in hospital following surgery. I accessed the hospital's system and ascertained that she is in a room with three other patients. A Frenchwoman and a Taiwanese."

"Okay ... but what—" Cord hauled in a breath. *French...* Could it be that easy? "What was the Frenchwoman's name?"

After a momentary frown, Wadi glanced at the laptop, scrolling and clicking. "Uh ... Ariane Chavasse."

"That's her." *Please don't ask how I know.* Heart thumping, he grabbed his phone. "What hos—"

"Already on it," Wadi said, lifting his own phone to his ear.

Cord faltered, wanting to do the work on this. Hated having to trust a man he didn't know.

"Hey." Auberon shouldered in, forcing Cord to shift his gaze to him. "Want to explain the name?"

Crap. "I—" Nope, not going to say he'd watched the movies. "She loves Audrey Hepburn." He didn't need to mention where the name came from—a character in the movie *Love in the Afternoon*—because they'd just ask how he knew that.

"That so?" Auberon's expression never wavered, but there was a glint of amusement in his eyes. "And you're a movie expert on this Aubrie—"

"Audrey."

"Huh." Pike smirked.

Cord had fallen right into that one. "Don't start w—"

"She's there!" Wadi announced, rising from his chair. "She's still there. We need to hurry—it looks like she's slated for discharge."

Auberon clapped Cord's shoulder as he turned to the guys. "Wheels-up, gents. Let's move!"

Kaohsiung City, Taiwan

"Okay, time to walk!"

Brooke groaned.

Nurse Min flicked her fingers at her, shooing Brooke off the bed. "You need to walk. Staying in bed is not good. We need you to walk so you can go home."

Home. If only that were possible right now … And getting discharged meant she'd be on her own. Out there. No money, no phone, no ID. She had no idea where to go … maybe find the U.S. Embassy.

No. No, she couldn't do that without the kids. Besides, they were probably monitoring it to see if she showed up. She'd been an idiot to think she could do this on her own, but Mazin had been so adamant about the family not finding out.

"Come on," Nurse Min insisted, coming around the other side of her bed. "I help you. Rotate your body."

Admittedly it was a relief to get out of bed, because she'd been forced to sleep upright, and the brace did little to alleviate the pain. She shifted to the side of the bed, gritting through the pain. Perched on the edge, she allowed Nurse Min to slip a pair of socks on her for the journey around the ward. The nurse's assistance hurt more than it helped, but as Brooke planted her feet on the cold floor, she felt the chill radiate through the material. Coming up, she spied her backpack on an open cabinet in the corner.

Standing, she felt Nurse Min grip her brace firmly. Thankfully, the velcroed brace kept her hospital gown shut. Though she would've preferred jeans and a sweater to ward off the perpetual chill that hung in the air. She shuffled her way through the halls, making a complete circuit of the third floor.

"Almost there," Nurse Min said, indicating to the room she'd shared with iPad girl.

Frantic Mandarin flew down the hall, asking for Min's help. Her nurse hesitated.

"Go ahead," Brooke said, bolstering her courage and strength. Eyeballed her room again. "I can get back on my own."

"You sure?"

"Of course. Go." Using the handrail that lined the wall, she covered the last twenty feet. At least she wasn't in tears this time but the pain was some kind of special. With an exhale, she moved to the cabinet, retrieved her backpack, and opened it. She dug through it and deflated—no idea what she'd thought she'd find in there. Just some vain hope that her wallet or phone would magically appear? Foolish. She knew better, since she'd discarded everything that could be traced. Whatever it took to interrupt their ability to track her. Once, she'd picked up a throw-away phone. But she'd used it, and it had to be discarded too. Even here, she'd used a false name to protect herself.

Easing onto the bed, she once again found herself wishing Cord was here. It was crazy how much she wanted to talk to him. He had a good mind. Quick wit. Made her smile. Body wasn't bad, but she'd long ago learned some of the cruelest personalities were bulked up behind hair gel and slick suits. Besides, she did not doubt that she'd get an earful from the MiLE founder with his knowing grin and pretty eyes that were marked with a sharp awareness of what happened in the world.

He's military, Brooke. Everything you despise.

Not everything. This nightmare with the kids showed her there was much worse than alpha heroes who thought every woman had to be rescued and every threat dealt with using violence.

A man's voice drew her attention down the hall. Her breath hitched, half thinking Cord had found her. But that was foolish. She'd hidden her every step. Used a false name. Nobody knew where she was.

Except …

Oh no.

Her gaze shot to the far end of the ward where—

Him! The man who'd chased her. Hunted her. She didn't know his name but she had his face memorized.

She had to get out of here. Heart pounding, Brooke jerked to the side—pain exploded through her ribs. She bit back a yelp and went rigid. Gritted as she stood and grabbed her backpack. Dug out her pants and sweater.

Side-eyed the man as he demanded someone help him. Brooke struggled and bit through the pain as she stuffed herself into the sweater. Thankfully, the nurses were unusually busy, likely annoyed by his rudeness. She threaded her legs into the jeans and pulled them up, silent tears sliding down her cheeks as she buttoned them, the compression on her ribs excruciating.

C'mon, c'mon … Too slow!

Shoes on the floor, she wiggled her feet into them. Bent to try and tie them, only to have the edges of her vision ghosting. Blast. She'd have to leave them untied. She snatched her pack and thanked God for adrenaline that was warding off some level of the pain so she could slip out of the room. She held her side to protect her ribs and kept her movements small and quiet.

Easing along the hall, she moved past the smaller nurse's desk—spotted a bottle of pills with her name on it, snagged it as she scouted the man, now leaning on the counter. Still waiting.

Good.

She headed to the elevator as she tucked the pills in her bag. Moving fast wasn't happening, so all she could do was put one foot in front of the other … slowly. Once inside, she knew temptation would exist to feel relieved, to relax. It'd be a terrible mistake. She'd learned that the hard way. Every time she had dropped her guard while looking for Caliyah and Jihan, that man had found her.

On the ground floor, she edged out of the elevator with care, meticulously picking the path of least jarring. She worried about the highly polished floor as she made her way to the glass doors.

Standing under the awning outside gave her a moment to catch her breath, scan the narrow street lined with cars. New York City had some anorexic streets, but this beat that by a mile. Cars … so many … What if the man wasn't alone? Her heart thumped at the thought. Scrutinizing the vehicles parked along the curb—was the man alone?—she was relieved to see only compact cars, as one would expect here.

She negotiated the steps and banked to the left.

Holy fires, it hurt to breathe. She wanted to slow down but knew she couldn't. He'd discover her gone soon enough and would rush down to find her. Time was short—and her breath even shorter. Merciful heavens, how had she gotten into such a mess? She tripped over a crack in the sidewalk and pitched forward. The punishing pain made her cry out.

Brooke bit her tongue as she forced herself to keep moving. Did he know she'd escaped yet? How on earth had he even found her? Again, she wondered if he was alone. Though she wanted to look back, she knew better.

Eyes forward, keep moving.

Cross the street. Staggering to the side, she looked for moving vehicles. Missed the edge of the curb and stepped down hard. Agony rattled up her spine. "Augh!" Tears rushed over her cheeks. She clenched her jaw and eyes. Batted at the tears as she took a steadying moment. Shuddered through the pain and urge to vomit. Forced one foot in front of the other.

The great challenge of hurrying yet being careful with her injury proved distracting and exhausting. All this effort and she was only halfway down the street.

Then she did the thing she told herself not to do—she looked back.

A blur swept out of the hospital and paused on the steps.

No! Panic shoved her around. Pain tangled her brain and legs. She felt herself going down. Caught herself on a car, the thud preternaturally loud to her own ringing ears. Used the hood to push herself onward.

Heard the thunder of his steps.

No … No no no …

She tried to run, but the pain was too blinding.

"Stop!" he barked from behind.

A car screeched to a halt on her left. She blurred in that direction, saw the luxury SUV. Doors opened.

"No."

Two men stepped out.

God, help me!

Brooke shoved onward, tears blinding her.

Hands grabbed her. Yanked her backward.

She screamed amid the excruciating fire radiating through her. Crumpled beneath the wave of torment. Felt herself being lifted … carried … shut in the back of the SUV. Drowned in black.

CHAPTER
FIVE

Flanked by Landry and Auberon, Cord stalked up the side steps into the hospital, where a handful of local police were waiting by the elevator. A call Jess had arranged. He really needed to pay her more. The familiar face of Lin Nai was framed with even more silver than Cord remembered.

"Thank you for coming," Cord said as they shook hands. "How's your daughter?"

The police chief gave an appreciative smile. "Healing, thanks to your organization."

They'd run an op here last year in which a dozen had been girls were on the verge of being shipped out of country. MiLE operators had worked with some SEALs to retrieve them on open water. "Glad to hear it," Cord said and angled to introduce OTG. "This is my friend, Pike Auberon, who is working with me on this mission. His men, Landry, Archer, Wadi, and Tycho."

Pike and Nai exchanged handshakes as they moved into the elevator.

"I've brought Chiu Yu-ting," the police chief said, motioning to the female officer wearing a dark blue jacket over a gray-blue shirt, "as the woman you seek is in the women's surgical ward."

Thin and pretty, the officer gave a half smile. "I have called ahead to the nurse who was attending Ms. Chavasse," Yu-ting said. "She is expecting us."

Cord nodded. "Thank you." He wouldn't give anyone Brooke's real name that didn't need to know.

On the third floor, they made their way to the nurse's station. The sights and smells of the sanitized facility grated. He'd been in too many hospitals, seen too many deaths—so many that he now had a permanent association between the two.

Yu-ting stepped out first and headed to the left, where a large semicircular desk sat like a sentry in front of a long hall. "Nurse Min."

A diminutive but stern nurse with her short, blunt hair stood and gave a sharp nod. "I am glad to help however I can," she said in English.

"These are the men I told you about," Yu-ting said.

"The patient, Ariane Chavasse—"

"You, too?" Nurse Min huffed a laugh. "Another man was just here, asking about her. She is very pretty to have so many handsome men looking for her."

Tension ratcheted.

"What room?" he demanded, afraid they were already too late.

Her gaze shifted down the hall, and before she could answer, he was already in motion.

"Two-thirty-five," she called after him.

He jogged past one room after another. Avoided an orderly with an empty food tray. Cord checked room placards with the number in Mandarin and English. Skidded to a stop at 235 and shot inside.

Three beds sat empty—two made, one in disarray. A

bathroom door was ajar, and he darted there. Vacant. He backed out and turned, saw a hospital gown on the floor. Crap.

"She was here not five minutes ago," Nurse Min said, distressed. "The other man say he a friend."

Pike and Cord shared a glance. Where had she gone? "She could've have gotten—"

A scream spiraled from outside.

Pike shot to the window and peered up the street, then down— "There! Black SUV."

Cord and Landry bolted down the hall. Skipped the elevator—too slow—and took the stairs, vaulting down them four and five at a time. Thirty seconds later, they busted out the front door and off the steps.

Cord paused, checking the street.

The peal of tires yanked his attention to the left. Saw the black SUV. Weapon out, he stalked forward as it barreled up the street. He moved between two cars and aimed as it raced toward him. Edging out, he firmed his stance and trained his reticle on the SUV.

Noted the burly driver, gaze suddenly diverted to him. In the passenger seat, a well-dressed man. The vehicle was closing the gap.

He didn't know where Brooke was in that Suburban, so he couldn't risk firing. And they were coming too fast. Cord shifted his aim to the tires. Squeezed off a round. The bullet ricocheted off the bumper.

The driver yanked the wheel toward Cord, the SUV accelerating with an angry roar.

Crap! Cord hurled himself backward. His spine struck a car as he hauled his legs up. The SUV skimmed the car, thrusting it sideways, effectively pitching Cord head over heels across the other side. He rolled into a landing and came up running after it. Could not let it get away. Not with Brooke.

When he saw it bank a hard left, tires screaming as it did, Cord knew he'd failed.

Then his gaze shifted to the mountain of muscle standing on the corner—Landry shifted and grinned at him. "You and your slow butt ..."

Cord cursed, kicked the nearest car. Left a dent. He punched it. Threw another in the air at the escaping SUV as it slid out of sight. In the street, he threw another air punch. "Augh!" Raking his hands over his face, Cord bent forward. Felt every place the car had impacted him. But none compared to the place this failure hit—his heart. And it'd hit hard.

"Chill, Big C."

"Chill?" Cord growled. "Are you kidding me—we lost her!"

Fingers threaded on his head, he turned a circle, as if she'd be there. Somehow hadn't gotten in the car. He'd be redeemed.

Son of—

Something in the street caught his attention. He stilled, then headed toward it, almost missing the small black sedan sliding up the street toward him. Cord angled to the side and moved toward the thing. A medication bottle. Mandarin characters were followed by English—Ariane Chavasse.

His heart clenched. *I failed you ...*

"Hey, Tag. I got you, man." Stalking toward him, Landry held up his phone. "Snagged pictures of them and the plates."

It was a thin hope that it'd get them any results.

"Hey." Auberon jogged toward him. "We've got some friends in-country. Let's head there. Wadi can dig into the hospital surveillance and hopefully get us some intel. We'll run the images Landry captured."

Swallowing his pride—he should've been the one thinking of those things and doing those things—Cord slid another hand over his bald head. "Yeah." He had to get it together or she'd end up dead. "Right. Let's go."

For the third time he scanned the street, unable to shake that erroneous hope that she was still here. That he hadn't been too late. Like he'd been with Fallon.

It seemed he blinked and they were pulling into a parking garage, took a spot on the second level that hugged a corner. They entered through a steel door, climbed a flight, then let themselves into a long, narrow hall that was complete fish-in-a-barrel. The three bulbous cameras matched the ones he'd seen in the garage.

The door at the far end clicked open before anyone knocked or pressed the button. Inside, they found a Command room with a handful of men and systems. Though Cord easily had forty pounds on the guy coming toward them, he had a feeling this man wasn't someone to mess with. Something about the way he held his hands to the side, chin up, challenge in his blue-green eyes.

"Chapel." Pike grasped the man's hand, bumped shoulders, and gave the guy's back a pat. "Thanks for the space to work." He swung aside. "You know Cord Taggart?"

The man had the moves of a preying tiger. "Not officially." Dark hair trimmed short had a wave to it. "Tyson Chapel."

"Saint," Cord uttered without thinking, recalling how word had spread the guy was anything *but* a saint. "Your reputation precedes you."

"I could say the same for you." The man had a grin that somehow felt lethal. He tucked his hands under his armpits. "Heard you've got some trouble."

Cord tightened his jaw as he took in the men at the various stations around the room—a cowboy, a Latino, a burly guy that reminded him of the actor from that TV show about SEALs, a man with more tattoos than muscles—maybe—and a blond-haired guy. "You heard of Canyon Metcalfe?"

Saint stilled, his gaze shifting to Pike and back. "Who hasn't?"

"His older sister thought she'd hunt down some kids that went missing."

A low whistle came from someone at the table where the cowboy and Latino were eating.

"That's … a problem," Saint said. "Do you realize—"

"Yes." Cord didn't mean to be rude, but he really didn't have the patience for a lecture.

Saint nodded. "Of course you do." He considered him for a long second. "I've heard about what MiLE's doing out there. Respect it on a deep level." He cocked his head. "You ever need operators"—he thrust his jaw over his shoulder—"give us a holler. Damocles will be there."

Surprise rippled through Cord, and he saw the same filter through Omen. "Appreciate it."

"Kiss up," Pike teased. "All talk, Saint. All talk. Put some action behind that like Omen's doing."

The team rivalry thing never got old.

"I'll show you talk." A lightning-fast pop to the back of Pike's head had laughter filtering through the bunker. Then Saint stepped back ready for a counterstrike, and when none came, he pointed to his right. "There's a conference room back there with all the plugs and screens you'll need." He thumbed over his shoulder. "Down the hall on the right is the galley, bunkroom on the left—showers are there, too. Use what you need. Can't find something, give me a shout and we'll get it for you."

"Again, appreciate it." Cord just wanted to get back on track.

An hour later, they were set up in the isolated room and digging into facial recognition on the photos taken by Landry, who was now reviewing all the footage from the hospital. On the far side, Tycho worked his magic to make connections in order to track down those plates on the SUV.

Cord stood over Landry, watching the footage.

"I swear—just going to the store for some feminine products."

Dang, he hated when she mentioned that stuff. "Just be back before dinner. You know Mom will blister us both if you're not here when she gets home from work."

"I know what she said," Fallon growled. "What do you want me to do—blee—"

"Go! Go already." He went back to his books, finished the assignment due tomorrow. After printing off the research paper, he glanced at the clock—did it really take that long to get what she needed? She was always messing around, though—and snatched his controller. Started the game he'd downloaded last night.

Without warning, a smack sent his headphones flying from his ears and onto the desk, clattering across his keyboard.

"What th—"

"Cord Wilson Taggart," Mama shouted as she stood over him. Shoved him out of the chair, causing a painful collision of his tailbone against the hardwood floor. "I've been hollering for you! Where is your sister?"

"You holding it together?"

The quiet question pulled Cord from the memory. "Yeah." It was more grunt than words, and more lie than truth. But both were better than coughing up the truth and falling prey to one of Pike's mentoring sessions.

"You sure about that?"

Cord faltered. Looked at the guy. What had he missed?

Pike nodded. "Thought so. Landry ID'd the guy who went into the hospital."

Gaze shooting to the screen in front of him, Cord registered the face. "That's him—the guy who was in the SUV."

"That," Landry said, backstepping over the chair and positioning himself at his side, thick arms folded over his chest, "is one Jürgen Volker. Age forty-five, Swiss-German, currently residing in Munich. Employed by Graben Pharmaceuticals."

Brain lagged, Cord frowned. "Why does that sound familiar?"

"It is owned by none other than"—Landry held the name

until they looked at him, and he lifted his eyebrows—"Gunnar Sauer."

Cord hissed a breath, his gut roiling. Just once—why couldn't he be wrong?

"Son of a—" Pike bit off his curse and shook his head. "So, this is definitely trafficking."

"*Ja, mein Freund,*" Landry said in butchered German.

There hadn't really been a doubt in Cord's mind that it was trafficking. What unsettled him more, what made him want to blow chunks, was that these threads, this happenstance of Brooke knowing kids who were taken, going after them—she had inadvertently drawn the ferocious attention of Gunnar Sauer, who had been implicated in Kasra Jazani's ordeal … and Willow Metcalfe's … likely even with Brighton Metcalfe's. Though he couldn't definitely draw the lines connecting the dots, Cord had a bad feeling.

It was a very real and terrible probability that Brooke had dropped down a rabbit hole right into one of history's most notorious and untouchable trafficking rings—the Trench.

CHAPTER
SIX

Unknown Location, Taiwan

Merciless and relentless, pain dragged her from the thick embrace of unconsciousness. A lowing echoed around her—what was that sound? Lifting her head, Brooke shifted—and tensed. Yelped. Pain throbbed in her side and head. She had been the sound—her own moaning of pain. Her cheeks were wet from tears she'd shed in her sleep.

Despite blinking, she could not see anything. Was she blind? Had she hit her head or something?

Clanging and a scraping of something against metal stilled her.

It all came back to her in a rush—the hospital, the man ... escaping ... then not.

With a groan, she slumped back down. Felt the cold, hard concrete beneath her palm. Where was she?

Chattering nearby made her hold her breath. Was she imagining that?

"Hello?" she said quietly, her voice croaking. "Is someone there?"

"Sh, miss," a child hissed in Mandarin.

"If they hear, they will hurt us," came another voice. Young. Too young.

Whimpers scampered around her.

Lord, have mercy—how many children were here with her? She was in trouble. So very much trouble. All those months of staying smart, avoiding trouble, evading those who wanted her to stop. That man. All for naught—Caliyah and Jihan ... Who would help them now? Nobody in the City had been willing, which was why she had to. What hope was there for them now? Precious, sweet Caliyah ... and so proud and independent Jihan ... So like his father. Who reminded her so much of Canyon.

She tried not to cry again, but this meant she wasn't going to be able to find or help Jihan and Caliyah. Grief struggled through her chest. Tightened her throat with raw emotion. *I just wanted to help them ...* They were such good children. Had such a hard life, their mother totally failing them.

Just as I failed Kaleigh.

She dragged her legs up closer, and tried to find the best way to sit up with the least amount of pain. She wasn't sure there was a way to accomplish that. The broken ribs were still too angry and newly broken. Pain would be constant. A hydrocodone would—

My backpack!

Even as her hand traced around her, she knew it was gone. The medication, too.

She wilted again. Knowing the statistics on ever seeing them again, she fell into silent tears once more.

"Are we going to die?" a small voice asked, a quaver in the question.

"No," Brooke said firmly, despite her own misgivings. "We will be fine," she replied in Mandarin. *Get up. Be an adult. They need you.*

"You do not know that," an older one bit out angrily.

Brooke learned long ago from her mother that anger was a masking emotion and hid what was beneath. And this time, it hid fear. So much fear she could almost taste it, because she was scared, too. Terrified. But time to get herself together. Think. Act.

Keeping herself stiff and careful with her moves, she pried herself off the concrete. Sat up, strained against the darkness to take in her surroundings. Pitch black defied her vision, forbade her from seeing.

Wait—what was that?

A tinge of gray stole into her awareness, a lightening of the ebony void. What ...? The thin thread of light glimmered somewhere in front of her, out of reach. What if it was a door or window? A way out ...?

Bracing her sides with her arms—trying to avoid using her core, which constricted her ab muscles and stabbed her through with more pain—Brooke struggled to stand with more than a few grunts or whimpers. On her feet, she wobbled, getting her balance a task without light. She shuffled forward.

"What are you doing?" someone—sounded like a teen—asked in Mandarin.

Brooke ignored the question and moved toward the spot that seemed to lighten the closer she got. Her vision must be adjusting to the darkness, because she could make out shapes and the forms against the wall.

Clanging and clinking echoed in the place. As she squinted and strained, an impression formed in her mind of the place they were being held—large, open, empty ... A warehouse?

Only as she stood there did she realize ... it was getting brighter ... and brighter. Her breath backed into her throat. It wasn't her vision that was adjusting. It was the light—headlamps. A vehicle getting closer.

She turned with more than a little jolt of pain even as a

pervasive groaning ruptured the quiet, black veil of the warehouse.

Light erupted from the side.

Brooke cringed away and her ribs punished her for it. She shifted and stumbled.

"What're you doing?" someone shouted in Mandarin as the thuds of car doors warned of incoming trouble.

Light clanked and popped overhead, illuminating the space— and their captors. Dressed in black tactical gear and carrying automatic rifles.

"Up!" the closest one shouted. "Everyone up. Against the wall. Hands on your head."

Brooke tried to count the number of men, gauge their weapons. Not that she had any training or ability to disarm them …

"You! Go!" A heavily bearded man held his weapon parallel to the ground and thrust it at her, knocking her sideways. "Hands on your head!"

With a yelp, Brooke took the cue. Stumbled toward the others, wincing as she lifted her hands slowly … so very slowly … could not reach her head without a searing rebuke from her ribs. Children. A dozen of them, ranging in age from four or five all the way up to teens. To her.

Three men rushed in with chains and began tethering the children's legs to one another.

"You will not escape!" Thick-Beard snarled. "Do not try. We will shoot and kill you. If you want to live, comply."

Lifting her chin, Brooke felt everything in her want to defy him. Stupidly. She had no hope of escaping with her broken ribs. Couldn't run. Couldn't fight.

I'm trapped …

No, worse. She was captive.

"Against the wall," snarled Thick-Beard—nearly in her ear. Used his fat chest to urge her away.

Not good. Not good at all. She moved toward the others, scanning the line to make sure she hadn't somehow missed Jihan or Caliyah. Even as she stepped into place, a man caught her ankle. Reflex jerked her foot—which stung her side—but the man's gaze snapped up at her. Chest rising and falling unevenly, she couldn't help but think about the decidedly dead-end nature of what was happening.

"The chain or two bullets," Thick-Beard barked. "Your choice."

Brooke swallowed, her gaze on the boss as the smaller guy slipped the cold, unforgiving steel around her ankle. Clacked it together. The trickling sensation of the chain being pulled through the loop rattled up her leg.

Panic swarmed her.

The nine-year-old girl next to her screamed and struggled against being chained.

Enraged at the outcry, Thick-Beard lifted his rifle and thinned his lips.

"No!" Brooke flung a hand in his direction even as she reached for the girl, the quick movement brutal, but she would not let this man kill the girl. "Hey." She cupped the girl's face, brought her gaze to hers. "It will be better if we are quiet ... for now."

Wide eyes pooled with tears begged her to make this stop. To save her.

Yes, be the adult, Brooke. Put your big-girl panties on and stop thinking of yourself for once.

She reached down and took the girl's hand in hers, gave her a nod. "What's your name?"

"Himeko."

Brooke smiled. "A very pretty name," she said in Mandarin. "We will stay together, yes?"

Himeko nodded mournfully.

Soon, all linked up, they were ordered to walk toward the

idling truck that had arrived. The men tossed the children up into the back of the white paneled delivery truck as if they were no more than sacks of grain. When they hoisted her up, Brooke fought through the pain. But her hand slipped. She thudded against the side. Screamed—and bit down on it.

The guard reared back to strike her with the weapon.

"No!" Thick-Beard shouted. "Look."

They glanced at her side and saw the brace she still sported.

Thick-Beard grunted. Jutted his jaw toward the truck. "Get in."

Brooke maneuvered up into the bed and scooched along, her chains clanging as she did. A man moved from one girl to the next, doing ... something. Only when he shifted to the girls on her side did Brooke catch sight of the hypodermic needle.

She drew in a breath and froze as he made his way toward her. God, help me ...

The girls on the far side were yawning, slumping into unconsciousness ... She strained to see their chests ... rising and falling. So, not dead.

Tensed, she watched as the needle swung toward her. Instinct had her lifting her hand to block it, but before she could even attempt to stop him, she saw the blur of a weapon slamming toward her head. Pain radiated through her neck and exploded through her side.

She dropped back with a shout, tears spilling out of their own volition. In the cacophony of pain came the prick of a needle. In minutes, the door was rolled down, locked, and the truck lurched into motion. Grief tore at her, knowing every minute, every mile took her farther from her intended purpose—to find Caliyah and Jihan. They were lost now. She was lost.

No, she was *captive.*

Was this about trafficking? Was that where they were

headed? Never before had she felt so powerless ... Fear stole in as she lost the battle of consciousness to the drug they'd injected.

CHAPTER
SEVEN

Judgment came in the form of three brothers with more tactical experience than most of the men in this room combined. Cord had worked with each of them at one time or another, but he'd never had a gut-level reaction to seeing them enter a room. Until now.

Maybe that was his guilty conscience quaking in its boots.

He smoothed a hand over his beard, then up over his bald head as Canyon, Range, and Leif strode toward him with all the confidence and intensity of a pack of wolves prowling enemy territory. He inclined his head to the eldest of three who had lasered in on him.

"It's been two days since she was taken," Canyon stated flatly, his lips tight. "What do you know?"

"Little." Cord indicated to Landry. "This is Luther Landry of Omen. He'll get you read in."

Gaze locked on Landry, Canyon swung a hand to Cord and pressed it against his chest. "No." He turned to face him and thumped his chest. "*You* tell us."

Why did this feel so much like getting dressed down by the

Brass? "I—" He choked on his own spit. Cleared his throat. "I—"

"What is this?" Stern-faced, Pike stood at the door, hands on his tac belt, glowering at Canyon. He stepped down into the Command area, scowling as he erased the gap between them. "You come up in here like you own the place—"

Range met him halfway. "Stand down, Auberon."

Pike faltered, holding his gaze, regret clearly scratched into his features. "I know I owe you an apology for Kandahar, but this—"

"Skip it," Range said with more than a little irritation. "We need answers and he's going to give them."

All three pairs of blue eyes blazed, taking him in. It was the silent one—Leif—who unnerved him most. He'd heard about the things this guy had been responsible for, the ops he'd carried out, the woman Ukrainian spy he'd married. Then again, he'd rarely seen Canyon ticked like this. So that had to be considered.

Nostrils flaring, the five-nine former Navy SEAL stared at them. "Using Taggart as a punching bag isn't going to help anyone's cause, especially not Brooke's. In fact, Taggart is your best chance of helping her."

"This punk," Canyon snarled, "had multiple chances to interdict and protect Brooke's *cause*, but he had his head in the wrong place and now she's MIA."

Enough. Cord palmed Canyon's wrist and closed his grip as he shoved it to the side. He swung around in a fluid move and pulled Canyon with him.

Weight plowed into him from the left. Range or Leif. Canyon plowed his shoulder into Cord's chest and rammed upward, knocking his throat. Though everything in Cord screamed to fight back, take Midas to ground, he knew that this ... this was what he deserved. The retaliation of Brooke's brothers. A swift punch or two in the gut.

In the split-second the guy pushed backward and Cord tried

to shift around to avoid the elbow to the gut, he felt both arms being hoisted. Hooked backward. He thudded against the wall, air punching from his chest. Range and Leif each pinned an arm, their expressions lethal.

Canyon moved in like a storm.

Cord braced for impact. Knew this would hurt. Knew this was good. He needed to be punished.

Face red with fury, Canyon barreled at him. Drew back his fist and slid in for the strike.

Calling on his training, one to take a punch, he closed his mouth and jaw, pulling his tongue from his teeth. Tucked his chin. Relaxed his posture and muscles.

Shoulder connecting—but not hurting—Canyon pressed into him.

Confusion rankled Cord. Why wasn't he hurting yet? He held himself still, tried to stay relaxed, anticipating the real strike. His head warred with him, told him that's what Midas was waiting for—a hard surface to crack.

Straightening, hand slapping Cord's cheek, Canyon edged back. "You are so easy, Taggart."

What ...? *What?*

Nervous jitters released in half-laughs around the room as the guys all considered one another.

"Glad you had the good sense to pull that punch, Midas," Landry said. "I sure hate to mess up a legend."

Cocky as ever, Canyon smirked. "Nah, that'd be my buddy, Griffin."

Landry frowned, clearly not getting the joke—Griffin Riddell of the original Nightshade team had earned the callsign Legend.

"So, you're not mad?" Cord clearly didn't have a brain today, asking that question, drawing attention back to himself and this fiasco. "I mean, I know all three of you want to rearrange my face."

Leif "Runt" Metcalfe jutted his jaw. "We've all been in ops

long enough to know it's unrealistic to place blame on one man. Even if he is entirely to blame."

Chagrined, Cord lowered his gaze. Rubbed the jaw they hadn't struck. "I own that."

"Nah," Canyon said. "I mean, fair level of blame rests on those log-thick shoulders of yours, but you forget—she was our sister. We know all too well that nobody can make Brooke stand down once her mind is set to something."

"And especially if it's a man telling her to do it," Range offered.

Leif snorted. "Really, it's anyone—she's never liked being told what to do. She raised most of us, so she's used to handing out the orders."

Canyon sidled closer. "You sure that's a fire you want to mess with?"

"Fire or not, I screwed up. If it's the last thing I ever do, I'll get her back—alive."

Nodding, Canyon skated his gaze up and down Cord. "That's why you aren't breathing through your mouth right now." He lifted his phone. "Mind if we loop in Stone to keep him abreast of the situation?"

Luther helped him cast the call onto a screen.

Once Stone was uplinked and introductions made, Canyon spoke. "So, like I asked when I first got here—what do you know?"

"Little," Cord repeated. "Omen ran some facial rec on a guy who showed at the hospital where Brooke had been taken—"

"Why was she in the hospital?" Range asked.

"Hit by a car. Two broken ribs. There was concern that one of the broken ribs had punctured an organ. Holiday weekend, short-staffed, the hospital couldn't run the tests right away, so they checked her in to monitor her."

"Back to the guy." Canyon notoriously stayed on mission.

"Jürgen Volker, CEO of Graben Pharmaceuticals, showed up minutes before we did."

"To kill her?"

Stretching his jaw, Cord hesitated, considered the brothers. Hated keeping a secret from them, but that wasn't relevant … yet. "I don't think so."

Blue eyes narrowed—on all three brothers. It was kind of creepy.

"If he wanted to kill her," he explained, "we'd have been picking up her body off the street. But they took her."

"Trafficking?" Stone asked, his connection sounding tinny.

"Most likely." For the next half hour Cord ran through their reasoning, showed the ley lines between the different cases— Brighton, Willow, Kasra, and now Brooke. The brothers listened intently, asked sharp questions, but they repeatedly came back to one question: Why Brooke?

"The missing kids," Cord posited, knowing it was opening the proverbial can of worms, but it couldn't be avoided.

"They were in the City, too?" Leif asked.

With a slow nod, Cord eyed Stone sitting at his desk back in Virginia, looking as noble and don't-mess-with-me as ever. Except … that expression. It flickered away so fast, Cord wasn't sure he saw it.

No, I know I saw it. I just don't know what it was.

"That's what's so whack," Range said. "Brooke doesn't give two wits about kids. Why on earth is she breaking her neck for these two?"

"What about the father?"

Over Canyon's shoulder, Stone again flinched. "What do you know about him, Taggart?"

"Less than I know about the kids." It was an honest-if-not-evasive answer. "Thirty-five, lived in the City, worked as a shift leader at an Italian eatery. Immigrated from"—*should probably keep it vague*—"the Middle East."

"The mother?" Range asked.

"Unknown. As far as I was able to figure, not in their lives. Possibly dead. Her name wasn't on any of the kids' school records." But Brooke's sure was.

Was it wrong to keep this from them?

You know dang well it is. But how could he violate the explicit request from Brooke? Yet … hadn't that been a request made when she'd been safe? He had to tell them. Though he'd not been able to do anything with the intel, hadn't unearthed anything … maybe they could.

"What?" Canyon demanded, blue gaze locked on Cord. "I know that look."

"Just sorting through what I've been told and processing my own confusion over why she dropped everything to look for these kids."

"Bullspit."

Cord's heart thumped hard at that challenge. He held Canyon's gaze.

"Give it to us," Canyon said, "because so help me God, if she dies and you could've done something to stop it, I will kill you."

"I'll do it for you." Cord sighed and decided there was nothing for it. "She was living with the kids … and father." He cocked his head. "More accurately, they were living with her at the penthouse."

"Hold up—my sister was living with this guy—as in *lovers*?" Leif snorted a laugh. "I suddenly feel the need to find the guy just to apologize to him."

"Shut up, man," Range said. "Remember, you're talking about our sister, who—"

"Yeah. Talking about our sister who never let us live down a single thing. And she's alive, so I'm not buying into this reverent-nice-guy act."

Canyon popped the back of his little brother's head.

"Taggart."

He flinched and bounced his gaze to the screen, where Stone was leaning in with a weighted expression. "Was the guy her lover?"

Cord wanted to argue, say there was no evidence of that, but those pictures of the four of them, laughing and having a good time ... the little girl's drawing of them all holding hands ... He shrugged. "I ... don't know."

"But you do. Cough it up."

Dang it all. Not the conversation he wanted to have. "I, uh, went to her penthouse, talked with her assistant-slash-housekeeper. There were pictures ... of them ... like they were a family. All indications suggest they were close."

Freak, it hurt to admit that. Gutted him. He'd thought he had a chance. Well, until he'd seen that luxury penthouse that must've cost millions and put her on a pedestal that made her unreachable.

Yet she's banging the guy working at the Italian restaurant?

Wasn't adding up.

Something in his field of vision snagged his attention—Stone. He hadn't missed that reaction.

"Chief! Wadi got something!" shouted Tycho from the phalanx of computer stations.

They all swung in that direction, hope struggling through the thick air.

"What d'you find?" Pike asked, moving to stand behind the guy.

Canyon angled the phone to make sure Stone was part of the convo, too.

"I've been poring over surveillance footage from cameras around the city from cell phones, various security cameras and satellite images. It is working in our favor that Taiwan hosts one of the freest online environments in Asia, with very high rates of internet access and no digital divides."

"In English, Wadi."

The man's thick eyebrows winged up as his dark eyes met the chief's, then skated around the faces of the others. "Since internet is so widely available, it's easy to ghost into devices in the area, see if we can find the van. The system's been scanning since we returned, and we've managed to track the van." He lifted his eyebrows in indication to the screen as he continued working. "The van left the hospital and zipped out to the highway. Traveled west ten klicks, then exited and pulled into this facility." He bobbed his head toward the screen. "Later that night, it emerged, and shortly after, the building exploded."

"Destroying evidence," Pike muttered.

Nodding, Wadi continued, clicking and changing screenshots. "I lost the van for a while but found it about forty klicks north entering a warehouse near the docks. It pulled up and …" His gaze rose to the screen.

Silently, they watched the feed as a stream of people were chained at the ankles and herded into the van one a—

"Slag me. Imma kill someone," Landry snarled. "They're loading *kids*."

"Teens, too," Pike countered as he studied the feed. "Maybe a couple of adults."

Canyon shouldered in, squinted at the grainy feed, and tapped a person helping a small child.

"There!" Cord barked at the same time Canyon said, "That's her—Brooke."

Her brothers gave him a long look.

"Okay, good, good," Pike noted, then indicated to the feed. "Where'd they go?"

Wadi deflated, hands moving deftly over the keyboard, clicking the mouse a dozen more times, all with the team watching over his shoulder. After an awkward sigh, he sagged. "I … can't find it. It's a newer van, so I will work to identify its registration, see if I can hack into the government systems and—"

"No," Cord said. "No back doors. It'll compromise our standing with the local authorities." He'd worked too hard and too long to sacrifice that now, no matter how much he wanted to so they could find Brooke. "Keep it aboveboard. I'll put in a call with my contacts to see if we can get some help."

"That's going to cost time," Canyon countered.

"Likely." Cord tightened his jaw. "I get that you are emotionally invested, but—"

"Emotionally invested?" Range shoved in between them and seemed to grow several inches. "My fist will show you—"

"Hey," Canyon said firmly, patting his brother's shoulder in a "stand-down" manner. "He can't use back doors, but he can't stop us."

The Metcalfes smirked. It was kind of creepy seeing all three brandish that trademark smug smile. And Canyon wasn't wrong. "I hoped you'd say that."

CHAPTER
EIGHT

Splat. Splat. Splat-splat.

The repetitive rhythm thumped Brooke into consciousness, the wet sliding down her face and neck bleeding into the awareness of pain … cold … So very much of both. Her throat was tight, stiff. A shiver wracked her body, yanking her from the last dregs of sleep. Realization rushed over her, reminding her she'd been drugged. That alone forced her to shake off the lingering effects of whatever it was they'd used to knock her and the ch—

The children! She lunged upward—and a violent jolt of agony pitched her back down. Whimpering, guarding her side, she stared up—splat! Something struck her forehead. Only then did she hear the rain … *thwap-thwap-thwapping* above her. The ceiling seemed … furry.

Wait. That couldn't be right. She blinked and her surroundings slowly came into focus. She squinted in the dim light, narrowly avoiding another splat on her face. The ceiling was a roof—a thatched roof. Cradling her side, she struggled to sit up. Angled to the side and rolled upward. Eyed the bamboo walls … Three walls and the one behind her … missing.

She shifted around and stared out the opening. Stretched her neck at the tightness. When she touched her throat, she sucked in a breath. Fingers met cold, hard steel. She frantically probed it, a terrible truth presenting itself—they'd put some kind of shackle on her throat.

She gripped it with both hands, trying to remove it. No. No no no. What were they doing with them? Why throat shackles when their legs were chained?

A whimper to the side drew her gaze there. The older children—teens—were waking, too. It seemed the smaller they were, the longer it was taking for their bodies to metabolize the drug and work it off. It seemed their captors weren't picky about race—there were Asian, Middle Eastern, and African children. Her own American heritage was likely an anomaly in this group, since she'd been captured hunting Caliyah and Jihan.

Two older teens—beautiful with their ebony skin and bright eyes—looked to her. Said something in their language that she couldn't make out. Mandarin she could do, but … "I'm sorry," she said in English. "I can't understand."

The more round-faced of the two smiled. "English. We speak English!"

Brooke started. "Oh." Relief slid through her. "Good." Considering the pain and their dire situation, she could not conjure the excitement the two girls showed, apparently happy to have an ally. Though, Brooke wasn't sure how much of a help she could be in her condition. First thing she needed to know … "Where are the guards?"

"The men," the round-faced girl said, "they go in the house up there."

Brooke frowned as she leaned—slowly, carefully to protect her ribs—to peer out the open side. Five or six huts huddled around a flat, open area. Beyond that the hill rose in steppes up to a flat plateau that boasted a small hut that was far more "home" than the hut she and the children were held in.

"We go now," a boy of probably ten said from the other side. "Hurry. While they are gone." He was shuffling out of the hut when Brooke noticed the shackles were gone.

Why would they unchain them?

Even as a thought formed, she looked up just in time to see the boy racing across the yard. Oh no. "No!" She tried to move fast, but her broken ribs slowed her. "Stop him! It's a—"

A blood-curdling scream rent the early morning.

They jerked in the direction of the terrible sound and saw the boy flopping on the ground like a fish out of water. Only, he wasn't out of the water. The entire field was flooded—he writhed and contorted as sparks sizzled in the chilly morning. "Look away," Brooke said, reaching for the smaller girls near her and covering their eyes as she drew them toward herself. "Don't look," she repeated in Mandarin.

The two little ones threw themselves at her, knocking her injured ribs hard—and hugged her. She gritted her teeth, but would not voice her pain. There were greater problems right now. As she held them close, she mentally touched the metal around her neck. Shock collars.

Dear Lord, what have I gotten myself into?

That boy's death would be seared into her memory for life. She held the girls and met the gazes of the two teens. "The collars," she said in English, knowing the smaller kids wouldn't understand. "They will shock you." Even swallowing had her throat rubbing the shock collar. Had to think about helping the children. She looked at the round-faced girl. "What are your names?"

"Ginika," the round-faced teen said. "She's Adesina. She doesn't want to talk anymore. Not after … what men did."

Brooke's heart squeezed.

"We know Mr. Chiji and Mama Willow will find us."

Brooke's heart spasmed. "Willow?" She widened her eyes. "Will—what did she look like?" This was too wild, too unbelievable. "I have a sister named Willow." Who was in Nigeria … with Chijike Okor— *Are you serious?* "Tall, pretty, blonde hair?"

Ginika gaped. "That is her! This must be God," the girl said. "He put us together here."

With a half smile, Brooke didn't contradict her, no matter the gut-level reaction those words elicited. Mom had been all about God, too, but that didn't stop her from being humiliated and shattered when Dad had his affair. Or stop her from having major back surgery that laid her up for months and contributed heavily to her decline that forced her to move into a stuffy lodge with Brooke's equally stuffy older brother.

Crack! Pop!

The kids recoiled and cried out—as did Brooke, her gaze flicking to the center area where she spotted about ten armed guards and a short, gray-haired woman.

"Let's go! Outside. Now!" It was Thick-Beard, weapon in the air as he fired two more shots.

Brooke bit back the urge to chew him out—shooting into the air was not a benign act and could be just as dangerous as aiming at someone. "Come on," she said, gingerly picking her way out of the small hut.

"You hurt?" Ginika asked.

Around a shaky smile, Brooke stiffened. "I'll be okay." She nodded. "Go on."

The girls headed out and Brooke brought up the rear, every step jarring and excruciating. When the man at the hospital had caught her, he'd further aggravated her injury from the accident. Worry niggled at the back of her brain. They'd held her at the hospital to run tests to check for possible damage to her liver, and she prayed being manhandled hadn't made that possible diagnosis more … definitive.

"I am Mrs. Cheng." The gray-haired woman's calculating gaze roved the gathered children and lingered on a brother-sister pair for a long moment. She lifted her chin and continued her perusal of those around her in a way that seemed to inspect them. "This land around you is my rice farm that has been in my family for many generations. It is time for harvest, and you will do this. The work is hard, but you will not stop until it is done. If you stop ..." She moved to the side and caught the brother of the pair she'd lingered on a moment ago, drew the boy into the circle. Rested her hands on his shoulders.

Brooke wanted to yank the boy from the woman's grip.

His wide eyes and quivering lip tore at her heart.

"Then Hsiao-Hun"—she indicate to Thick-Beard and then the shorter, lankier man—"and Youliang will make an example of you." She released the boy and stepped back with a nearly imperceptible nod as she took the boy's sister by the shoulders.

A move that tightened Brooke's core.

The brother screamed and fell to the ground, writhing. Reaching to the collar, then yanked his hands away. Tears fell as his face reddened.

Beneath the grasp of the cruel woman, the sister twitched and tried to break free. Tried to get to her brother, her own cries melding with his.

Mrs. Cheng gripped the small face and held it in what looked like a painfully tight grip. "No, you watch! All of you watch, or you will be next!" Once more her gaze roved the circle of victims, her narrowed eyes scanning ... assessing ...

Taking note, Brooke realized, of connections.

Instinct had her close the last few feet—and deliberately insert herself between Ginika and Adesina. The girls whimpered, but Brooke stood firm. "Watch her," she instructed the Nigerian girls. "Or she will hurt you, too."

Mrs. Cheng, who couldn't stand taller than five-four, lasered in on Brooke. "You think you too pretty for fields, yes?" She shoved aside the child and strutted toward her. Maybe we make you better for beds. Mm?"

Something in Brooke warned the woman wanted to elicit a response. She would not satisfy her.

As the boy's cries continued to strain the air, the woman stared harder at Brooke. Without warning, she struck.

Voltage seared through Brooke, fiery tendrils zapping her throat and charging down her neck and shoulders. She jerked—and her ribs screamed in protest. The violence of the agony nearly dropped her to the mucky ground.

"When I talk, you answer with 'yes, Mrs. Cheng. No, Mrs. Cheng.' Always. You answer this way." She scowled as she leaned in. "Am I clear?"

Brooke looked down at her—in many ways. "Yes, Mrs. Cheng," she gritted out. Pain and humiliation she could endure, especially if it meant these children were not the focus of this woman's excruciating cruelty.

CHAPTER
NINE

Safehouse, Kaohsiung City, Taiwan

"I'm pretty sure someone is following me. I bumped into the same man in my hotel lobby when I suddenly switched directions, realizing I'd forgotten my phone. Which isn't really like me to be so careless, but I'd spilled water on my blouse, so I'd tossed it aside to change and, since I was already late to connect with our sister firm here in Kaohsiung City, I rushed right out.

"Anyway … later that day, after the meeting with Gerard, I went down to the local market. I'd learned that this particular one was known for trafficking, prostitutes—"

"How on earth did you learn that?" Cord muttered to himself.

"—so I wanted to get a lay of the land before I could start making inquiries."

Cord groaned and roughed a hand over his face and beard. Though her intentions were admirable, she was a kid playing with matches. The people he and his operators indicted against were not people who took "inquiries" lightly. In fact, they were viewed as a threat to their very lucrative, very dark industry.

It wasn't the first time he'd listened to the recordings, but each time he dug deeper, he grew more irritated. He couldn't find anything to help. The only name she'd really mentioned was this Gerard. She'd used descriptors as names—Thick-Beard, Scrunchface, Baldie …

Which frustrated the heck out of him. If she couldn't get names and figure out what their roles were—as in, head-chopper, sniper, garroter—she shouldn't be messing around in this terror-scape.

With another growl, he rolled upright and stopped the replay.

Danggit, Brooke. Why couldn't you just leave it alone? Or better yet—actually, I don't know, talk to me *about this?*

Pinching the bridge of his nose, he sat there. His phone rang. He eyed the screen and bit back another groan. Answered it. "Yeah."

"Taggart. Stone Metcalfe."

"Yep." Moseying to the far wall and boarded-up window, he steeled himself. Stared through the hair-thin sliver between the slats.

"Wanted to talk to you about something."

He'd seen this coming. The look on the guy's face during the briefing yesterday warned something was up.

"What do you know about Daghestani?"

Playing dumb would only tick off the guy, and they were past that, especially with him all but dumping Brighton on him—though with the ring on her finger and a bun in the oven, it would seem he'd done the guy a favor there. "You know something about him," he suggested.

"That he has two kids and was living with my sister, yeah."

No, there was more to it. "Other than the fact he immigrated last year, not much."

"From where?"

"Afghanistan."

A grunt stabbed through the line. "Where in Afghanistan?" He almost sounded disappointed. Or was that relief?

"Uh ... hang on." Frowning, Cord opened his laptop, wondering what Stone was trying to dig up. "What're you thinking?"

"A few things, but is there a connection between Kandahar and this guy?"

"You mean between Kasra's brothel and him?"

"Your words, not mine."

"Because you're too cowardly to speak them."

"I have to live with Range after this; you don't."

With a grunt of concession, he opened the file he'd gotten from the ASAC. "So, Daghestani—Oh, hold up. Not Afghanistan. It was Saudi." How had he mixed that up?

"Where?" Stone's razor-edged tone had a dark lethality to it that warned to cut through the crap.

For a second, Cord toyed with pushing back, asking him what was going on. Pin him on the way he acted on that last call. He eyed the place of birth again, holding it hostage to his suspicious nature. But there wasn't time for games—Brooke's life was on the line. "Riyadh."

What came through the connection was not a word or a grunt, but what Cord would've sworn was an under-the-breath curse.

"You've figured something out. Brooke's life could depend—"

"Later."

"Stone?" Cord tucked his chin, straining to hear. "Stone?" He glanced at the phone. The guy freakin' hung up on him. "What the heck?" So ... what had he figured out? And why hadn't he shared the revelation?

"That's usually the reaction I have after my brother calls, too."

Cord pivoted. "Canyon."

"Good guess." The sarcasm was thick with these Metcalfes. Canyon jutted his jaw. "What'd he want?"

Digging through that call, Cord furrowed his brow. Shrugged. "No idea. He asked about Daghestani."

Canyon mulled that for a moment. "It probably hit him hard that our sister never told us about a guy she's living with. That's a major step, especially for her."

"I think it's major for most people."

Wizened blue eyes considered him. "You really have it bad for her?"

Another quip danced on his tongue. "I do, but I … I'm learning to accept it's a one-way street."

"Because of this Daghestani guy."

Cord swallowed. Nodded.

"But she had the diary sent to you."

That argument didn't work—he'd tried more than once. "Daghestani was already MIA. She only—"

Canyon grunted. "Missing my point, Mr. Clean."

His brain lagged and his hand was lifting toward his shaved head when he caught himself. "Cute. But you missed mine—she only sent it to me because I own MiLE. Tracking down people is what I do."

"Same is true of myself, Range, and Leif, and she sure didn't send it to any of us. All of us could've interdicted, and as blood relatives, we'd have more incentive."

Cord shook his head. "Doesn't make sense. I mean, I know y'all weren't on the best of terms—"

"Back that truck up, chief."

"That'd be Pike. Here, I'm 'boss.'"

Brows drawn together, Canyon threw him a stiff scowl. "You don't know squat about me and my family."

"Except that every one of you has an attitude as big as Auberon's chest, and all have been impacted firsthand by trafficking of one form or another."

The guy drew up. His mouth opened. Closed. Then bobbed his head. "I'll give you that one."

Pretty sure I gave it to you.

"Just because I couldn't tell you what she had for breakfast doesn't mean we were at odds. Fact is, Brooke didn't communicate with us much, but when we were together, all those weeks or months of silence vanished," Canyon said. "Which is why I can't figure this one. She had to have known she was out of her depth, that Range, Leif, and I would've dropped everything to assist."

"I think she didn't care." Cord tucked his hands beneath his armpits. "Whoever this guy was to her, whatever their relationship, she must've felt a singular obligation to do what the authorities didn't—go find those kids."

"Which—again—is not like her. The only thing I saw her fight hard for was her career."

"A career she abandoned to go on this hunt."

Canyon frowned. "Do what?"

"She took a sabbatical. Of sorts. Left New York nearly six months ago, looking for these kids and their dad. She's been back a couple of times. About six weeks ago, dumb luck had me flying out at Newark. I'd just cleared security when I saw her coming toward me. We had dinner there in the terminal. Like always, she was vague. I applied pressure, trying to get her to tell me what was going on. But she said she had to go or she'd miss her flight. Never gave a hint of what was going on. But it bugged me—she looked gaunt, tired, so I knew something was going on. That woman was a vault."

"Never was a chatty Cathy."

"According to the digital entries"—he wasn't sure why *diary* sounded wrong—"once she landed here in the city, she made some in-person visits to her law firm's sister company, met with a man named Gerard—"

"D'you check him out?"

"Digitally," he said with a nod. "The CEO there is one Gerard Frost."

"Guess I'll do it *facially*."

"What're you doing with that face?" Range asked as he joined them. "Besides scaring kids."

"Look who's talking," Canyon taunted back.

"Good, go," Cord said. "That's not something I can do, since I'm too well-known here and amongst this trafficking ring. They see me ..." He gave a cockeyed nod.

"They'll get skittish. Brooke'll pay."

"Yeah, but don't think this organization will panic and make mistakes. And as soon as I can figure out who's at the top of this org chart, I'll take his head." Cord was so ready to end this ring. "They've been in control a very long time, and they're used to making their problems disappear."

"Like Brooke."

And yet, something bugged Cord but he was still trying to get it sorted and solidified in his head. Make it actionable.

"Out with it." Though the guy's expression didn't change, there was a clear challenge lit by fury in it.

"They took her."

"And?" Canyon held his gaze. The guy was not only smart, but street smart. Combat smart. He knew what this meant, which also meant he just wanted to hear it spoken. Apparently so did Range because he wasn't talking. But the guy had that drilling stare down to a science.

The very thing Cord had been avoiding. "It would've been easy to finish her off, get rid of a problem when she got hit by the car."

"But they didn't."

With a slow nod, Cord went on. "Yet they tracked her down … could've easily killed her there at the hospital."

"Again, they didn't."

"That footage we found with the kids and Brooke bound—classic MO for this ring to relocate their victims."

"Thought we already had the trafficking talk," Range said. "I mean, we did agree this is likely trafficking. Right?"

"Volker is involved, so this goes beyond putting someone on the street or in a brothel. Too, Brooke's older than their typical *merchandise*, but she's beautiful, fit, …"

"Careful," both brothers said, almost in unison.

"Appreciate the concern for your sister, but you need to aim those attitudes in the right direction. Am I interested in Brooke? Yeah, but that's not the point here." The more Cord thought about it, the more he wondered if they'd ever find her alive.

"*And?*" Canyon demanded. "Your earlier sentence is dangling unfinished. She's not their standard fare, and …?"

"I think they have a specific … purpose for her. But what concerns me …" Cord met the brothers' gazes one at a time. Exhaled heavily. "If they find out—or already know—that she's the sister of the operator who dealt a blow to the Trench …" His gaze struck Range. Thank God Cord hadn't started dating her, or once they realized she was connected to him it'd be lights out.

"You blaming me?"

"I'm saying, this entire industry capitalizes on connections, on threatening humiliation and harm to the family and loved ones of those trapped in it."

Swiping a hand over his mouth, Canyon uttered an oath and turned away. Without warning, he pivoted back, his gaze narrowed. "So … you're thinking they took her"—his gaze bounced to his little brother—"to get back at him?"

"No," Cord said. "To *get* him, me—us. Wipe out whoever is standing in their way. They will use her to draw him, to draw me, out. To kill us."

Both Metcalfes answered, "They can try."

"And they will," Cord assured. "And don't think the government or military will help. The Trench has its name for a reason—they have dug in hard and fast across governments and military branches. Nobody wants them angry because their blackmail material is vast, and their reach bigger."

"Okay, so playing by that 'if' you lobbed," Canyon said and jutted his jaw, "does that mean they knew the kids were with Brooke, so they took them …?" His brow furrowed. "That's … a stretch."

"Agreed. I don't think that's it at all. Brooke didn't make herself a threat until she started looking for the kids."

"And the dad," Range added with a shrug. "I mean they were living together, so relationship level is elevated."

Shoulders tight, Cord didn't respond. Couldn't trust himself not to reveal how much that rankled. "The kids are here—or were, last Brooke could decipher. The dad is an unknown, both identity and location. Not worrying about him right now."

"Agreed," Canyon said. "Focus on Brooke, and if we're lucky—we'll find the kids, too."

"Think I'll dig deeper into the dad."

Not him, too. Why was everyone in the Metcalfe family obsessed with that guy? But … "That works. I have things I need to do, including briefing local authorities. The entire purpose of MiLE is to interdict with the victims. Find them, secure them, help them rebuild their lives."

Canyon gave him a bemused look. "And it has nothing to do with my sister."

Cord clenched his jaw. "She trusted me enough to send me that digital diary. I'm not going anywhere until I find her."

The Metcalfe with the golden touch planted that hand on Cord's chest. Patted it. Then his cheek. "Never asked you to." He took a step, then backstepped. Caught the collar of Cord's shirt. "I know you got this, you've done this a hundred times, saving kids from pervs." His lips thinned. "But this is my sister. And if you screw it up …"

"You already said you'd kill me. Can't be any more dead than dead."

Canyon's eyebrows lifted. "There's the afterlife."

CHAPTER
TEN

"WHAT'VE YOU GOT?" Canyon spoke calmly into the comms as he walked the market Brooke had mentioned in her diary. He stopped at a stall that had taro balls.

"Headed deep into the devil's den," Range said from farther down the street, where he tailed the man their sister had named—Gerard.

Canyon bit into the taro ball with pork floss. Almost groaned.

"You realize that's probably cat you're eating," Leif taunted.

Buying another, he moved away from the stall, tracking the CEO's assistant, who was at a stall buying boxed dinners for his boss. "They banned the consumption or sale of dog and cat meat back in 2017, dude. Do your diligence before you run an op."

"Yes, Mother," Leif muttered. "Car and driver are still here. Probably as bored as I am."

"Target entered a building," Range reported. "A hotel."

Canyon eyed the assistant. Curled his lip. "How anyone eats octopus is beyond me."

"Says the man eating pig."

"Hey, never ask me to turn down bacon."

"I thought Dani cured you of that."

"She's not here is she?" Canyon said around the bite of another taro ball as he paid, then wandered to a stall with bamboo wares.

"Wait till I tell her."

"Always were a brat."

"Going in," Range muttered.

"Leif, back him up," Canyon said, tossing aside the last taro ball and shifting his position to keep an eye on the assistant. However, this vantage also gave him a bird's-eye view of the alley Range and the executive had gone down. "Guessing CEO Gerard has some side business going on."

"It would be my opinion," Range said, his words coming slow—likely clearing doors and corners, "he's the reason she got captured."

Those Metcalfe instincts had always been razor-sharp. "Talk to me, Mini-me."

"Only thing I'll do is double-tap you if you call me that again."

Canyon smirked, watching the assistant take the bag of food and start back to the SUV. "Sit-rep," he chastised his brother as he edged closer to the vehicle and paused at a vendor selling cheap toys. He lifted a small pink beanie pig. There was something about the air, the busyness of the vendor, that threw him back to his days as a Special Forces grunt and living in the Philippines. Married the chief's daughter. He'd been an egotistical punk who hadn't thought through the long-term repercussions. Thought she'd died ... only to have their daughter delivered to him years later. A daughter he hadn't known about. Now, Tala was a teenager, giving him grief every which way from Sunday. Dani had been understanding and forgiving. Even though he'd knocked her up, too.

Stellar record there, Midas.

But he had turned from his swaggering days. Father to three now. Fourth on the way. And all he wanted was to get back to them.

Voices skated through the feed, yanking his attention back to the present. To his brother in the hotel. He resisted the urge to press a hand over his comms piece to hear better. The tinny sounds told him Range was inside. And he hadn't given a sit-rep.

Crack! Pop! Pop!

Screams and shouts erupted throughout the market. Canyon tossed the toy and snatched a ballcap. Tucked it at the back of his belt. Weapon out, Canyon stalked forward, toward the sounds. The end of the alley where he'd seen his brother vanish. A sea of people swarming away from that brothel told him those shots were related to his brother.

"Range, what's your situation?"

He caught sight of Leif darting around a car, weapon out and thrust in the direction of the hotel. Half his heart thudded with pride at his kid brother. The other pounded out panic—that was his kid brother. Who'd been running ops for the last decade. Probably had more skill in his little pinky than Canyon and Range had combined.

And here was Canyon, bringing up the rear. *Too old, too slow.*

Leif glanced over his shoulder to him.

"Any sign of him?"

"Negative."

He did not want to have to go into the building, but he was not losing another sibling to this trafficking ring. Even as he met up with his kid brother and they moved together toward the entry, he was bemused at the thought of anyone trying to make grumpy Range do anything he didn't want to do. True, Kasra had grounded him some, but Range was still Range.

"Take point," Leif said, shifting back to allow Canyon to go first.

At the door, he held up his fingers, one … two … On three, he shoved the heel of his boot into the door. Wished for his M4. Not the best for close-quarters, but he favored it regardless. Moved into the building, glad he'd thought to don a tac vest. Wished he had his brain bowl. He'd eat it if double-tapped.

So, shut up and keep moving.

The long dank hall struggled against the dim lighting, giving off a bad vibe. He paused before approaching a juncture, both listening and regretting not inviting Colton or Griffin to the party.

"Midas, Omen Actual coming up your six."

Surprise lit through him—where had they come from? "Good copy," he muttered, the presence of more operators reassuring.

A firm pat came to his shoulder. Leif.

Canyon did a quick look-see around the corner of the juncture. The far end gaped darkness and ominous threat. Even as he pulled back, he registered the form slumped against the wall. Range! He surged on, sweeping and clearing doors and junctures, moving swiftly, silently. He hurried to Range's side. "Hey."

Leaning against the door, hand to his chest that spewed blood, he grimaced a smile. "Getting slow, old man."

"Tell me about it." Canyon went to a knee and swung his backpack in front of him. He had a small medkit, but not his full kit. "Operator down. Medic needed." Checking his brother's pupils, he asked, "What happened?"

Range lifted his arm that hung loose to the side. He held a camera. "Caught me taking pictures. Guess they thought I got his bad side."

"Who?"

Another grimaced smile. "Gerard and another playboy." With

care, he eased his brother forward and checked for an exit wound. "Made a mess, Mini-me."

"If I could hold my gun, I'd make good on my promise."

"No doubt."

"Kasra will kill you for me."

"No," Canyon said, carefully packing the wound. "She likes me, remember?"

"They always like you," Range growled.

"Charming good looks."

"Except Kasra. She thinks you look like shriveled leather."

"And she probably thinks your moisturized face looks heavenly."

"Delicious, she said."

"I really didn't need to know that." Once they had Range field dressed, Canyon helped him up. Even as he did, he caught sight of a weapon. Rolling so Range was pinned between his backside and the wall, Canyon took aim. Fired. Once, twice, three times.

A man stumbled backward, eyes wide. He slid down the wall with a guttural wheeze.

"Crap," he muttered, anticipating more threats.

A stream of operators in tac gear swept past him to clear the rooms, check on the guy.

"You were supposed to keep him alive," came the stiff voice of Luther Landry. "Questioning him would've been helpful."

"Not if I'd eaten lead."

Landry grunted. "Guess that depends on who would've been helped." Sarcasm ran thick among operators, a necessary outlet for the dark, violent deeds they meted out and dealt with.

"Any sign of the playboy?"

"Negative," said one of the operators, a lanky dude with too much attitude. "Girls, children, a raspy-voiced woman who probably smokes more than my grandpa, but no men."

Once more supporting his brother, Canyon and Leif helped

him out of the building and back to their vehicle. As he opened the door to climb behind the wheel, he spotted the CEO's vehicle just as they tore away—and not before the window, which had been rolled down as the assistant took a photo of Canyon, rolled up.

Crap! Now his face would be all over the place. He'd need to lie low. Keep his head down.

Too old, dude. I'm too freakin' old for this.

SAFEHOUSE, KAOHSIUNG CITY, TAIWAN

"Taggart."

Cord whipped around from his station in the Command room.

Pike Auberon thumbed him in his direction. "Check it out."

On his feet, he moved to the hub where Pike, Low, Jess, and another girl were working fastidiously. "What is it?"

Wadi took a sip of his bottled water then motioned to the screens on the wall. "Found that truck." He tucked a caramel into his mouth and nodded as he went to work.

"It's holed up at a warehouse on the north side of the city," Pike explained.

"I'll go," Cord said, already moving.

"Negative, negative." Pike sniffed. "You're some serious crap, man, but no. The Metcalfes and the rest of my team are there, checking into the CEO. We'll divert them."

"But they're busy."

"It'll save time. Or do you want to hold up a possible interdiction so you can do it?" Pike thumbed toward his phone. "Because I can do that. Tell everyone to stand down, slow down everything, so you can be the top dog."

Cord stilled, disbelief choking him at the punches the Omen founder didn't pull. He clenched his jaw. "Fine. Send them."

Pike's chiseled cheek twitched. "You sure?"

"Enough, just do it. I get your point."

Lifting a phone, he nodded. "Good." He focused on the call, sending the team north. But he hesitated … paused, concern creasing his brow. "You sure?" Again, he nodded. "Okay. Keep me posted."

Edging closer, Cord cocked his head. "What was that about?"

"Range got hit. They've patched him up and will proceed north."

"You're sending a wounded—"

"I'm sending Tycho, Archer, and Landry." Pike planted his hands on his tac belt and stared at him. "You think I'm handling my team wrong?"

Cord huffed. Lowered his head and gaze. He and Pike weren't subordinates but equals. And he'd asked for the guy's help, hadn't he? "No. I just …"

"Good, because I've got something you and I need to check out."

Heart perked up, he adjusted his attitude and stance. "How's that?"

"Check it out." He pointed to the screen and moved around the hub to stand closer to it. "While searching for the truck, Wadi noticed a strange sudden and large increase in radio communications in this area." He used his finger to circle an area in the northwest. One that looked like hills and remote farms. "Rice paddies."

Cord frowned. Rice paddies … and an uptick in radio waves …

"It's too remote for surveillance footage, but Wadi managed to trace a possible route to and from this area, and when he did, he found this vehicle heading in that direction from the city two days ago."

"Farmers transporting their harvest."

"Too early. Harvesting is just starting."

"Supplies?"

"Most in this rural area don't use combines or large equipment. By and large, this area is dominated by poorer, family-operated paddies."

This was the way—throwing out ideas in order to talk through possibilities and rule out plausible reasons for such activity. All in an effort to keep them from acting on rash suppositions and bad intel.

"Too," Wadi said with a jut of his jaw, "that truck was much heavier—see its bed to wheel height ratio? And here, it is returning … lighter."

"It should be the opposite, if they're harvesting. Unless it's pesticides."

Wadi snorted. "It would be an ungodly amount to weigh the truck down that much. Enough to level a city."

Cord stared at the aerial map of the area of stepped paddies. "Those huts …"

Pike gave him a knowing look. "Would make good shelters for forced labor." He almost seemed to smile. "Show him the next image."

Wadi switched the images.

Frowning, Cord squinted at the image. "What am I—" He lifted his jaw. Stepped back. "Camouflage." The farm now had camo netting hung over the huts. Hiding what was beneath it.

"Installed this morning."

Was that where they'd taken them? Where Brooke was now? "We need to check it out."

"There you go," Pike said with a grin. "You're a bit slower than I'd anticipated."

Not easily offended, Cord rolled with it. "Slow is smooth …"

"And smooth is fast."

"I'll grab some gear."

CHAPTER ELEVEN

OUTSIDE KAOHSIUNG CITY, TAIWAN

NEVER HAD she taken knocks lying down. She had four brothers, for pity's sake. So this … this wasn't going to be her lot in life. She wasn't going to be worked to death or whatever they intended. There had to be a way out of this place.

Under the guise of needing to use the outhouse, she took a stroll in the dark, damp night. It was hard to believe that Christmas was so close when humidity plastered her clothes to her body. Her hair felt like it had doubled its density, the humidity puffing it out. At least she'd had a scrunchie with her when taken.

Mama had said she ate like a rabbit, and in part, it'd been true. She hadn't been one to enjoy food, mostly because of the intolerances she'd developed. Stress-induced. Dairy was out, cruciferous vegetables. Rice tended to burn like the dickens—well, so did wine, but she refused to surrender that. It was the only thing that helped her calm down enough each night to work or sleep. Mama would beat her for that, but it was a vice Brooke wasn't ready to give up.

Well, guess this forces me to give it up.

Hugging herself, she walked the perimeter. Checked on the children in the huts. It tugged at her heart, seeing them huddled, scared. Dirty. She already could smell herself, and let's not even talk about all the stains on her pink sweater Or the way her once-white sneakers now looked like brown-leather loafers. Ugh.

The stench of cigarette smoke pushed her in the other direction. Last thing she wanted was for Hsiao-Hun to see her. He hadn't made any inappropriate comments, but the man reeked of lecherous intent.

There was a part of her that ached with relief that they weren't shipped off to some other part of the world for sex trafficking. She'd seen that happen with Willow, and even the two Nigerian girls—she gave a small wave to the girls as she ambled to the far side of the camp. But this was no joy ride. It'd been two days and they'd been roused before dawn, given a rice ball with very little meat, some rice milk, then sent to the paddy, where they'd trenched the area so the water would drain. Well after dark they returned to their shelters, exhausted. Hands and back aching. The first day, the kids had ended up sunburned because of the sun glare off the water.

Then Youliang and another man had installed army netting over the shelters. Though, she was fairly certain that wasn't for their benefit. Nothing was. Mrs. Cheng wanted her rice harvested and she had proved more than once she would punish those who weren't working.

She stepped into the outhouse, took care of business—and peered through the slats out the back. Up the slope. Moonlight gave little help. And her view was too limited. She stepped out and slipped to the side. Stayed close, knowing there was a perimeter sensor somewhere nearby. One of the girls had discovered it the other day on accident.

She had to be smart. She leaned against the wall and peered out at the hills in the other direction. Up ... up ... maybe a mile or more there was a band of trees. If they could somehow make it there ...

Right. You want children to run for a mile or more ...

What about the shock collars?

Brooke rubbed her forehead. Yeah, what about the collars? How could they escape with those on? If only Cord—Canyon were here. Her brothers were operators. So was Cord. Well, surely the diary had been sent to him by now. Was he figuring things out? Would he find her?

After the way you treated him?

So. Help wouldn't be coming. Not that she was blaming Cord—he wasn't the vengeful kind, she didn't think. But it'd been days ... they'd been relocated ... and were beyond the reach of technology. Canyon had taught her a few things. She just wasn't sure her fledgling knowledge could be put into action to effect an escape. Not with twelve kids.

"What are you doing?" came the surly voice of Hsiao-Hun as he thudded toward her.

Startled, Brooke hurried around the side of the outhouse, ignoring the pinch in her side. If only she'd managed to keep her backpack—the pain meds would be dreamy right now. Nearly rammed straight into the large form of the man. She attempted to move past him. "I wanted to see the moon." Pain ricocheted through her scalp, then her side as he yanked her backward. Slammed her into the wall. Though she tried not to, she cried out.

Though she didn't have the skills of her brothers—or Cord— she did know self-defense. She raised her arm as she wheeled around. Shoved her arm up and over his, then—took a breath to brace herself—dropped hard.

Her move broke his hold—and any semblance of sanity as pain severed her thread-thin hold on breathing without fire.

His fist connected with her head. He reared back to punch again.

Something thudded against his chest. Then another against his head.

Rage lit his face. "Who did that?" he demanded, stalking toward the huts.

Biting through the agony, Brooke struggled to her feet. As he yelled at the others, she again moved to slip past him.

His meaty paw swung for her with a demand to know where she thought she was going.

He missed, but as she attempted to pivot away from his grip, her shoe slipped on the mucky ground. Went out from under her. She landed brutally on her hip. Fell back.

Hsiao-Hun laughed. Smacked her head. "That will teach you!"

"Leave her alone!" It was Ginika.

"No!" Brooke said to the girl, flashing her palm so she'd stay in her hut.

But Thick-Beard thought she was telling him no. And he targeted her again.

At least he isn't going after the kids.

She braced herself for more impact, more pain … but another sound and an explosion of light intervened. The noisy joists of a vehicle lumbering up to the paddy proved her saving grace.

"Get inside," Hsiao-Hun barked, practically dragging her up and pitching her at the hut.

With relish, Brooke climbed into the hut and scrambled to the corner. Braced, tensed, she watched through the open wall as shapes moved in the headlamps that glared against her eyes. She turned her face to the bamboo wall and battled the desperation she felt. It would not be as bad if she did not have broken ribs. She could do nothing but be a victim. And if they kept battering her, they would puncture her liver and she'd die.

The thought ripped hope from her hands.

Cord ... Cord, please tell me you've listened to the diary. Find me ... please.

When the wind caught the tree limbs and twitched them aside, as if working in cooperation with Cord and Pike—the hand of God?—to scope out the farm, a flash of wood peeked through. No way to get a good look-see on that location without being seen, not from this vantage inside the truck on the side of the hill.

"We'll need to split up," Pike said, "go up and around the hill, come in from opposite directions."

It'd eliminate chances of them getting caught together. Cord nodded, knowing it'd also help them get a lay of the land on both sides. About a half klick farther up, he got out, grabbed his ruck, and headed to the hills, trusting Pike to conceal the truck somewhere and hoof it up to the middle. Cord stopped about halfway there, retrieved his pack shovel and dug a hole. Buried the ruck and weapon. Continued on, crawling into a prone position next to Pike who was already scouting from the overlook.

"This is a lot to go through for someone else's girl," Pike noted quietly.

From any other buddy, that comment would've irked Cord. But he knew Pike. Almost anticipated the probing remark, a move designed to get a bead on Cord's thoughts and feelings.

But that ... that was the wrong tack. And it wasn't like Pike to be shallow in his queries. The Special Forces legend was always keyed into the mission, objectives and outcomes. Though he cared about his team, he—like Cord—knew greater purpose was not one individual, and in this case, who they dated or didn't.

"That's just it," Cord said as he settled in, "she's someone's girl." Molten lava had nothing on the irritation burning in his gut at saying that. "She matters. It's why I do what I do—they matter, the people. Whether someone's son or daughter, brother or sister, aunt or uncle, niece or nephew, grandkid. If they're alone in the world and caught in this net … it's the 'one lost sheep.'" He cocked a look at Omen's team leader. "We're the sheepdogs, remember?"

As expected, Pike merely nodded. They all knew the saying that there were three types of people: sheep, the wolves who seek to devour the sheep, and the sheepdogs who do what it takes to protect the sheep. Many times, that wasn't pretty. In fact, it was often downright bloody.

Silence carried them the last few yards before they went to a low-crawl, straight up to the small overlook amid some thick vegetation and bamboo stalks that gave them a view down on the lower-lying elevation, and there, as they'd anticipated from the truck an hour ago, they spied a rice paddy. Due to the dark hour and cam netting over the buildings, getting a visual wasn't going to be done with nocs.

Cord grabbed his thermals and scanned the area. First spied the five small huts with thatched roofs and bamboo walls— looked more like storage than dwellings. Set in a U-shape around a central area that abutted a very large rice paddy. No moonlight glinted, so he'd guessed it'd already been drained.

"To our eleven—likely the main structure huddled with two smaller ones."

Verifying with his own sweep, Cord grunted. "Thinking the small huts near the paddies for our captives."

Pike returned the thoughtful grunt. "So why aren't they running? It's dark, hut is easily seven, eight hundred yards ba—" He fell silent as thermals showed a change in pattern at several huts.

"Movement," Cord said.

"Copy."

Cord monitored the shifting pattern, that suggested someone moving on the other side of that hut. Unless a farmer sealed between each stalk, the huts weren't weatherproof. Which meant they had gaps. Through those gaps, the thermals picked up the heat variance.

Using his sat phone and the app that required no GPS, Pike worked to map the farm of interest, then the surrounding tracts. Hopefully the moon afforded enough light to give an accurate reading. At this point, even semi-accurate would be a boon.

While his buddy mapped, Cord continued to surveil, get a feel for the lay of the land. As he studied, he picked up two forms—a child and an adult—crossing the space between the huts toward the smallest structure. An outhouse? "Visual on two persons. Child confirmation."

"Farmer and his kid?"

Cord traced the adult visually and hooked on one aspect that told him this wasn't a farmer. "It's a very well-armed farmer." How many farmers walked their kids to an outhouse with a T91.

As he monitored their movement, more shapes bled into the visual field. Two more came from their two, then another from ten.

"Uncles making sure the kid knows how to flush?" Pike had a wicked sense of humor, and the poker face to go with it.

"Or to bring extra TP." The jokes were necessary to keep them from delving deep into rage or despair. Seeing things like this never got easier.

"What the ...?" Pike muttered, adjusting his thermals. "You gotta be kidding me."

"What?"

"Check that kid's throat."

Cord zeroed in and zoomed more, tightening on the smaller outline of color that revealed a male child ... He bit back a curse at the way the thermal seemed to glare off a band across the kid's neck. "*What* is that?"

He knew. Had no doubt, but did not want to voice it. Didn't want it to be real, because if Brooke was here, too …

"Shock collar."

Ticked, Cord had to fight to stem the rush of anger that demanded he storm down there. But they had confirmation of what? One kid. "I count four armed combatants … and one kid."

"Seems kinda inverted."

Yeah … "Need a closer look."

"Negative," Pike snapped. "No plan, no backup, means a major snafu."

Though he knew the chief was right, Cord didn't want to sit still any longer. He'd spent weeks searching for Brooke.

"And you have no confirmation that your girl is down there—"

"She's not my girl."

"—and until then, you keep your butt planted."

A child's cry scampered up the hillside and straight into Cord's chest, beating against his stationary mode. It was eerie the way his cry wafted all the way from those structures.

Livid, Cord watched as the combatant rough-handed the kids back to a hut. Another form emerged from the hut. Stepped onto the ground. Reached for the kid.

Cord's breath backed into his throat. Thermal imaging wasn't the same as looking through a regular lens, but this gave him enough to know. "It's her." Ha! "Visual confirmation."

He dropped his nocs and launched up from the spot. Sprinted down the hillside, drawing the Sig holstered at his spine.

Well, that's what he *wanted* to do. But if Pike didn't kill him first, the combatants would've. It was bad enough he flinched— not out of fear but out of having to restrain that instinct to go in *now*.

"Not your girl, huh?" Perceptive Pike taunted.

"She's living with a guy."

"I'd say she's living with six …"

Truth. And those were only the ones they could see. The din down there slowly rose as more shapes appeared. Not close enough to hear, Cord could only watch and guess what was happening. Seemed Brooke wanted to protect the kid—was that one of the Daghestani kids?—and the guards didn't want her out of the hut. Their interaction drew others from the blank void of the heat imaging.

Though everything in him screamed he do something now, Cord knew they needed to gather more intel—how many, what were their rotation patterns, number of kids, possible infil/exfil options, weapon-to-person ratio.

"Counting a half dozen unfriendlies," Cord muttered.

"So far," Pike agreed.

A good reminder that they'd just started.

Exfil'ing in daylight would expose them, destroy any chance of helping the victims. So they remained in position as night surrendered its hold to dawn, which revealed numerous forms pouring from the huts. Stumbling around. Brooke appeared again, this time with two others, almost the same height. At Brooke's five-nine, she seemed more adult … but maybe, in this case, that was true.

"Two teens." The strange color pattern of the thermals distorted faces, but— "Hold up." He tried to tighten and clean it up some, which was impossible. "That's…" He swept his gaze over the other teen. "Willow's kids—from Nigeria. They're here."

"Along with at least two dozen kids," Pike growled.

The captives were herded into a single file line that queued past a table. Hands cupped, they were given a small round rice ball, then moved another ten paces and received a tin cup.

"Freakin' concentration camp right there," Pike hissed.

This wasn't the Holocaust, but this was cruelty defined. The kids gulped down whatever was in the cup and kept moving, eating the rice ball as they were forced out to the rice paddy.

Anger churned and writhed like the rice paddy snakes common in the flooded fields. Thank God this paddy had been drained already for harvest. "We end this," he hissed. "Only six armed guards—we can do this. End them."

"Get your head out of your pants," Pike hissed. "Look at it, Taggart. What're you missing?"

The rebuke was unusually harsh for the Omen founder and drove Cord's attention back down the hill. What ...? Kids working to bundle the rice. Brooke—apparently the only adult among this group—chopping the stalks. Guards lazily walking the perimeter tossing the occasional shout at a kid who was probably working too slow for their liking.

"I'm not missing anything—they're forcing the kids to work the fields."

Pike's gray gaze hit his. "Wide open fields."

"Yeah." Though irritation punctuated Cord's answer, he then faltered. "Like they're not worried."

The chief gave him a cockeyed nod. "And why wouldn't they be worried?"

Crap. "They're watching ..."

"I think it goes beyond that." Pike gave another nod. "Let's test my theory." He pulled out a switch and hit the button.

An explosion halfway between the main property and the paddy sent screams and shouts scurrying through the early morning. A secondary sent a ball of flame into the sky.

"Huh," Pike said as he glanced at his watch, even as the guards were rushing toward the chaos. "Guess I planted that too close to the pesticides ..." As if it'd been a mistake.

Returning his attention to the chaos, Cord knew two things: Pike didn't make mistakes like that, and the events playing out were crucial to any potential exfil strategy, so he'd better keep is eyes on the farm.

A couple of kids seized the distraction of the explosion and sprinted in the opposite direction.

No no no. Don't do that. His gut reactions were almost never wrong and Cord willed them back.

And sure enough both kids dropped and writhed in the field—sparks and flashes sparkled around them, turning his insides to lead. The paddy they'd fallen in … it hadn't been drained yet.

Oh, God … please …

From the side, Brooke started toward them, shouting. Miraculously managed to intercept one of the boys, but the other …

No!

Pike cursed.

Brooke slowed … stopped. Hand to her mouth, first pulled to her, shielding his face so he wasn't forced to watch his friend's—brother's?—gruesome death.

Cord wanted to close his eyes, not watch the kid's final moments, but he'd vowed long ago he'd never turn a blind eye to the suffering of the children. Too many did that, discomfited by the pain, sensibilities offended by uncomfortable realities. It was easier to shut it out and pretend it didn't happen than to do something about it.

"When we go in," Pike hissed, "we're cleared and *hot*."

"One-hundred percent," Cord vowed. Meaning none of the unfriendlies would make it out alive. He knew God had a very special place in Hell for the lowlife scum who hurt kids. And Cord had the distinct pleasure of being the delivery mechanism to expedite that journey.

As the men worked to put out the fire that consumed one of the smaller structures on the main part of the farm, Brooke did her best to corral the children, keep them from the horror of what happened. By the time they were refocused, black SUVs swarmed the farm's dirt road.

"Twenty-three and change," Pike mumbled.

Cord should've anticipated it. "They're watching the farm."

"Very closely."

Which meant they could likely see Cord or Pike if they attempted to intervene. They wouldn't have a prayer.

"Think they'll search the hills for the cause?" Cord asked, a little unsettled by the number of professional guns those SUVs disgorged."Negative. I planted a pressure plate. They'll think it's an old mine." The chief gave a dangerous grin around that beard. "Hopefully."

Amid their number, Cord spotted a familiar, and it took a second for him to register the face. "Slag me—that's the partner Brooke met with in the city."

Pike grunted. "Explains how and why she got captured."

If someone inside the sister company was working with the Trench, did it follow that someone in New York was collaborating as well? He needed to get Jess on that ASAP. Maybe leave a tip for that ASAC, since this might establish an international connection.

Inside an hour, the SUVs were gone, having left behind four extra heavy hitters to replace the unlucky sap who'd triggered the pressure plate. They'd learned a lot at the cost of two lives. One he could release to God, but the other ... another black mark on his soul.

Let me never *forget, Lord.*

Dusk hugged the land, ready to put the world to bed for the night. So far, three things were obvious: the traffickers were watching the place, there were perimeter sensors for the collars in addition to controls the guards had, and last ... *I have to go in.*

Pike wouldn't let him. Not without a plan and backup. But that'd take too long. He had to even the odds a little for her and the kids ...

After dinner—another rice ball, another cup of what he guessed to be rice milk—Brooke and the kids were ordered back to the hut. As she had last night, she went to the outhouse, did her business, and afterward, lingered on the side, staring up into the hills …

She's looking for me.

"Let's get moving so we can—"

"No."

Pike stilled, gaze locked on him in the scant moonlight.

"I have an idea."

The chief hesitated. "I'm not going to like this, am I?"

"You never do."

CHAPTER
TWELVE

His name, she learned, was Guang, and he was eight years old. Or would have been tomorrow. Or was it today? She had lost track of time, a futile effort when confronted with pain that far outweighed the pain in her side.

Brushing the straight black hair from Akio's tear-stained face, Brooke did her best to help the six-year-old evade the terrors that robbed his peace.

She was done seeing kids electrocuted and abused. Even as she had the thought, Brooke fingered the hard collar around her throat. She'd thought it metal, but she realized they were plastic. Still, seeing that little, scared boy race toward freedom …and die a cruel, senseless death …

Back against the wall, she hugged her knees. Breaths were coming marginally easier in regards to the broken ribs, but the mental and psychological toll was ruthless. Agonizing.

To her right lay Ginika and Adesina. The former had her arms wrapped about her sister, who slept fitfully. Brooke rubbed her forehead where a headache had been browbeating her all day. Where were Caliyah and Jihan? What good was she to them now? She'd failed—miserably. Dear, sweet Caliyah …

"Dad, my teacher said our next story was due before Christmas," Jihan noted from where he sat at the kitchen table, working on the iPad the school had checked out to him for schoolwork. *"Can you help me?"*

Mazin's dark eyebrows rose as he appraised his son. "What is it about this time?"

Eating her vegan bowl quietly, Brooke watched the father-son interaction. Jihan had a knack for writing stories—each on a topic specified by his teacher—which his father did not seem to take seriously.

"A place we've visited. I want to do it on Saudi Arabia."

Shifting in his chair, Mazin met her gaze, then his son's. "What about the zoo? You like—"

"Mrs. Harris said it has to be a location—like a city or country."

Apparently needing time to digest this, Mazin took a sip of his water and set down his fork. "Okay, Jihan. I will help you."

"Yes!"

"On one condition."

The boy faltered.

"No mention of our family or where you were born. Mention Saudi, yes, but nothing specific." His large hand engulfed his son's. "You are old enough to remember … yes?"

Large, brown eyes pooled with unshed tears as he gave a forlorn nod.

"Can we get a Christmas tree this year?" Caliyah asked, her cheeks flushed with the excitement of the idea. "We've never had one. I want one. I want a lot of different colored lights and glitter on it."

"You don't put glitter on a tree, dummy," Jihan groused.

"Yes, you do! I saw it—it's all sparkling." She turned her pleading expression to Brooke, whom she knew to be a soft touch. "Can we, please?"

"My home is always decorated for Christmas," Brooke admitted with a tentative glance at Mazin, hoping for a nod of approval. She hadn't thought to ask him if he celebrated the holidays.

"Yay!" Caliyah hopped to her knees on her chair and pumped her fists in the air. "I want to go pick it out." Exuberance and innocence wreathed the fiery little one. "Can you go with us, Daddy?"

Mazin held Brooke's gaze, then finally sighed. "Okay, I suppose it can't be avoided."

Though he sounded chagrined, she saw the amusement in his beautiful dark eyes, which flared at the exultant squeal of his daughter.

Brooke couldn't suppress her own smile, though her stomach tightened a bit. Christmas will be very different this year.

She had definitely called it with that thought. But she hadn't seen ... this. Elbow on her knee, she rubbed her forehead. Focused on the beauty of that memory. Recalled how for the first time in more than a decade, she had looked forward to Christmas. Before, it had been a holiday of painful memories and invariably led to arguments between her and Mark. And Canyon .. and ... well, all family members.

"Do you think Mr. Chiji and Mama Willow will find us?" Adesina whispered to her sister.

"Remember what Mr. Chiji always say?" Ginika spoke softly into the darkness of their hut. "God will make a way."

Except when He doesn't.

"When we let Him, He likes to show off." Ginika laughed—a beautiful sound. Yet ... so naïve a comment.

Biting down on her derision, Brooke tilted her head back against the bamboo. Mama would be so disappointed in her lack of faith. But what could she say? She'd seen too many things and been the brunt of—

First World problems, Brooke.

"Right, Missus Brooke?"

She twitched at her name and forced a smile. Didn't want to lie to them, give the girls false hope. "I'll be right back." She scooted to the edge of the hut and let her feet dangle, waiting for a guard to notice her. Hsiao-Hun wasn't on duty tonight. A different, more intent one patrolled. Maybe she should just—

"You! What are you doing?" the man demanded in Mandarin.

Donning contrition and silently begging him not to shock her into submission, she lifted her hands and tucked her chin. Asked to use the outhouse. The god-awful-smelling thing had somehow become a respite.

Wary and irritated, he stomped to her. Grabbed her by the arm, muttering things to her that no decent person should speak to another. He meant to rile her, anger her so she'd resist and he'd have a reason to beat her senseless. As he'd already done to one of the girls.

She let him lead her across the compound toward the stench of waste. In the week that they had been here, she'd learned to use the toilet quickly to avoid humiliation or having one of the guards yank open the door to mock or ridicule. Once the guards had grown bored and knocked over the hut while one of the boys was inside.

Just the memory of Guang, whom she hadn't been able to reach in time. At the time, she hadn't known his name. Hadn't been able to call him by name and stop him. But she'd managed to pull his brother back just in time. Akio had screamed, then those turned to sobs that persisted through their rigorous work, despite her staying at his side with one hand on him. He then cried through their paltry rice-ball dinner. And the "free time" they'd had before being ordered to the huts for the night where, with more of the same, he'd fallen into a fitful sleep.

She was so tired. So weary.

The guard banged on the wall, ordering her to hurry up.

Sapped of strength and will, she drew in a deep breath—and instantly regretted it. Coughed as she emerged from the refuse. To her surprise, the guard wasn't there. She glanced around, confused. Stole that moment to look to the hills.

Where was Cord? Why hadn't he come yet?

Because you kept your secrets and protected Mazin. And now, she would suffer the consequences. The children were gone, he was gone, and even she was gone—as far as her family was concerned. Though, they wouldn't know to look for her since she hadn't really kept up a solid line of communication with them. Though she talked with Mom every week ... Okay, every other week, then—

Every third week?

Good grief, I'm a terrible daughter.

Mom could just be so overbearingly positive and ... Christian. Had all the answers, all the verses ... But it got where it felt like empathizing, understanding ... acknowledging didn't matter. Only fixing Brooke mattered. That's what everyone wanted to do. Fix all the parts of her that weren't up to code.

Either way, the painful truth was that this was her own doing. Nobody was coming. Nobody cared. She hadn't talked to her mom in ages, and God even longer.

Quid pro quo.

If she wanted God's help, maybe she should've kept open the lines of communication.

Serves me right.

Light bobbed and stabbed at the field. Confused at its source, Brooke eased around the back of the outhouse, covering her nose and mouth as she peered down a path that had been worn down by vehicle usage. Joists and metal creaked and groaned as a large-bed truck clambered up the makeshift road.

What ...?

Crunching from behind gave little warning of the hand that grabbed her by the hair and yanked her back. "Get back to the hut!" the man snarled, his breath foul as he hauled her backward.

Stumbling and tripping, she cried out. Tears stung—from her

scalp but more so from her broken ribs. A flare of rage jerked her upright.

"Do not test me, whore," he hissed around a mustache that was evidence of his struggle in manhood. Not thick enough to be one, it looked more like a kid had scribbled it on his lip.

But what she saw in his eyes, in his curled lip, yanked her back. Warned her not to push him. That mustache was not the only place he'd lacked in life, and he'd apparently developed a mean streak a mile wide to make up for it.

"Lee, leave her!" instructed Hsiao-Hun, who was not her ally, but she suddenly found herself grateful for him.

Lee bared his teeth as he hovered closer. "One day, I will teach you how to respect men."

To do that, you'd have to be one.

Swallowing her retort, she yanked back. And though she felt the fire of that through her midsection, she cared not. It'd freed her of the beast. She shoved away, hurrying toward the hut as she hugged herself and kept her gaze to the ground.

"Brooke!" a child cried out.

No. Not just a child.

She stopped short of the hut. Pivoted—mercy, the pain in her side—and spotted the fiery six-year-old flying at her. Brooke caught her—not without a little pain—and exultation shot through her. "Caliyah!"

Oh, mercy. If Mrs. Cheng saw this ...

Instinct shoved Caliyah back. "Quiet. Keep still." She gave the little one a stern look. "They are not nice here. Understand?"

Lower lip trembling, Caliyah nodded.

"Inside, quickly." She glanced toward the truck and saw Hsiao-Hun holding Jihan by the neck. Swallowing, she did her very best not to react. If she did, the man would hurt or kill the boy. "Stay against the far wall," she ordered Caliyah as she eased to the edge of the open doorway and sat, watching the other children—Jihan included—as they were unloaded ... and collared.

There were at least twenty more. This group had more teens, more boys. But still ... so many ... How could nobody know? How did so many go missing and end up in a place like this without anyone finding out?

What was going on in the world that this went on unhindered? How had children become a commodity to be traded and exploited?

Lee started toward her, and Brooke felt her stomach quaver.

But someone drew the wiry man around—Hsiao-Hun. He ordered the guy away, then turned that thick beard in her direction. It was then she noticed his hand on was Jihan's shoulder. He walked the pre-teen toward her.

"You know him? And the girl?"

Brooke stared at the round-faced man but did not answer.

Hsiao-Hun thrust Jihan toward her. "He has been a problem. Tell him what happened to the boy today, the one who tried to run."

He wanted her to scare Jihan into compliance. And merciful heavens, she wanted that, too. She met the hardened expression of Mazin's son. "They shocked him"—she nodded to the collar—"and he fell into the paddy. Died of electrocution."

Hsiao-Hun huffed a laugh. "You can still smell his burning flesh."

"I thought that was you," Jihan spat back.

Which earned him his initiation into shock therapy.

Brooke wanted to grab hold of him, but the current would transfer.

He flopped against the wood floor of the hut, arms curled to his chest as he let out a gargled cry that crushed her soul.

"Stop," she pleaded with Thick-Beard. "Please!"

Hsiao-Hun grunted and walked away.

Brooke scooted into the hut and Caliyah scrambled to her

side, grabbing at her. Brooke did her best not to cringe or pull away but the pain was nearly unbearable.

"Hold me," Caliyah whimpered. "I'm scared. It was so awful. The men were so mean. They did bad things to—"

"Shut up!" Jihan yelled. "Shut up, shut up. She doesn't care. She doesn't need to know."

"Hey." Arm around a now-crying Caliyah, Brooke touched Jihan's shoulder. "Enough. Okay? It's terrible for all of us."

"You have no idea. What do you know—"

"They broke her ribs," Ginika said, smoothing Caliyah's hair back. "Be careful, okay. She's hurt."

The sensitivity of the Nigerian girl stunned Brooke but she was so relieved to have the children with her. "It's okay ..." She hugged Caliyah, who snuggled in closer.

"You're hurt, too?" Caliyah asked around a whine.

"Shh," Brooke reassured her. "I'll be okay, especially now that I've found you again."

"You didn't find us," Jihan growled. "They brought us here!"

Technically ... but wow, he was so angry. Worry niggled at what had happened to him since they'd been separated. "You're right, Jihan, but regardless of how it happened, I am very glad we are back together."

"A'cus we're family," Caliyah pronounced, her words scrunched like her cheek against Brooke's chest.

A steady fire burned across her side, but she bent down to press a kiss to the little head. "That's right—family."

"But where is Daddy?"

Heart aching, Brooke wished she had an answer. "I think he's looking for you ..." It was a lie she hated speaking, but she could not bear to tell them he had been attacked, too. The video footage had shown all three of them vanishing in that van.

"No, he's not," Jihan snapped. "He's dead. They killed him."

Startled at both his vicious anger and words, she stared at

him. "No." She swallowed around a thick throat. "No … he's not—"

"They took him just like they took us. Then he was gone. And the only time people are gone is when they are dead. Like my friend."

"Your friend?"

"Jem."

"Oh … was she with—"

"*He!*" Jihan all but growled.

"Oh, sorry."

"Jem was at the warehouse with us. They took him … and he never came back. But I saw the blood on the man's hands. They killed Jem. It's what they do. Same thing happened with Dad."

"That's not true," Caliyah cried loudly, sobbing and soaking Brooke's shirt. "Tell him it's not true."

"It's not," she said, hugging the little girl. She leaned around a wince of pain to touch Jihan, who yanked away. "Your father is strong. Trust him, believe in him to find his way back to us. Okay?"

"It's stupid to believe that!" Arms crossed, he huffed and flopped onto his side, ending the conversation. Slowly, face to the wall, he curled into a ball. Though he tried to hide them, his quiet sobs reached out and strangled the last of her emotional reserve because he had always been a confident, strong-willed boy, but this bitterness …

In court, she had seen instances like this. Kids lashing out, actions cruel, words as sharp as glass that was broken … like their souls.

Merciful heavens, what had happened to him?

She curled up with Caliyah, putting her back to Jihan's, hopefully giving him a sense of protection. Sleep was an uncooperative foe despite her bone-deep physical and mental exhaustion. And though sleep would not come, the tears did. Tears of desperation. Tears of defeat. Tears of fear. Finding the children hadn't given her the sense of completion she'd anticipated, hoped for … Instead, it'd just made her more aware of the impossibility of their situation. There would be no rescue.

And silently, she found herself thanking God that Cord hadn't come. The last thing she wanted was for him to get trapped here, too.

Don't come. Stay safe—and very far away.

CHAPTER
THIRTEEN

Outside Kaohsiung City, Taiwan

Light and shouts ruptured the thick veil of night, along with the thread-thin grasp she had on sleep. Alert and awake in an instant, Brooke kept her midsection stiff as she scooted to the edge, both to protect the children and to see what was happening.

Beams of light bobbed in the waist-high fields. Guards ran in that direction, though some hung back, likely to keep the captives in line. A group had gathered at the far edge of the rice paddy, huddling around something. Hsiao-Hun cast his beam ahead as he trudged down the small incline with Mrs. Cheng, who looked angry and ready to deal with whatever miscreant intruded on her property, time, and sleep.

"What is wrong?" whispered Ginika.

Brooke shook her head, shifting for a better line of sight on the scene. When that didn't improve her ability to figure out what was going on, what could draw the cruel woman from her tower, Brooke stood. Wrapped her arms around herself as she took a step forward, aware all the guards were focused on the disturbance as well. Caliyah hooked her arms around Brooke's legs. After shooting a glower at them both, Jihan pushed to the front.

Meaty thuds of punches being thrown drew her attention back to the huddled group just beyond the rice paddy where she and the kids had worked yesterday. Had one of the children tried to escape? But … they would just die, like Guang. And since the boy's death hadn't drawn out the madam … this had to be more significant, right?

In the perfect timing of two men shifting to look at the approaching Mrs. Cheng, a head turning, and a narrow stream of illumination—a face made itself known. A bald head. Beard.

Sucking in a sharp breath, Brooke stepped back as her view was once more blocked. No. No, he couldn't be here. Please, don't be here. Don't be Cord. Swallowing, she told herself to find out. Learn the truth.

"Brooke?"

Caliyah's sweet, tired voice startled her.

"Stay there," she instructed the girl. "The guards don't like when the children leave huts."

"What's going on?" Ginika asked.

"We're not babies," Jihan protested. "Tell us."

The huddle of guards swelled. Erupted backward. Bodies collided. Cracks and thuds echoed in the still morning.

Unable to take her next breath or step, Brooke waited … knew that Cord was lethal and cunning. She'd seen how he dealt with problems, and feared what would happen here if he tried something. Those weapons worked, though the guards relied more on the shock collars.

"What are you fools doing?" Mrs. Cheng demanded as she finally reached the chaos.

The huddle parted, and to her shock, Brooke saw Lee straddling Cord, who …

What on earth …?

He held his arms crossed over his face, shielding himself.

She had totally expected to see that reversed. Or rather, that Lee would be dead, with Cord standing over the lifeless body.

"Get off him," Mrs. Cheng snapped. "Touch one of my workers again and I will have you shot."

"He is not a worker. We f—"

"Shut up! Here, I am your boss and don't care who your uncle is—you obey me!"

Lee snapped his chin down in a submissive posture.

The short, stocky woman flicked her hand at Hsiao-Hun and Youliang. "Get him up."

The two men hauled Cord upright, and when they did, the bloodied face shocked.

"Who are you?" Mrs. Cheng demanded. "What are you doing on my farm?"

Cord inclined his head. Smart man. "S-sorry. I was just hiking ..." He kept his head down as he gave a grin and thumbed over his shoulder. "I was just trying to find that mountain everyone talks about, y'know?" His Southern accent sounded painfully thick.

Like his idiotic skull!

"I was just trying to get lucky and find that—"

"There is nothing lucky about you being on my land." Mrs. Cheng clasped her hands in front of her. "Well, maybe not lucky for you, but it is for me. The children are too slow, the woman too weak. So, now I have a strong back to work my rice paddy."

Cord cocked his head. Frowned. "I ... what?" He took a step closer and with a finger, turned his ear toward her as if he had hearing problems. "Sorry. Come again?"

You are not that stupid, Cord Taggart.

No, he wasn't ... All he had to do was look around him, which she was sure he already had. That meant he knew exactly what was he doing—his best to convince this woman to let him go.

Brooke cupped her hands over her mouth and nose. *Please*

please please don't ... Could she will Mrs. Cheng to send him away? Not—

"You're trespassing."

"Shoot him," someone said.

"What? No—ain't no tres-ing, ma'am. Just *passing*"—he motioned with his hands as if diving into water—"through. *Hiking.*"

"He's a spy," Lee spat.

"Spy?" Cord chuckled—then faltered. "W-why? What would I spy? I don't care about your rice fields." He indicated to a backpack that one of the guards held. "Look in there. Y-you'll find a map, water, jerky—if I was a spy, wouldn't I have ... I don't know, cool gadgets or tech!" His eyes widened. "Or a gun." Idiot smiled. "I don't have a gun." He glanced at one of the rifles aimed at him but cringed away.

Believe him. Please believe him. Make him leave ...

Mrs. Cheng watched with more sick pleasure than should be allowed as Hsiao-Hun quickly put Cord in a hold that immobilized him while another guard secured one of the collars around his neck. "Good." She seemed entirely too proud of herself.

When the woman's gaze swung to the huts, Brooke realized most of the children were awake and witness to Cord's capture. Which meant the Shrew saw it, too.

"Tie him at the stake," Mrs. Cheng ordered. "Do not move him until I say."

"I thought you wanted him to work—"

"I want those children to understand who is in charge. That this man will *not* save them or change their situation." She gave a firm snap of her head as if to make her point. "Then you will make him work, even if it means beating his back bloody." As she started for the house, Mrs. Cheng again looked to the huts. "Go to sleep or you will work now!"

Hsiao-Hun and Youliang held Cord by the arms, forcing him

to the center of the compound where two guards were already preparing a rope.

Hand on her mouth, then resting at her throat, Brooke watched. Made eye contact with him. She felt herself twinge toward him.

Cord gave her an imperceptible shake of his head, then stumbled.

Deliberately. Hsiao-Hun yanked him upward, cuffed his hands and tied his arms up over his head.

Grief-stricken, angry that he was here—it would do no good. He was as much at their mercy as she and the children—she turned back.

"I know him," Ginika whispered.

Brooke startled. Pushed the girl back into the hut. "Time to sleep." But the girl wouldn't move and Brooke nearly knocked her over.

"But I know—"

"Quiet," she hissed. "If they see you know him, he is dead. You are dead." She leaned closer, wanting her point to be clear. "Do you understand?"

Ginika seemed to pale beneath the words. Gave a half nod as she stumbled toward the hut.

"Who is he, Brooke?" Caliyah asked around a yawn as they lay back down in their hut.

Hugging the girl to herself again, Brooke propped her head on her arm so she could see past the children, out into the night, and to the tethered man she had wanted—secretly begged—to come. Now, she felt responsible for his predicament. Because she knew how Mrs. Cheng worked—the woman liked to find and milk connections. Work one person against another. If the Shrew figured out Brooke knew him, she'd beat one of them. Possibly both.

Which was fine. Brooke wanted to beat Cord herself. What good was he here, captive? Why hadn't he been more careful?

And the worst of all ... why did she suddenly feel as if everything was going to be okay?

Color him confused, but Cord couldn't figure out the scowl Brooke kept shooting at him. And dang, if his knee wasn't killing him from standing on the mucky ground that afforded no resistance. Made his muscles work harder to stay upright. Said muscles were now trembling.

But as the black of night—which wasn't exactly black considering the floodlight glaring down on him—gave up the ghost, he'd started assessing the encampment, glad to put an eye on what the camo netting hid from plain sight. Thermals had been helpful, but this was better. Already a plan simmered in the back of his mind. Just prayed that Pike got back to the team without a hitch because this was not a one-man job.

Not long after dawn cracked open another day, the bearded guy—clearly had military training—showed up, dragging a metal baton along the bamboo huts, waking the children, teens, and Brooke.

Brooke. It'd been good to see her face even in the haze of darkness. And that's what had confused him—she'd looked ticked. That didn't make a lick of sense, so he must've misread that.

He hadn't, however, misread the goons. Men who used power to make up for manhood that seemed to evade their sorry selves ... But there were more kids than expected, and since his arrival, more guards had trickled in. He spotted one or two scouring the hills beyond Cheng's paddies. Again, he hoped Pike had put enough distance between him and this chaos before the fire ants flooded out of their nest.

In a matter of minutes, the kids were up, moving to use the restroom, then getting in a single, long line. Brooke—man, she still did a number on his good sense, even with bruises and dirt-and-blood-stained clothes—stood in line with the kids. In front of her … yeah, that was the Daghestani girl. The boy behind her. He'd half expected her to hold the girl close, but she wasn't. Hands at her side, she kept her gaze down.

Had to hand it to her—likely smart considering that hag who'd ordered him tied up.

"You okay?" one little kid asked as he paused to stare up at him.

"Sure." Cord nodded.

Another boy grabbed his friend's shoulders and spun him toward the line, and just as quick, dropped his hands to his sides. "Don't talk to him. They'll hurt you."

Cord slid his gaze down the queue that ended at a table. Nobody was touching. Heads down. Hands to self. It was quiet. Eerily—*wrongly*—quiet. Kids shouldn't be this quiet. He felt the anger, the violence, thrumming in his veins, washing away the whole dumber-than-dumb-hick act that had kept him from eating lead last night.

Calm … calm …

But somehow his gaze again found Brooke. Traced her form—the dingy pink sweater, mud-stained jeans that seemed… baggy. Her once-white tennis shoes … the freakin' dog collar around her neck. Around everyone's necks.

Even mine.

Quick intakes of breath shifted his attention to the captive children, the line—the table where two guards delivered food, just like he'd seen through the thermals. But being this close, watching up close and personal leant a kind of macabre feel to the wretchedness of it all. The kids moved through the line methodically. He watched, though feigned as if he weren't—no need to encourage the wannabes to test their strength on him again—as they walked away, sipping from a tin cup, which they then deposited in a barrel and cupped their hands to their mouths, eating sticky rice.

While the rice was better than nothing, it wouldn't provide enough sustenance for bodies sent out to work in the fields.

No matter how much he wanted to rip these thugs apart limb by limb, he had to play nice so they'd believe he was no threat, untie him, and pitch him in with the others. At least that way—for now, until the others came—he could do the heavy labor and grant Brooke some relief from the pain.

Sun beat on them as they headed into the paddies. Ginika and Adesina appeared to be the eldest and were given direction over kids in one paddy, while Brooke worked the largest field. His gut cinched each time she whacked at the stalks with that scythe—the pain had to be wicked with broken ribs. As the day progressed, so did the heavy clouds. They moved in and hung thick and threatening.

KAOHSIUNG CITY, TAIWAN

"Anyone got the twenty on Auberon?"

Canyon looked up from the table where he and Leif sat with Range, freshly stitched, popping some ibuprofen and working the photos from the market brothel. "He was with Taggart."

"Yeah," Luther Landry gruffed, a mannerism that conjured up memories of Griffin Riddell. "Due back this morning, and unless I forgot my secret decoder glasses, they ain't here."

The burly mass of man known as Lowell Reisinger rose from his seat. Log-thick arms seemed to beg to put someone in a chokehold. "So the boss got himself in trouble. Again."

"We don't know," Landry countered, but then shrugged. "Just that they aren't here."

Canyon moved around the table and joined the Omen team. "Last-known?"

Landry tapped a glass that held a projection of a map. "North of the city. Scoping out an area that had unusually high radio frequency traffic bouncing around."

"Track their phones?"

Wadi uncrossed his arms where he sat at his station. "Nothing. They either turned them off—"

"Wouldn't be the first time," Low noted.

But it could also mean the phones or people were dead.

"Where did the phones last ping?" Range joined them, guarding his abdominal wound from the altercation at the brothel.

"Hey," Canyon said, pointing him back to the conference area, "sit down and rest."

"I want to hear this."

"You can *hear* from the chair."

"If I wanted Mom to babysit me, I'd have gone to the lodge." Range shoved a fierce expression to Wadi. "Last ping?"

Wadi and Landry shared a look before the former sighed around an aggrieved expression. "Chief told us to stay put, even if we didn't hear from them for a while."

"So why are you worrying?" Range had more than a little gruff in his tone.

Landry seemed to grow a few inches—and in diameter, that chest broadening. "Because he's the boss."

Brick Archer lifted his chin. "Chief is notorious for overcommunicating, even when he says he won't. It's rare to go this long without some signal or message."

They all looked to Lowell, who seemed confused at first as to why they were eyeballing him. "Boss is known for going silent when he feels it's necessary."

"Okay." Canyon nodded, processing the intel. "My brothers

and I are working an angle that I know Taggart wouldn't want us to let up on. What about you?"

Landry considered him, then cocked his head. "Waiting. On the chief." Curiosity glinted in his gaze. "What trail are you on?"

"Putting histories to faces that Range captured at the market. Already thinking we might have something—doubt the guy with the CFO was just a john or a VIP customer. Plan to run it past the MiLE operators to see if he's familiar."

Landry nodded. "Good. We keep this thing moving while we wait."

"Agreed, but I think … " Canyon smirked at the guy. "Seems a perfect time for a drive in the country then, wouldn't you agree?"

A slow grin brightened Landry's gray-green eyes. "That it does. Fresh air will help me think clearer."

"Well, not sure about that," Tycho taunted. "But it's worth a shot."

Landry popped the other guy so fast nobody had time to react—except to laugh at the belly-birthed *oof* that gusted out.

"I'll go with you," Lowell said, moving toward the Omen team.

"Negative." Canyon felt very much the old man here. "We could use your help to work through the images Range caught at the brothel. You're the only MiLE operator we have access to right now."

The barrel-chested guy hesitated, then acquiesced. "Makes sense."

Once Landry and Tycho left for that Sunday drive, Canyon and his brothers made room for the moose-of-an-operator to join them.

"Wish I'd been on the ground before Cord went out there," Lowell muttered. "He knows better. Always thinks he's invincible."

Canyon considered the guy. The negative talk about his boss … which was laden with concern. "Doubt he's worried—not with someone like you watching his six."

The guy's brown eyes took him in. "Dang straight." He clicked his tongue. "But you don't have to give me platitudes."

"Wouldn't dream of it."

"Now you're just yanking my chain."

"Here," Range gruffed, sliding over a picture. "That's the CEO at the firm. Same guy who met with Brooke."

Lowell crowded up to the table, his brick chest bumping it. "Never seen him before."

"Name's Gerard Frost." Range slid another photo in as a peal of thunder rumbled overhead. "And this is the driver of the car that delivered Frost."

Thick arms on the table, Lowell shook his head. "Same—unknown." He raked his hand over his shorn scalp. "Gotta be high-level to come up empty.

"Hey, Metcalfe," Landry called from the far side of the safehouse.

Canyon and his brothers looked in that direction.

Landry snorted. "Sorry, *Old Man*."

"Hey, no need to get personal." Canyon felt every one of his nearly forty years, though. And he had another kid on the way? God, help him. "Car's in the way," Landry said, thumbing toward the door. "Can you move it?"

Canyon looked to Leif, who'd been driving.

His little brother frowned. "I parked against the wall. No car in front of—"

"Grenade!" came a feral shout from just outside the door.

Lightning-fast reflexes honed in more than fifteen years of operating pitched Canyon away from the shout. He dove for cover on the other side of the table, crashing into Leif, who'd grabbed wounded Range and taken him to ground.

Boom!

The concussion punched Canyon in the back. He dove into a roll, scrambled toward his brothers as he drew his weapon. Aimed in the direction of the explosion.

The barrage of bullets forced him to stay down.

"Bomb!" came another shout.

A whistle. Shriek. As Canyon hauled Range up with Leif, he heard the clap of silence. Knew one thing—this was not going to end well.

CHAPTER
FOURTEEN

AN UNEXPECTED DOWNPOUR last night tore at her heart, made it hard to sleep, knowing Cord was out there beneath the unrelenting drive of pelting rain. She lay in the hut, the thatched roof providing more protection than she'd imagined possible. Holding Caliyah, staring out at the post, she ached for him. Two full days tied to that stake.

At the end of the work day, as she trudged back from the fields, handing off the scythe—which she'd so wanted to use on these monsters-of-guards—Brooke ached and hurt, not only in her body, but in her heart. Even though he slumped against it, with the way the rain soaked his shirt to his torso, his muscles seemed strained—as if he were holding up the post, not the other way around.

"He has a lot of tattoos," Jihan murmured, arms crossed, scowl fixed. But more so—his attention fixed on the thick-skulled operator.

Despite her attempts to school her thoughts, to tell herself it was inappropriate and ridiculous, she fell asleep thinking about those tattoos and arms. Morning brought an end to the rain and a thick layer of humidity that lingered beneath a sun that seemed unfairly bright, even with the canopy overhead.

"Is he alive?" Ginika asked. "He's not moving. What if he got sick and died."

"It wouldn't happen that fast." Right? Yet when she realized the girl was right—he *wasn't* moving—Brooke sucked in a breath and took an involuntary step toward him. "Cord."

His head lifted and his gaze swung in her direction. Where she expected exhaustion to hood his gray eyes or puff out bags under them, he looked at her with sharp awareness and again a warning that vaulted across the camp, telling her not to do anything.

"He's okay," she murmured. "Time to eat and get to the fields."

Caliyah stomped her foot and groaned a whine. "But I'm so tired of working."

"I know," Brooke said, sagging beneath the oppressive circumstances.

Jihan shoved toward her, palms up and out. "And I have blisters! This is all your fault."

Brooke said nothing of her own broken-rib agony, feeling all-to-keenly the sharp edges of his words. "We are all hurting, but the guards will hurt us more than our aches if we don't do the work." She cupped the little one's face. "We are warriors, yes?"

"No," Caliyah pouted with another stomp, lower lip stuck out. "I'm a little girl!"

Seeing Lee moving their way out of the corner of her eye, Brooke had to think fast. "Let's"—think, think, think—"plan a game. For tonight. After work."

Caliyah eyed her speculatively. "I like games ..."

"Me, too." Brooke managed a smile. "Tonight, a silent game to celebrate another victory of a day finished. Yes?"

It was barely enough to keep the peace, to convince the children to move to the tables to get their rice ball. Allowing herself one brief glance at Cord, who was now on his feet again and staring out to the fields, she got her own breakfast and herded the children to the field. The humidity made it hard to breathe and the downpour last night had once again flooded the field. Still, she and the kids worked.

Brooke gripped a clump of stalks, braced herself against the inevitable pain in her side—and swung the scythe at it. Gritted her teeth. The wet stalks were stubborn, but she determined to finish this field. She'd seen a documentary once and knew the next step was letting the stalks dry out … then beating them to loosen the grains.

Laborious, back-breaking work.

Maybe she should take her time with this one …

A ripple in the slowly draining rainwater snagged her attention. She glanced there even as a shriek came from her right.

The shriek become unholy terror. A rice paddy snake shot at Caliyah.

Brooke lunged and snatched her out of the water, swinging her around. Her knees buckled under the excruciating pain, but she didn't care. "Out! Everyone out!" She tripped, Caliyah spider-melded to her chest and waist, and landed on all fours.

The terrorized child arched her body toward Brooke's, screaming.

Guards came running, shouting for them to get back to work.

She managed to get back on her feet, Caliyah terrified and unwilling to release her. "A snake," Brooke breathed as the guards reached them. "It attacked the child."

Hsiao-Hun considered her, the kids, then the paddy. His eyes narrowed and in a flash a dagger flicked out of his hands. With a *thwish*, it thumped between some stalks. Water erupted, the snake thrashing until it died.

"Back to the field," Lee barked.

"Please," Brooke pleaded. "It's the end of the day—"

"Back in!"

She turned to Hsiao-Hun. "There is only a little. Can the children go rest and eat, and I will finish?" She nodded to the paddy.

He again considered her. "In the field," he barked to her. "Kids to the huts."

"I will stay," Ginika offered bravely, her sister pawing at her, frantic at being separated from her.

"No," Brooke said.

"I will help," the Nigerian girl insisted. "You—"

"The children need a strong person to help them," she said with a slow nod, hoping she would bite on the praise.

Swallowing, Ginika slowly agreed. Guided the children back up to the huts and past Cord, who—

Brooke took in a sudden breath, finding him staring at her. Even with the distance, she somehow sensed his anger, his fury—not at her, but on behalf of her. Using the back of her hand, she swiped her hair from her face and sludged to the paddy.

An hour later, every cell in her body livid with pain, she trudged back.

Hsiao-Hun took the scythe. "That was brave."

Watching his hulk retreat, she argued his comment—it wasn't brave. It was necessary. The children wouldn't last much longer. She wouldn't …

Ginika came to her, hands extended with a ball of rice.

Brooke shook her head. She wasn't taking the girl's food.

"Extra," Ginika said softly with a half smile.

Unsure whether to believe her, Brooke faltered.

"Take." Ginika lifted Brooke's hand and rolled the ball into it, then urged it to her mouth. "Eat."

Unbelievably, she salivated at the thought. Goes to show

what hunger can do ... And that thought drove her gaze to Cord.

Head down again, he wasn't watching her. Enough. She'd had enough. As she stood there, resolve hardened in her breast. "He needs it more," she whispered.

"The guard won't like it," Ginika said with wide eyes.

"He doesn't have to." Brooke slid her gaze to the thick-skulled operator. "But we need him, and after being in the rain all night . . ." She took the rice ball and cup of rice milk and moved away from the tables. "Here."

Cord's head came up, his broad shoulders widened. He glanced around the compound. "You shouldn't—"

Heart thundering, expecting a shout or bullet or beating any second, she put the rice ball to his mouth. "Eat. Now."

He locked gazes with her and chomped into it. Drew it back as he chewed. Gulped. "You," he said with a nod.

"No." She held it up to him. "Another. Now. Before—"

"What are you doing?"

"Go," he hissed.

Brooke shoved the rice at his mouth. "Take it."

"Go—"

The rice smooshed into his mouth and she drew her hand away, closing it quickly into a fist, doing her best to lose as few grains as possible. She swung around and faced the guard storming toward them. "Mrs. Cheng said he was to work—how will he work for you if he dies of dehydration or malnutrition?" she said in Mandarin.

The guard thrust her aside. "To your hut!"

Monitoring the movement behind the guard, she pleaded with him. "But he needs—"

"Get back!"

Ginika was cupping the rice milk to Cord's lips.

"I will if you will take care of him!"

The butt of the guard's rifle rammed her face.

She ducked to avoid the blow, not caring about the pain in her side. Glad that the ruse had worked. "Okay, okay." She cowered away, moved to the hut.

"What is going on here?"

Oh no. Brooke tucked her chin and cast a sidelong look toward the voice of Mrs. Cheng. The woman was storming toward her, outrage in her round face.

Brooke thought to cower again, but no ... she had made a stand, and now she needed to hold her ground.

"What happened, Lee?" Mrs. Cheng demanded.

"The woman fed the man her food."

Appraising eyes narrowed on Brooke. "Did she?" She tilted her head as she moved toward Brooke. "You care about this man so much you give him your food?"

Standing straight—at least a foot taller than the Shrew—Brooke told herself not to look at Cord. "What I care about is a break." Offering her blistered hands as proof seemed smart. "The work is brutal and I am tired. You said the man would work, so I would have him work. It has been two days since he was tied there. He smells, and much longer, he will die."

Mrs. Cheng smirked. "Those hands are not used to hard labor, I think."

"I had an office and a desk," Brooke conceded.

"I suppose you want him in the hut with you. Do you think you will be safe if I put him in there with you?"

"Put him wherever you want." Just get him off that stake. "I don't need a man to make me feel safe." She made a point to look at the guards. "In fact, I find most men to be animals. They need to be kept in line."

Mrs. Cheng laughed. "You are funny. But this man"—she pointed to Cord—"will not get you out of work."

Brooke couldn't help but swallow. She inclined her head, accepting the Shrew's words and will.

"Unchain him." She curled her lip. "She is right—he stinks.

Take him to a paddy and make him wash." Her head snapped back in Brooke's direction. "Why you wear that thing on your waist?"

This was the last thing she wanted to admit, afraid the men here would take advantage of her injury and make her life worse. "I was hit by a car. Broke two ribs. Your man took me from the hospital."

Mrs. Cheng's gaze raked over her. "I know not why he take you—you too old." She flicked Brooke's hair. "Black hair boring! Men want blondes or redheads."

"Then let me go."

The woman cackled. Shook a finger at her, then shuffled away.

Arms coiled around Brooke's legs, and she reached down, holding Caliyah close as she stole a glance past the guards ushering the Shrew away.

Cord's gaze connected with hers. Gratefulness swam in his gray eyes. An imperceptible nod as the guards roughly shoved him toward the paddy.

At least he wasn't tied up anymore. She turned toward the hut when a tin cup appeared in front of her. Brooke glanced at the proffering.

Ginika smiled. "He took a gulp, then said to give you the rest."

With a huff, Brooke rolled her eyes. "Thick-headed oaf ..." But she finished off the rice milk and let Ginika return it for cleaning. In the hut, she sat with Caliyah, who held on for dear life. Poor kid.

"Who is he?" Jihan asked, his voice tinged with awe. "He's ... big."

"A strong back," she said, not wanting to betray their connection to anyone, even the kids. It would be too easy to extract the truth from them with the right threat. "And a person—nobody should be treated like that."

Darkness had fallen and the guards still had not brought Cord back. Had Mrs. Cheng changed her mind, had them kill him?

Oh, Lord …

She swallowed the prayer. What could she do if that'd happened? Nothing, except blame herself. Which she was already doing because he wouldn't even be here if she hadn't gone after the kids …

But how could she not?

She glanced down at the little one lying on her lap and drew her aching hands over Caliyah's hair.

Black hair is boring!

Well, thank God for that—at least in this situation.

"Is he coming back?" Ginika whispered in the darkening hut.

"Maybe they put him in a different hut," Jihan said. "I want him in here—it's all girls, and all you do is cry, cry, cry. Or sing that stupid song!"

"Jihan," Brooke chided.

"Well, it's tr—"

Ginika gasped. "There he is."

Her heart was getting quite the workout today. It skittered through the dark, right alongside each step he took. But then the guards shoved him to the right, out of sight.

At least he's alive. For that she would be grateful. With his presence here swelled hope … They might just get out alive.

As night swooped in, Ginika started humming a song quietly that eventually drew Adesina into the rhythm … and soon it was paired with a very quiet hand-clapping game, a more sophisticated version of patty cake. It had been their pattern the last two days, a game they'd taught the other girls.

Caliyah shifted on her back and held up her palms to Brooke. "You do it with me."

Habit had "no" perched on her tongue but … why not? "Okay …" She shifted, as did Caliyah, and they hummed and patted palms. Laughter started softly, but then a burst of giggles startled everyone. They covered their mouths and huddled, giggling even more.

A large shape broke up the scant light coming from the light post.

Brooke stilled, pushing Caliyah's hands down, knowing the guards rebuked any form of merriment.

Youliang and Lee clambered in. "Over, move to the side."

What were they doing?

She and the girls obeyed, crowding themselves to the far side as the men erected what looked like a fence—no, like bars on a jail cell. What on earth?

They tied it in place, partitioning off one-fifth of the space, then left. "What are they doing?" Caliyah asked.

"Sh-sh," Brooke said, hugging the little one closer. "I don't know."

A few minutes later, the men returned—with Cord. They shoved him into the narrow sliver of space and secured it tight. So, yes—a jail cell. They, apparently, didn't trust the man to not attempt an escape.

Cord sat against the wall, legs out straight, head resting as he stared at the opposite side where boots met bamboo.

She wanted to say something. Had the strangest compulsion to touch him, verify he was really there. But the Shrew capitalized on any emotional connection.

So, Brooke returned to her position against the wall. Stretched out her legs, mirroring the way Cord sat. Inches and bamboo "bars" separated their shoulders.

"What's your name?" Shufen, a nine-year-old asked.

Cord didn't answer.

"We should rest," Brooke urged the children in Mandarin.

"Why won't he talk to us?" Kaili asked.

"I think he's tired," Shufen said.

"We all are," Brooke agreed. "Now, sleep."

With the space Cord's cell took up, she did not have the same amount of room to stretch out as before. And that was okay. Lying down and trying to sit up hurt. A lot.

Rubbing her shoulder, she took comfort in the snores and steady breathing of the children. More than once, Jihan grunted or whimpered. What had they done to him?

"Thanks."

Brooke stilled at the sound from Cord. It was so subtle and quick, she wasn't sure it'd been spoken. She nodded, her words held hostage behind the fear of being discovered. Of being hurt. Shouldn't she be the one thanking him? She'd told the Shrew she didn't need a man to feel safe, but it'd been an outright lie because having him here … she very much felt safe. And it kind of angered her. "I—"

His long snore silenced her.

She stole a look in the cell. Night had fallen and shielded his side from the light. But she could see his thick beard. His bald head. That muscular chest. Where had he been the last two days when she'd had to cut rice stalks? How her hands and shoulders ached.

But he was here. Right next to her. He …

He found me.

Comfort in that revelation wrapped her tight, allowing sleep to take a strong hold.

CHAPTER
FIFTEEN

If she realized she'd fallen asleep with her head on his shoulder—of a sorts—he was pretty sure she'd sue him into eternity. Or throw him off that millions-dollar balcony she owned.

He actually had a mind to do that to her—

She shifted—and cried out. Stiffened and came upright, awareness stabbing into those blue eyes of hers that swung in his direction.

"Yeah, you slept with me."

She scowled. "There are children—"

"Still sleeping, but not much longer if you keep barking."

Brooke huffed. Shook her head as she scooted back against the wall, holding her side where a black brace didn't seem to be doing her much good. "What is your problem?"

"You!" he hissed. "You're smarter than to show me any sympathy."

"Oh, sorry, was it too inhumane of me to want you cut down already? Should I have waited till you ripped your arms out of your sockets?"

"I had control—"

She sniffed. "By that stench roiling off you, you really didn't."

Humiliation crowded him. He'd done his best to scrub the waste from his pants. "My point," he said in a low growl, "is that if you show them you care about me—"

"Caring about you would mean I had you cut down the first day."

"—they will use it against you."

"They already have," she spat. "Why do you think they locked you in here!" She let out a growl-purr, which to her was probably a growl-shriek, but it was cute. And he loved getting a rile out of her. "Besides, if you want to nitpick mistakes, let's start with you not being careful enough and getting yourself caught. Lord knows how you survived as an operator." She snorted. "Now you're stuck in here, and that helps nobody!"

Man, she was a spitfire. At least she had some color in her cheeks that had been pale the last two days. "You think it was an accident I ended up in here?"

Her mouth opened, blue eyes took in his face, then the mouth closed again. She looked toward the kids, then snapped back to him, a grimace telling him those ribs were hurting more than she let on.

"*How,*" she hissed, "does this help, you being in here?"

"You have my shoulder to sleep on now."

Brooke shoved her dirty, black hair from her face. "Merciful heavens, you are thick."

Cord puffed his chest. "Thanks. I didn't think you'd—"

"Stop." Fire in her eyes and fury in her tone, she was not messing around.

He donned contrition like an ill-fitting shirt, one where the buttons would pop if he twitched wrong.

"The lives of these children depend on using intelligence and shrewd moves, not idiotic heroics or your bloated ego."

Properly chastised, Cord nodded. But did she really think so little of him? "You think I didn't have a plan?"

Those pink lips parted. Surprise rippled through her pretty features as those blues settled on him again, like the warmth of a clear blue sky that he could soak in all day long.

"You have a plan?" she said with more than a little disbelief.

"Yeah." *C'mon, Taggart—lies don't become you.* "Like maybe eighty percent of one."

She stared at him, and it was an expression he couldn't read. Scratch that—he could read it. Felt a whole lot like that stank-eye thing Momma mastered and used to put the fear of God into him. "Possibly seventy." Dang, he had to give it to her. "You're right."

Brooke huffed her exasperation and shook her head, which she tilted back against the bamboo wall. "I can't believe I actually hoped you'd come."

Do what? Cord jerked his gaze to her, felt his heart do a little mamba at those words. "You did?" Probably shouldn't get too excited when she was this ticked. "You hoped I'd come?" *Me.* Not some other operator. Him. Cord Taggart.

"I *hoped,*" she growled at him, "that you'd bring in a team of operators, gun all the bad guys down, and get these kids to safety. Isn't that what you do—what MiLE does?"

Dumbstruck still over the fact she was hoping for him to come in and rescue her ... he didn't have a response.

"Or do you always screw it up?"

Cord grinned, and thanked God there were bamboo bars separating them or she'd probably have slapped him into next week. But he saw through her anger. "Oh, I'm pretty good at screwing things up, but do you really think I'd screw up something so important as rescuing you?"

"Who said I need rescuing?"

Okay, he'd let her sort that one out for herself.

And she did. Gaze jerked down. She shifted. "Point made."

"Wasn't trying to make one." He watched as the little girl next to her curled closer, hands tucked beneath her chin, and shuddered.

That was the Daghestani girl, wasn't it?

"I was on the hill with a buddy. He went for help. I came down here."

Hesitation guarded her as she stroked the little girl's hair. With the remnant of light catching the movement of her eyes, Cord knew she was thinking things through.

"Your brothers are in-country, too."

Brooke snapped her gaze to his. "Canyon?"

He inclined his head. "Range and Leif, too. Working with my team and a black-ops team."

Expression now thoughtful, she turned her attention back to the fields. She sighed. It was a sound of release. A familiar sound he'd encountered in his years of liberating trafficking victims.

"Can you get me up to speed on what's happening, what you've seen? How many, etc.?"

She inclined her head. "The number of guards keeps changing—every time I think there's eight, then there's ten. Mrs. Cheng owns the place and she lives up the hill. There are more guards there."

"Yeah, noticed the barn has more human dung than cattle dung."

"What's dung?" the little girl's voice spiraled out.

Brooke glowered at Cord.

He gave her a sheepish shrug.

"Like I needed another child to take care of."

"But you *will* take care of me, right?" Oops—there was that stank-eye again. He rubbed his shoulder and stretched the joints, which were still sore from two days of him strung up like a fish on a line. "What's the routine?"

"Daylight's coming, so the Thick-Bearded guard is Hsiao-Hun. He's not … bad."

"Thick-Beard." He nodded. "Favors you."

Her gaze shot to his.

His shoulder lifted. "Scouting my competition."

She sniffed. "He will shock the kids or me if he feels it's warranted, but he's not psychotic—that's Lee. Tall, skinny absolutely demented."

Cord nodded, remembering that guy. "Also has a thing for you."

"It's because I'm the only female here of age."

He cringed, hating that she thought like that. It was sick, but she was right—men high on power wanted to show women how much power they had. "I won't let it happen."

"What? Is that part of your fifty-percent plan?"

Now she was sweet-talking him. "Seventy, remember?"

She sagged and looked around the hut. With nine or ten kids scattered on the floor, there wasn't much room, but they had made the best of it as they possibly could. "They need help. To get out of here."

Pike should've made it back to the safehouse. The team would get together, work up a plan, contact local authorities, and work with them to execute said plan. It usually took a few days … "It will happen."

He folded his arms, crossed his legs, and glanced out at the field. Recalled her saving the girl from the snake. Seeing Brooke collapse in pain yet fight to protect the kid … he'd nearly snapped the rope in two at that point.

"They make us work the fields—the stalks are cut, so now we'll lay them out to dry. Then we'll beat them to free the grain from the stalk."

"That sounds painful in your condition."

"My *condition* is I'm captive. Injuries are a luxury I can't afford."

Maybe with his back in the mix, he could offset some of the labor-intensive work, or at least shorten the duration of said labor. Ginika woke next, and slowly, she began rousing the other kids as the day began.

"Will they let him out?" a boy of about nine or ten—was that Daghestani's boy?—asked as they took turns using the bathroom.

"He has a collar, too," Ginika said. "And he's strong."

"They want strong people to work," Jihan said as he shifted toward the bars, looking at Cord as if he were an ape at the zoo. He leaned in. "Can you help us break out?" he whispered conspiratorially.

"Jihan," Brooke chided. "The guards will hear you."

"He has a collar, too," the little girl said as she leaned against Brooke. "He can't help us because he's a prisoner, too. Right?" She peered up at Brooke.

They seemed pretty close, looked to Brooke for answers and direction. Like they would a mother …

"Don't worry about that, Caliyah. It's time to use the bathroom, then food."

"It's not food," the girl said, exasperated. "It's *rice*. I want apples."

"I want shakshuka," the boy said.

"Daddy said you can't have that because you got sick from the spices last time."

"No, I didn't." Affronted, the boy turned toward the open door. Hopped down. "I'm going to the bathroom."

Cord watched as the guards started showing up again, milling about, monitoring the movement of the kids to and from the outhouse. Took note of the four who carried a large bowl of rice balls on poles down the hillside.

The kids filtered out of the hut and headed for the tables to get what could loosely be called breakfast, and only because of the time of day it was being delivered.

Brooke scooted across the floor, then let her legs dangle off the edge. It was cute, but it was also probably to avoid the jarring pain of hopping down out of the hut. She sat there for a moment, watching the kids, then glanced over her shoulder.

Concern etched those blue eyes. She seemed to want to say something, but then she pushed to her feet and joined the line with the children. At the table, he heard her voice—but it was all soft and gooey like. And she was talking to the freaking guard.

No … no no no.

Even as she moved away with her rice ball and a tin cup, Cord saw the thick-bearded guard headed his way.

He relaxed himself, closed his eyes.

A string of Mandarin peppered the air.

Cord debated looking at the guy.

"Hey."

Best not tick off the one holding your leash. Cord finally looked at him. Saw the guy motioning him on his feet.

He stood. The guy turned his finger in a circle, indicating for Cord to face the other direction. He complied. Heard the chain unlock.

This would hurt. But recon wasn't always benign.

Cord steadied himself. Fisted his hands. Breathed in … breathed out.

Hose-One, or whatever his name was, barked something.

Steeling himself, Cord came around.

"No! Cord, don't!" Brooke's voice sailed between him and the guard, followed by a rapid stream of Mandarin. But then, wasn't Mandarin always spoken rapid-fire style? He stumbled out of his confrontation effort.

But still found the beefy guy warned by Brooke's shout, so he put him in a chokehold. Which Cord knew how to get out of, but across the open yard of the compound, he saw the other guard had Brooke. The sick guard. Lee.

Son of a blister.

He was going to get himself—and them—killed.

Maybe she should've let Lee shock Cord. Maybe it'd teach the thick-skulled operator that his actions would have repercussions on the rest of them.

Restraining and holding her close—inappropriately close— Lee hissed in her ear all the horrible things he would do to her. That one night, she would not be expecting it, and he would be there.

Then he thrust her forward and shocks riddled her body. She dropped onto all fours, then slumped to the side, her teeth clacking. Every nerve ending on fire. Warmth squirted across her tongue. Tears sliding down her cheeks, she begged God for it to stop.

Slowly, the fire and volts receded, leaving her on the mucky ground. Shudders wracked her body, reminding her of the broken ribs, the aches in her back …

"To the fields," Hsiao-Hun ordered.

Peeling herself off the ground, Brooke had to focus hard on putting her feet under her. Standing. Following the children—

A touch came at her elbow.

She yanked it away from the offender. "Don't," she growled, still thrumming from the shock collar. Felt the raw flesh beneath it.

"What—why did you do that?" Cord asked, his tone … odd.

Hurting so fiercely, she shoved him away. Stepped into line with Caliyah and Jihan, catching their hands, trying to steady themselves.

A half dozen guards hauled bamboo stalks and set them over benches. Large blue tarps covered the ground.

"Grab a bundle of stalks and beat them across the slats so the rice falls to the tarp," Hsiao-Hun barked.

The kids glanced around, the instructions having little meaning to children who had never done this work. Brooke wasn't sure herself, but she wasn't going to give the guards a reason to shock anyone again. She headed over to the easel-style set-up where the stalks had been hanging to dry and took a bundle. Ignored the twinge in her side, and returned to the bamboo.

"Go ahead," she said to the others in Mandarin with a nod. She glanced at Hsiao-Hun, wondering if she was doing this right, then swung the stalk at the bamboo poles. It was incredibly more rigorous than she'd expected. Her knees buckled, and she swayed. Struggled to stay on her feet. Upright. Fearing another shock, she glanced at the guards, who were distracted ... by something to her right.

Thank goodness, they hadn't seen her. They'd have beaten her or worse for being lazy. Instead, a series of repetitive thwaps drew her attention to the side.

There, Cord and Jihan were taking turns beating the stalks.

"Me ... you ... me ... you ..." Cord huffed as they alternated, the words eventually sliding into a cadence that unbelievably managed to get all the kids into working.

With the kids working and Cord in all his strength and vigor encouraging them and chanting a cadence, the burden that had been on her shoulders the last week faded. She lifted the bundle, glancing again to where he was working with the kids. It wasn't really a rigorous pace but a steady one. Slow and steady.

Slow and steady wins the race. How many times had her brothers said that?

Brooke fell into rhythm, surprised to find the cadence he taught the kids helped her as well. Not just improving the rhythm of work, but the chant—which she said in her head, it was too much like breathing fire to say it out loud while she was beating the stalks—relieved stress. Helped her focus, calm.

They made it through dinner without an incident. She wasn't sure that had ever happened before, and somehow, all her frustrations with him being stuck here with them rather than effecting an escape, and the earlier shocking lesson ... they melted away.

After dinner and restroom breaks, they settled back in the hut. The atmosphere was different tonight, and she knew it was because of Cord. There was a part of her that did not want to admit how much he'd affected them—positively—but at the same time, she was done with jockeying for control. Tired of being the one to hold it all together, especially since she'd obviously done a terrible job. A job she'd been doing all her life.

All day the guards had kept Cord separate during times that were typically communal—eating and moving back/forth from the fields, using the restroom. Even now, she and the kids had settled in the hut, and Hsiao-Hun stood with Cord, hands tied. They really were worried about him attempting some escape, weren't they?

Finally, he was escorted over and delivered to his three-by-five foot space, crammed between the bamboo walls and the bars.

Nodding to the guard who secured the bars with a thick padlock, Cord settled in. Closed his eyes and folded his arms.

Brooke wanted to look at Cord, wanted to talk to him, but she dared not draw the guard's attention. So, she waited ... afraid to speak, afraid to feel that shock again ...

The girls were playing their hand-clapping games again in near-silence, huddling close so their whispered verses weren't overheard. Jihan had managed to wrangle himself toward the bars, toward Cord.

"How's the wrist?" Cord asked the boy.

Brooke glanced between them, wondering what he meant.

"Better," Jihan mumbled. "I did what you said and it doesn't hurt as much."

"Good. By morning, you shouldn't feel anything."

"What happened?" Brooke whispered into the dark.

"Slight sprain—got a little exuberant with the stalks," Cord said. "But he's tough. Pretty sure he did as many stalks as I did."

Jihan's chin lifted a little higher. "He taught me how to hold it so it doesn't hurt as much."

"Technique is everything." Cord gave a smile that defied the darkness.

Quiet settled in. The rustle of fabric and shoes stilled. The near-silence was nice, almost peaceful. It seemed so counter to their circumstances.

"I'm sorry," Cord said, his voice stealthy and deep.

Brooke shifted her gaze to the side, to where he sat in the inky darkness. What was he apologizing for?

"Whatever I did this morning that set you off … I'm sorry."

Ah. That. She'd nearly forgotten about it. In captivity, the gap from morning to evening seemed as weeks. "Your actions—our actions—affect all these children. Trying to take out one guard to escape—"

"I wasn't trying to escape."

Brooke huffed and deflated. "But you dove into Hsiao-Hun."

"It's recon. Gauging response times, figuring out what their plans are when situations arise. How many come to assist. How many don't. It's all part of being able to formulate an exit strategy." He sighed. "I thought they would shock me … I had no idea they'd hurt you."

"That's the method here—if someone does something, they hurt someone else."

"Wickedly cruel, but effective." His gaze shifted to hers, barely visible in the light from the center post in the camp. "I'm sorry. I wanted to kill someone when I saw you …"

"I can handle myself. I'm okay."

"But you weren't. I saw—"

"I've survived a week without you, Cord. And I can survive longer if need be."

"I know."

She stared into the blackness, and thanks to his baldness, she could make out the outline of his head. Where his face delved into the thick beard was harder to discern. But she felt the sincerity of his words, though it surprised her.

"But you don't have to," he said softly. "I'm here for a reason. On purpose. No accident. For the kids, for you."

"Then be smart about it, okay? Getting into a brawl doesn't help."

"I never meant for you to get hurt, but it did give me vital intel on how things work here."

"My electrocuted body was happy to oblige," she bit out.

"I swear, Brooke—I am so sor—"

"Don't," she said around a sigh. "But now you know, so ... be smarter?"

"Scout's honor."

A near-smile creased her heavy mood. "You're sure your friend is coming, my brothers ...?"

"I wouldn't have infil'd otherwise. It's not a one-person job."

"Then why are you here?"

Cord shifted. "You."

Brooke's chest seized. "That's... that's stupid. There are children here who—"

"Like the Daghestani kids? That's them, right? Why you're here—you went looking for them."

How did he know ...? "I ... yes."

"And it was okay for you to put yourself in jeopardy for them?"

She saw where he was headed with that. "It's different—they're children. Mazin's children, family."

"Right, and I'm nothing but a thick-headed oaf."

"At least we got that straight."

He sniffed.

And somehow she heard the hurt, the irritation.

"Can we just … pretend to be friends, so we can get the kids out of here?"

Now her feelings were hurt. "I … I thought we were friends."

"I'm not really sure you know how to do that. You've been leading me on with all these clues for months, and now that I'm here, managed to put the pieces together and figure out how to find you, you're treating me like *I* am the enemy. This—saving kids, getting them out—it's what I do. What my team does."

"I didn't give you clues. What're you—"

"Play dumb with yourself if it helps you process things, Rapunzel, but don't expect me to buy it. In Nigeria"—his finger stabbed through the bars—"where those girls came from—you made a point to let me see you. More than once, reached out to me, to ask questions. If you didn't want me to know, you would've shut me out in the cold like you do to your family."

Indignation carved through her. "You know nothing about me and my family."

"I know none of them even knew you were out of the country. None of them knew you were living with Daghestani and raising his kids."

Brooke startled. Frowned into the darkness. "Living with …"

He considered for a second. "Your assistant invited me to your condo—saw the pictures. She told me how much they mean to you."

"What were you doing there? How did she get hold of you?"

"I was looking for you," he all but growled. "You weren't answering messages, and then I caught wind of the kids' kidnapping … Then I got the digital diary."

"Journal," she corrected. "And I tried to stop that from

sending." She rubbed her forehead, wondering what he thought of her unfiltered thoughts being poured out in a journal she'd never expected anyone else to hear.

A long pause struggled between them. "So you didn't want my help after all?"

"I …" Boy, this got complicated fast. Every instinct in her wanted to cry "no," but … "As I said in one of the entries, if something happened to me, then I knew the one person who would intervene would be you."

"You didn't answer my question."

"What do you want from me, Cord? I'm tired. I'm in pain. I—"

"Just a straight answer."

"Does it matter now? You're here—trapped like the rest of us."

"It matters to me." For such a big guy, he sounded very small with that one line. "Don't mean to make you feel cornered. Would just like some truth sprinkled into this."

"But my feelings don't matter. What matters is getting the kids to safety."

"What matters," Cord said, his tone firm, almost sharp, "is getting *everyone* to safety. It's why I'm here. You're why I'm here."

Rattled at the intensity he put behind those words, Brooke had no doubt it wasn't about everyday work for Cord. Yes, he was an operator combating human trafficking. Yes, he'd go to the ends of the earth for the victims. But this … this was about … more … And she just wasn't sure she could go there again.

"You … you said you knew about the kidnappings." She glanced at Jihan and Caliyah, sound asleep. "What about Mazin? Did you find anything about him? I could never get any information on him."

"He's important to you …?"

Brooke turned her gaze toward him, probed the darkness in an attempt to see his face. His eyes. "Yes," she said. "I told you—they're family."

"Right."

What on earth? He sounded … jealous.

"No," he bit out. "Never found anything. Even talked with the ASAIC there in New York. Guy's been missing since they took him." The sound of him shifting filled the quiet gap for a moment.

"It's so odd," Brooke muttered. "Why is he missing, but the kids are here?"

"Pretty standard to split up family groups. Gives them less emotional support, fewer allies so they don't get ideas in their heads."

"I suspected as much, which is why I've tried not to show too much favoritism toward them."

A grunted carried between the bars.

"I know I've failed, but … I guess I'm not strong enough for this. I thought maybe I could do it, that I'd do what law enforcement agencies wouldn't do … But these kids, especially Caliyah …" She couldn't help but smooth the little girl's hair. "She's like a daughter to me. Like—"

"Family. I know."

Were this any other situation, she would be simultaneously amused and annoyed at his blatant jealousy. But this time … it just made her sad. Things were already so irrevocably complicated, and there just wasn't any hope for her. Not anymore.

Where was the Omen team? Or the Metcalfes?

Cord worked through the day, doing his best to carry a bigger portion of the load. It was eating at him—the kids were gaunt, thin, weak. Brooke even had lost weight, and the broken ribs had never had time to heal. What the heck was taking Pike so long?

He worked with the boys and kept them on task, did his best to help them keep their noses out of trouble. The Daghestani boy showed his intelligence and an aptitude for operating. It wasn't often Cord could see it in a kid this young, but the boy had it. He didn't miss a thing.

The perv that had set off Brooke's collar a couple of days ago was paying a little too much attention to her. This might be a forced labor camp, but it didn't necessarily dictate that was all that happened here. Cord prayed he didn't have to hurt someone. Or kill. Not with all the kids around.

"I don't like that man," Jihan said as he filled another basket with the rice grain. "I'm afraid he'll hurt Brooke."

Cord wondered if he could get some intel from the kid on how his dad and Brooke met. "You really like her, huh?"

Nodding, the boy continued the mindless task of separating the rice from the stray bits of stalk, then scooping the quarter-inch grains into the baskets. "Dad says we're family. We live at her house—it's huge and up high in a building. I can see everything from the windows."

Cord hoisted a full basket and moved it to the side. Picked up the two the boys had filled, then delivered them both to the store room, halfway between the encampment and where the woman owner—Mrs. Sheng? Chang?—lived. Each step he took, he counted. Each guard identified, counted. Each trip, he used a different route, learning the lay of the land, where cars were positioned. Was there a gate? He recalled, too, watching with Pike the response to a believed attack and how rapidly they'd been on scene. It meant the others were close. Considering the time and distance, on the edge of the city maybe.

Why hadn't he thought of that before?

Used to beating his body into shape, Cord could admit to

still feeling exhausted. It was one thing to work out, another to work from sunup to sundown with the stress of shock collars and guards all too happy to punish them.

That night as they ate sticky rice—he vowed to never touch the stuff once free of this place—and drank the rice milk—which was some kind of nasty—Cord stole more than one glance at Brooke, who sat with the girls and ate.

"Do you know what happened to my dad?" Jihan asked around his rice as he eyed Cord.

Right in the ticker, kid. "I … don't. An FBI agent showed me a video all three of y'all being taken, but your dad hasn't been located yet."

Another bite, some grains slipping down his chin, which he caught and stuffed in his mouth, too. "Maybe Jaddi has him."

Cord frowned. "Who?"

"My jaddi—Mom's baba." The kid shrugged and scrunched his face. "He is a bad man. He killed my mom and tried to kill us. Jaddi made people do bad things to other people. Made them pay, so did my mom. That's why Baba took us to America."

A sick knot formed in Cord's gut. "Why would he want to kill you or your dad?"

"Jaddi said Baba stole Mom from him—and us. But that isn't true. Bad things were happening all the time at Jaddi's. He and Mom had a big fight—that's when she died. The imam blame Baba, so we all left."

"What kind of bad things?" Cord hated asking the tricky question, but he prayed the boy didn't have more than a passing knowledge of what Cord guessed was prostitution or trafficking.

Jihan cocked his head thoughtfully. "I don't know. Men would come all the time and they would go with Jaddi and Mom to the other house."

"Jihan." The crack of his name by Brooke drew Cord up straight. "Time to rest." Once the boy hurried over and climbed into the house, she stomped closer. "What're you doing?"

"Talking," he said, trying to act nonchalant. "He brought up living in Saudi."

"He's a *child*," she hissed. "Interrogate someone else!"

Hello. That was a loaded reaction. What roused all that animosity? "So, you know his family was messed up in trafficking? This ... Daghestani, his dad—he was—"

"What do you want from me, Cord? What can you possibly do with information about his terrible, abused life in Saudi?"

"Considering I'm working to take down the Trench, which has branches dug in all across that country, maybe a lot." He shouldered in closer and lowered his voice. "Why are you so against me talking to him? It could help—"

"It helps nobody," she bit out. "As you pointed out, his dad isn't here."

"But he knows things about—"

"Enough!"

He pulled back, surprised at the vitriol. Seemed so unlike her. "What are you so afraid of, Brooke? What do you think I'll do or figure out? Because this—"

His nerve-endings crackled. The smell of burned flesh registered the same time searing pain zapped through his body, heated his neck to the point he expected it to blow off.

He dropped to the ground. "Augh!" He heard a yelp.

"Cord!" Brooke reached for him.

He yanked away, not wanting her to get shocked, too. Even as the shocks zipped down his arms and spine, he realized it wasn't as strong as he'd expected. Painful, heck yeah. But ... not debilitating. Save possibly cracking a tooth. Could he use that somehow?

How, genius? They still have guns and you don't.

Valid.

A stream of Mandarin flew from the side, and Cord spied the too-thin perv-guard standing over him. Wished the paddies were still flooded. He'd take the guy into the water during one of these shock-therapy sessions. Fry that sick brain into oblivion. It'd be worth it.

On a knee, Cord slowed his breathing as the fire dissipated. Pushed upright and wavered. Groaning, he forced his trembling muscles to support him.

Gentle hands steadied him, and he found Brooke assisting him. And with more care than he'd expected to find in those blue eyes. Okay, this was worth it, too.

He gave her an appreciative look.

She frowned. "What?"

"Should've asked him to shock me sooner."

Rolling her eyes, she led him to the hut. And blessedly, the guards didn't order him into the cow-stall, but he didn't want to draw attention to the lapse, so he stepped inside and pulled it closed.

Brooke's lips parted, clearly having noticed the same thing.

Stretching his neck, feeling the singe of that shock tingling through his shoulders, he touched it. Moved to the other side and sat down.

"I'm sorry," she whispered.

"Don't be."

"I … I should be." She joined him, sitting close to the bars as evening drew the curtains on another day. "I overreacted and you ended up getting hurt. We need our strength and we're on the same side."

"Are we?"

"Of course we are." She sighed, then pinched the bridge of her nose. "It's probably best if we just …"

"Play nice? Act like you *don't* want to rip my throat out?"

Her gaze met his. "I'm sorry. I know I haven't been … nice."

"And the Understatement of the Year Award goes to—"

"Please. I'm trying." That defensiveness fell away. She sagged, leaned her forehead against the bar marginally. "I'm so tired, Cord. So very tired. I just want it over …"

"The path to freedom is intel and recon."

She groaned. "Can we just … rest?"

"When we're dead."

"Already there."

His finger itched to touch her shoulder, to touch her, let her know it'd be okay, but he had a feeling this stronger-than-steel woman would rebuff his words as platitudes. And she'd likely be right, because he couldn't guarantee anything beyond this right here.

"How'd you meet Daghestani?"

Brooke lifted her head and considered him, seemed to want to challenge him, but then she relented. "My dad. When I was like … fourteen," she practically scoffed. "He took me on a ski trip. That's when I met Mazin."

Was that irritation in her tone? "You've known him that long?"

She nodded. "Sort of—it wasn't really until about four years ago that we got to know each other. Believe it or not, we reconnected via social media. And I'd told him that if he was ever in the City, to reach out. Told him he always had a place to stay."

"And that is some place …" He felt petty saying that.

Hesitation slowed her response. "Thanks. I … it's … I like to host parties for the firm."

"Killer views."

Her face brightened. "Isn't it incredible? Many times after a long trial or deposition, I'll sit in my pajamas on the floor with a glass of wine and just stare …"

He shuddered.

"What?" She cocked her head. "Are you … afraid of heights?"

"Baby, I HALO and HILO jump."

She gave him an incredulous look. "You just shuddered when I mentioned sitting on the floor by the windows."

"They could break."

She laughed. "You *are* afraid of heights."

"No, I'm not afraid of heights." He shifted his position. "I'm afraid of falling from them or that three-thousand-miles-an-hour-to-zero deceleration."

Brooke angled around to face him, sitting cross-legged. "The big, muscular operator is afraid of heights."

"I just said—wait, muscular?"

She scoffed. "The muscle that counts most is the one you're lacking."

He knew there was a jibe coming.

"Your brain."

"That's uncalled for, Rapunzel. Now, I've been nice and done my best—"

"Why'd you call me that? My hair is neither blonde nor long."

"And my brain muscle"—he tapped his head—"*isn't* lacking. After all, look who I'm sitting with right now, rather than in some dank safehouse."

Resting her forehead against the bars again, she tilted her head, the stringy black hair framing her face. "I can't figure you out, Cord Taggart."

"I'm pretty simple, Punz. Give me my Bible, a Dr. Pepper, the woman I'm staring at, and I'm golden."

"Give *me* to you?" She arched an eyebrow.

He shrugged. "I'm not above begging or spending the rest of my life working off the debt."

"Debt?" She huffed a laugh. "What are you—"

"But I know you got this other fella, and he's staying at your swanky million-dollar mansion—"

"Penthouse."

"—so there's some history there and I imagine he means a lot to you, since you live with him and his kids are like your own to you. And I'm just a grungy, hard-hitting operator." When he saw her mouth open to object, he waved her off. "Yeah, I already know you don't date military types, but I can prove that's a mistake."

"Cord." She sighed and shook her head. "Look—"

"There's one thing I can't figure—"

"Only one?"

"Why you kept that guy from your family, if he's living with you, sleeping in your bed—"

"Cord!"

"I know it ain't none of my business—"

"Cord."

"But it just seems … beneath you to go around in secret like this and—"

"He's my brother."

"But I have my values. Biblical val—" Her words finally struck his brain. "Canyon? Who mentioned him?"

"No," she said softly and looked at her hands, then back to him. "Mazin Daghestani is my brother—my *half* brother."

CHAPTER SIXTEEN

Outside Kaohsiung City, Taiwan

"You wanna back that 747 up?" Cord ran a hand over his shiny head, staring at her. Eyes wide. "He … Wait, *what*?"

She sighed and weighed how bad this could get if she came clean. But she *hated* the idea that Cord thought she was intimate with Mazin. And honestly, it'd be nice to have someone to share that secret with, bear that burden. "My … father had an affair."

"Whoa. Didn't see that coming. How did you end up living with your … half brother?"

"Mazin showed up about a year ago, scared out of his mind—his ex-wife's father was trying to kill him and the kids, saying they had destroyed his business and name." Brooke fought the tears at the memory of that incredibly overwhelming moment. "I'll never forget it—getting a call from Bertram in the lobby—"

"Oh! Yeah, met Mall-cop." Cord cringed. "Dude judged me harsh."

Brooke laughed. "Betram is good at what he does. He called, said my brother was in the lobby with his kids. Shocked that any of my brothers would come up to the City to see me—let alone with his kids—I told him to send him up. Imagine my shock when the elevator opened and I found Mazin standing there." She shook her head with a wry-but-sorrowful expression. "Seeing the condition of the kids … his absolute despair."

"How'd he get stateside?"

She sniffed. "He knew I was a lawyer and refused to tell me. He said it was because of my job, but I think it was more about shame. What he had gone through …" She shook her head. "They showed up with nothing—not a bag, toothbrush, nothing. Just the clothes on their backs. Not a dime to his name. Ishwin helped me get toiletries and clothes for them, we fed them. The first night, Caliyah and Jihan wouldn't leave Mazin's side. They all slept in one room together. It broke my heart."

Cord looked at her, his gaze steady. No judgment. Actually there seemed some sorrow. "I've had to do those last-minute arrangements for kids. Not easy." A rare moment of contrition and realism. "You did good, Brooke."

She couldn't recall the last time he gave praise. Not that he was a hard man, but he simply rolled with things. "Thank you, but it was just something I knew had to be done. Part of me felt I was making right over thirty years of wrong done to him. They were family in need, and I had the money, my home was big enough …"

"Taj Mahal has nothing on that place."

Sharp words deftly applied. Brooke couldn't believe how much that hurt. "I … I can't tell if you're trying to make me feel bad about the penthouse—"

"No. No, I just …" He seemed to reconsider, then plowed ahead. "Sorry, it's just hard to see that level of extravagance and not think what MiLE could do with all the pretty pennies that cost."

Level of extravagance? Admittedly, she had a very nice home and life. She supposed some might call it extravagant. But hadn't she earned it? Worked hard for it? "I won't feel bad for having made a successful career that pays well."

"Didn't ask you to. And I'm sorry my words made you think that, Punz."

Punz. Rapunzel. What was with that?

"Hey." He scooted forward. "So, when I met with the ASAIC, he mentioned the kids were in private school ..."

Brooke eyed him through the slats. "Cross-examination of the witness?"

"Negative. I just didn't want our conversation to end on a negative note, but our wheels seemed locked in that icy direction."

It took her a few minutes to tuck aside the quick offense, know that Cord Taggart was probably one of the best men she'd ever met. Most genuine, caring ... That's what she had to remember when he handed out truth with a tank versus a teaspoon.

"Central Prep is the best high school in the City," she explained. "The board president is the brother of our firm's CEO, so I pulled some strings to enroll Caliyah and Jihan. Being a powerful attorney in New York has its benefits and helped me call in favors to secure a work visa for Mazin. They approved it quickly because he had a management job offer at the Italian eatery."

"I know how hard it is to get those things through all the red tape. Government isn't known for expediency." He nodded. "Nicely done. And doing it for people in need ..."

His words were a balm, an encouragement. She hadn't expected that. "It's actually been really wonderful having them live with me." It was a second chance at family she'd never expected to have.

"But your brothers—the real ones. I mean, Canyon and—"

"They don't know about Mazin. Stone knows Dad had an

affair, but I think he's the only one. Nobody knows about Mazin."

"Except you."

This thick-skulled operator was somehow worming his way into her heart. "And you."

"Yeah." His gaze shifted to the children. "Niece and nephew. Explains why you went all over creation to find them."

"Nobody would do anything, nobody cared. Not the authorities, not anyone. And it was mortifying as an attorney to see the level of ambivalence within the law enforcement communities—"

"I wouldn't call it ambivalence," Cord argued. "I have a lot of LEO friends and connections. The number of kids who go missing is astronomical. And authorities are short-staffed and bound by red tape, procedures, laws ..."

She leaned forward, her heart thumping. "But I found them, Cord. If I could do that—"

"And look where we are."

Recoiling, she could not believe he said that. "*You* put yourself here."

"If you want to be technical, so did you."

"I—"

He held up a hand. "I'm not arguing, but I don't want you to fairytale this either. Brooke, there are over two-hundred kids MiLE is actively looking for, and that's just my team. Dozens of other orgs are out there searching. Next time you have cell connectivity, look up the story 'Find Gardy.' His father, Guesno, has been searching for him for over *eight years*. What you did here"—he motioned around them—"and the success you experience is not typical. In fact, it's pretty abnormal. And very dangerous."

She drew back, heart thumping. "I worked my rear—"

"Yes. You did." He touched her hand. "And I want to say this with as much gentleness and reassurance as I can muster, because I do not mean to wound, but this … the search for kids, the battle to protect them, it's not about you. Or about your efforts." He nodded to Jihan and the others. "It's about them."

Brooke drew up. Swallowed her sharp words … and her pride.

"Because what they've gone through, what has been done to them—that they're still living and breathing? They're the heroes."

They were words she needed to hear, needed to correct her path. "You're right."

A strange tenderness filled his rugged features. "Don't get me wrong—what you did, leaving everything, tracking them down? I'm …" He seemed to search for a word. "Moved. Impressed. Most people sit on their couches or behind a laptop or phone, remarking how terrible trafficking is. Share a photo or two. And go to bed and sleep peacefully."

Convicted, she peered up at him, heart stirred. "I did that … for weeks …" Her hand slid to Caliyah. "But I couldn't take it any longer. Not after what happened to Brighton …" A breath shuddered through her. "Seeing what you did for her inspired me."

He groaned. "So you nearly getting killed is my fault."

She smirked. "You know my brothers. Fairly sure they told you it wasn't easy to dissuade me."

"They, uh, had more colorful words to describe it."

She laughed. "I am sure." But then her heart twisted again as she considered the kids and their father. "It pains me that none of the family knows about these two or Mazin—who is mistakeably a Metcalfe. But that is a secret long sealed in the vault of All Things That Should Not Be Spoken."

"You should tell your brothers—they're legit focused on right and wrong, but they're also very devoted to God, family, and country."

"I can't," Brooke admitted, her heart hurting. "Mazin did not want sympathy relationships, nor did he want to impugn our father's reputation, damage the family name, or hurt my mother. And for that I am—was—grateful. But ... when we connected on social media, we talked ... a lot. We were both black sheep of the Metcalfes—me for one reason, him for another. But I could relate to what he felt as an outsider looking in."

"Black sheep? You? Cuz of the dark hair?"

"Ha." Had to admit, she really liked how he tended to make her smile or laugh. "No ... I ... my family didn't understand what was happening with me and Mark, they were always saying what a great husband he was. That I didn't know what I had."

Cord's expression took on a gentle, discerning shade. "But you didn't tell them ..."

She frowned. "How do you—"

"Seems to be your MO—keeping things close to your vest, dealing with hard stuff on your own." Again, no judgment. Just that hefty dose of truth.

"It's difficult to share things with those you look up to when they assume the worst of you, or blame you when incidents happen." She felt the hollow emptiness that had been a common occurrence at every family gathering.

"So he did ... stuff?"

Did his words have an edge to them or was that her imagination?"Not him, his cousin Craig," she said. "Quite an alpha guy. I consider myself strong, but when he was around ... Anyway, he resented me, my career or life in New York. Detested that I took Mark away—they were best friends growing up. Every time we saw each other, he'd somehow corner me or pull me aside, tell me what was I doing wrong, tell me I didn't know how this or that felt, or that I was ruining Kaleigh or Mark. Even when the psychiatrist said Kaleigh was bipolar, he argued with me that she didn't have the symptoms."

"Was this Craig a psychiatrist or psychologist?"

"Accountant."

"Ah. Sounds like a real joy to be around."

She appreciated his reaction more than she'd admit. "Yeah. I got to where I dreaded getting together with all the cousins. He always had one thing or another to take me to task about. Yet, the tension was blamed on me. I was told that *I* had a problem with Craig, but I should try to get along. I couldn't believe it—all those years of being brow beaten by this person, bullied regarding everything I did … and I got blamed."

"What did Mark say? Tell me he pummeled the guy."

"Mark said Craig was Craig, and he was family, so …"

Cord huffed. "The one who should've been protecting you …"

Brooke studied him, surprised at how well he'd pinpointed what she'd felt all those years. "The whole situation drove me more into my career and Mark back to his family. Kaleigh hated the City. Considering her anxiety issues and diagnoses, I had to admit the slower pace of suburbia was better for her." She shrugged and rubbed her arms. "Eventually, Mark stayed there and I stayed in the City. He filed a year later." She pursed her lips and bunched her shoulders. "I still avoid get-togethers like the plague. Got to where I started believing something was wrong with me, since everyone else could get along."

"Who wants to be a part of something that makes you feel bad or alone?"

How did he always get it?

Cord roughed a hand over his face. "After Fallon's death … that was pretty much my whole life." He eyed her again. "Hard to believe Canyon and Stone treated you that way."

"My brothers could get behind one thing: military. I couldn't sort out how I felt and why I was always ambushed at gatherings, so I never told them."

"Called it," Cord teased.

"Just stayed away. Didn't need to feel worse about myself.

And of course, knowing about Dad's affair and Mazin ... I just couldn't pretend anymore. Swore off anyone remotely connected to the military."

"Yep, already heard that acerbic vow."

She touched his arm. "I am sorry." Should she admit she didn't feel that way ... about him ... anymore?

"So, Canyon, Range, Leif—they don't know about Mazin, and you're keeping it that way."

She shook her head. "I will respect Mazin's wish not to tell the family. For now."

"Well, they know he's sleeping with you." Cord flinched, seemingly chagrined at how he'd said that. "Sleeping—at. The. House. *Living* with you." With a groan, he muttered an oath.

"Leave it to you to have *that* slip of a tongue."

"Hey, I've never been shy about my feelings for you. But look, I ain't gonna lie—they had big questions about why you went after this guy and his kids, why they were living with you." He hesitated, as if making sure what he'd said had come out right this time, then shook his head. "Stone and Canyon both called, knew something was off, so I don't reckon that'll stay a secret for much longer."

"Once Mazin is found, then we'll re-evaluate. I think ... I hope things will be good. He's so much like them. Really hated taking me up on the offer, he had absolutely zero options outside of me. And my name wasn't connected to his, so it provided a modicum of safety for him and the kids." She pursed her lips. "Mazin would tell me every day how much he'd saved, all with plans to get out on his own. I'd insisted he not worry, told him I loved having them with me—it was nice to come home to family rather than an empty penthouse. It was like a second chance ..."

Why was she telling him all this?

"This is why you've been so protective of the kids and angry when I pushed the little guy about—"

"I'm sorry, but yes. I know it wasn't easy for Mazin to trust me with the terrible truth of what was happening in Saudi—"

"And that was?"

Brooke swallowed. "Forced prostitution. He had no idea his wife and her family were involved, and when he tried to stop it—they were cruel. Threatened the kids."

Cord fisted his hands, his expression fierce.

"As you can see, their backstory is pretty complicated. Who they are, what was happening back there ... Mazin didn't want anyone knowing about his connection to the Metcalfe name or the past." She shrugged. "He didn't want the kids to feel rejected like he had. He said the only relationship that could come out of that was one of obligation, and he wouldn't subject them to that."

"That's unfair, isn't it?" Cord asked. "Your family didn't know he existed ..."

"Dad did. But he just went on with his life and career, that chest puffed out with all those medals and prestige, leading troops—and even my brothers—into war."

"All while ignoring his own flesh and blood."

Brooke bobbed her head. "I couldn't stand my dad. Take all the female teenage angst and heap onto that this revelation ..." She grunted. "I was so disgusted by Dad's hypocrisy, that I ... snapped. Graduated high school, got a full scholarship, and moved to New York. Never looked back. Married Mark, had the requisite two kids, lost myself in building a career." She seemed chagrined, then sad. Swallowed. "Lost my kids ... my husband."

That was a lot of raw flooding out of her veins right now, and it scared her. She'd never been that honest with anyone, and she was already wishing she hadn't divulged all that information about Mazin.

"This is why you don't date military."

She met his gaze but said nothing. Somehow regretted ever voicing that to the one man who *had* come searching for her.

Just as he'd said about Mazin, holding a grudge toward her brothers wasn't fair since she'd withheld the information from them.

Just like Dad.

"I … I've changed since then."

"Since the last six months."

Since you. She lifted a shoulder, wondering if he could tell her heart was racing. "I'm a fast learner." Her stomach swirled with the absurdity of her own comments. This was very inappropriate considering the circ—

"Don't do that."

Her gaze bounced to his. "What?"

"Whatever argument you were just having in that head of yours, the one that was making that sunbeam smile turn into a gray cloud? It affects me, those around you."

"You're ridiculous."

"About you? Yes." He motioned around them. "I mean, I am sitting in a prison, having walked in here all on my own."

"But you have that seventy-percent plan."

Cord smoothed his large hand over his beard. "Maybe should've said sixty."

She huffed an objection. "You're kidding."

"Yes and no." He looked out at the camp, glad their convo hadn't drawn the guards. "Omen should've already been here."

Her eyes widened. "What're you saying?"

"We need to put our heads together and come up with a plan if we want to get out of here."

CHAPTER
SEVENTEEN

HER GAZE NARROWED. "YOU'RE SERIOUS."

"As a heart attack. Pike was supposed to head back to the safehouse and get the others. They should've been here night before last at the latest. I have to guess something went wrong."

"Wrong?" Brooke challenged. "Be very careful what you're insinuating, because you told me my brothers were here, and if they're not rescuing us, then ..."

"Either way, we need a plan. Sitting here playing good slave isn't going to get us anything except more time in the pen. And when rice harvest is over? What then?"

She swallowed.

"Problem is, this camp is being monitored. Within a half hour of our last diversion, the place was swarming with vehicles and guns."

Her eyes widened, neck craning forward. "That was you? You did that?"

"So," he said with a nod, "at most, we'd have thirty mikes to get clear of this place. And we believe that the fast response indicates there is some kind of surveillance tech—cameras, drones, whatever—out there. So, even if we escaped on foot, they'd figure out our direction and would have a reasonable chance of intervening."

All but hugging the boards, she leaned in. "But since you've already thought through all this, I would guess you have a plan or idea."

He cocked his head. "'Or.'"

She tucked her chin, staring through those eyebrows. "*Or?*"

"I can list possibilities, but I'm not excited about any of them. Top of my list is stealing a truck when it makes a delivery."

"Stealing a—" She shook her head. "But that wouldn't hold thirty kids."

He held her gaze firmly. "Stack 'em high, stack 'em deep?"

"You've got to be kidding me."

"Mostly. But desperate times … or … not everyone goes." Wouldn't be the first time he'd had to make that decision.

She drew back. "We are *not* leaving anyone behind."

He clicked his tongue and winked. "Girl after my own heart."

Despite the way her heart stirred at his words, she rebuffed it. "Are you always such an insatiable flirt?"

"Only with the ones that matter."

One*s*? Why did that irritate her, that there had been more than one? "How many mattered?"

He eyeballed her. "Counting you, Rapunzel?"

Now her cheeks warmed, but thank goodness he couldn't see the blush. "Are there so many you have to count them—and why do you keep calling me that?"

He smirked. "A few …"

"So there *are* too many to count."

"Is that what you think of me?"

"Hey, military, tattoos, muscles, good looks."

"Well, don't stop there …"

She wanted throw her shoe at him. "Tell me about the most important one—not counting me."

Cord winced. "Maybe a story for another time."

"Hey, I just poured out my darkest secret …"

He groaned and ran his hand over his mouth again. "A'right." He huffed and shook his head. "Fallon."

Nice name. She was already jealous somehow.

"My kid sister."

Why was she so relieved?

"Fair was in town, so I made plans with my buddies and our girlfriends. Only, when I head out, Mom orders me to take Fallon. She's ten, can't drive, not even sure she could count money, and the last thing I wanted was to be saddled babysitting when I had plans with my girlfriend." He gave her a long look. "Don't judge me—I see you sitting there thinking the worst of me."

She laughed and held up her hands. "I am not. Just listening. Though why on earth you'd plan a date at an amusement park is beyond me."

"Not everyone was raised rich and on ski slopes."

Brooke faltered. "How …"

"Saw the picture on your mantel."

"One of my favorite photos of my mom and I." With a guilty shrug, she hunched her shoulders. "Dad couldn't go, which made me very happy. Mom and I had a wonderful time. Skied, went shopping in town, and ate sushi. It was wonderful. We haven't had a trip like that since."

Cord groaned. "Any trip with sushi is one I wouldn't repeat either."

"You're being childish."

"No, I'm being medically serious—besides the nasty taste in your mouth from raw fish, I'm allergic to shellfish."

"If you don't eat shellfish, how do you know it's nasty?"

"How do you think I discovered I'm allergic to it?"

She grimaced.

Thunder rumbled in the skies and lightning splintered its brightness across the black blanket of stars.

"Rain at Christmas." Brooke sighed. "Can it get any worse?"

"Considering our situation, I really wouldn't ask that."

Unfortunately, rain did not come, and they were forced back out to resume threshing. Extra tarps had been laid out, likely anticipating the rain. As they made it to the area, Cord turned to her.

"Hey. You do the scooping."

She frowned. "Why? I can—"

"Rest your injury."

The woman flat-out bristled. "I am perfectly capable—"

"You *are* perfect, and you are capable, but your ribs are broken." He leaned, probably more intimately than necessary, and peered over her shoulder, feeling her cheek brush against his beard. "And when we break out of here, you need to be strong enough to run, maybe even carry a kid or two."

Though she pulled straight, she did not pull *away*.

That was a first. And he pushed his gaze to hers, her blue eyes once more throwing warmth in his direction. Those lips … and man, if she didn't have the same thoughts written all over her flushed face as what danced in his head.

"So, you're planning an escape?"

Okay, so maybe not the *exact* same thoughts. "Yeah." Right. Of course.

Mandarin bit into their quiet aside.

Brooke sucked in a breath and shifted away as Sho-gun or whatever his name was stalked toward them, a baton in one hand, remote in another.

Well, crap.

Cord backstepped. Made eye contact with the perv-guard and saw the warning there. Though his protective-warrior side rose to the fore, he acquiesced. Turned and picked up a bundle of stalks. Spotted Jihan working his way toward him with his arms full as well. The kid had a good heart, and Cord appreciated the way he sought him out. What he didn't appreciate was the way the guard looked at the kid, who threshed with the precise moves Cord had taught him.

His gut tightened, hoping Lee didn't realize that technique had nothing to do with threshing rice and everything to do with self-defense. By repeating the motion over and over, day after day, Jihan was developing muscle memory. That'd serve the boy well.

Crack-crack-boom!

Cord felt that peal of thunder in his chest. The next instant, he was drenched by the sudden downpour. In under ten minutes, they were standing in ankle-deep water.

Shouting came from the guards, and Cord hesitated, wondering what was going on.

The Daghestani girl cried and clung to Brooke, who squinted around beneath the driving rain. In her face was the hope of everyone—that the guards would send them back to the huts.

A moment later, Sho-gun shouted something in Mandarin. Though Cord didn't speak the language, he let the kids moving back to the huts tell him their wish had been granted. God had put him here for a reason, a thought he took seriously. So he stood in the center of the campground, rain drenching him, until all the kids were safely in the huts, but most importantly, that Perv-Guard headed back to their pens uphill.

"Go!" Sho-gun jutted his jaw toward the hut, urging Cord back to the shelter.

And he wanted to curse. This guy had a fondness for Brooke but didn't have that same affinity for Cord, so he'd likely lock that barrier in place. And though it wasn't a solid wall, the bars created a tight space. Not suffocating, but not fun either. He stepped inside and turned.

Sho-gun stood there, staring at Cord, who returned the

favor. Amid the standoff, Cord could feel the room grow still. Tension ratcheted as the children watched.

To his left, Brooke shifted Caliyah behind her and came to her feet.

Cord felt the water sliding off him and plopping onto the wood floor, but he dared not move. This felt … intentional. Important.

Expressionless, Sho-gun spoke something in Mandarin, low and quiet, and back-knuckled where the lock wasn't secured.

What was Cord supposed to do with that?

Brooke shifted closer.

He stiffened. "No—"

"Hsiao-Hun"—Brooke nodded to the bushy-bearded guard— "says it is clear you are a soldier, so why do you just sit here? Why do you not try to break out?"

Huh. How exactly was he supposed to answer that? Not wanting his intentional pause to be taken as rebellion—they had shocking solutions for that—Cord gave a nod. "Tell him it's probably for the same reason he didn't lock the cell or shock me back into this prison."

"You can't say that," Brooke hissed.

"Tell him."

"What if—"

"*Tell him.*"

By now, the guard seemed half amused, half annoyed.

Brooke exhaled heavily. Spoke in Mandarin repeating what he said. At least, he hoped she wasn't editing his words. Then she swung her gaze back to him. "What are you doing?"

"Hopefully securing an ally." Hopefully not getting zapped into the next life. When Sho-gun whacked his hand against the bars, Cord flinched. Heard the big guy mutter something.

Then the big guy left the hut.

Holy Mother … Cord expelled a thick breath and shifted to—

Brooke slapped the bars. "What are you doing? What if he wasn't an ally? He could've hurt you!"

"What's this, Punz? Worried about me?"

She growled. "You're a thick-skulled idiot."

"About you, yes."

Another growl … that had a smile hidden in it.

The entire afternoon was spent in the huts, the driving rain relentless—and provided a much-needed break for the kids and for Brooke.

Cord drew off his shirt and wrung the water from it.

Titters and giggles filtered through the hut.

"If I didn't know better, I'd say you commanded the rain so you could get your shirt off."

Cord winked. "Worked, didn't it?" He strained back into the soaked shirt, but at least he didn't have water streaming down his back and legs, making him feel like he was peeing himself. He skated a look at her. "Appreciating the view?"

"Wondering why on earth you've scribbled all over your body."

"Each one has meaning."

That made her take a longer, more in-depth look at them, and he didn't mind the attention. "Military …"

"Fifth Group."

She angled her head to see the one over his left ribcage. "Eagle for … patriotism."

"'Merica."

Across his back lay an anchor. "What …?"

"Best friend from high school—Navy SEAL. Died in Iraq." He really wanted her to stop investigating the tattoos, because she would no doubt come to the one crawling up his left arm.

She wrinkled her pert nose. "A snake?"

"Close." He thrust his arms through the sleeves and tugged it down.

Her eyes flashed to his. "What …?"

"Nothing."

The kids, thankfully, pulled her away—to a circle they had formed to play games. Propped against the wall, Cord watched them and kept a bead on what was happening outside the hut. He had a pretty good feel for how these guards operated.

With the guards tucked away and no work for the weary, games and merriment seemed the order of the day. Laughter and songs filled the air. It was a nice change. Really nice. This ... this was how a kid's day should be spent, what they should experience. Not pain or abuse.

While daylight still afforded a view—though marred, thanks to the storm—he scanned the hillside. Wondered how Pike was coming with the extraction plan. Slowly, an idea began to percolate ... He left the shelter of the hut and traipsed around in the rain, skating his gaze up and around. Testing angles. Lines of sight. Twenty minutes later, he returned to the hut. Noticed there were more kids in here now. More come to play.

When the cats are away ...

Positioned at the edge, he leaned against the opening and monitored the camp. Tried to let his brain work contingencies. Exfil routes. Realized there was probably enough water in the paddies now to drown someone ...

Warmth pressed against his back, and he tensed. Glanced to his left where Brooke's ivory face appeared. Lord, have mercy, she was beautiful.

She set her chin on his shoulder and peered up him. "What're you thinking?"

Dang, he was thinking all kinds of things he couldn't voice. Least, not without getting smacked. And did she know how hard it was to think with her doing that? He could take down an ISIS base, fight traffickers, destroy a Trench stronghold, but think while looking into Brooke Metcalfe's beautiful eyes? China had a better chance of becoming a constitutional republic.

He jutted his jaw toward the open area. "Guards are in the

barn on the hill. All of them. If I'm reading it right, they have no line of sight past the outhouse. Perfectly blocks this hut and the one to our nine."

"That's our … left?"

Cord nodded. But … there had to be cameras or drones—the response time when Pike had tested it was too fast not to be. Did condensation from the rain build on the camera lenses? Would it be too much to hope that the lenses might fog up or the downpour would make it too hard to see?

Her hands settled on his sides. "You think we can—"

Kiss? Make-out? Absolutely. But that wasn't what she was going to ask. Was it? She was more sensible. Intelligent. Unlike him. She was asking about … what—

Oh. Right. Escaping.

"Unknown." He couldn't give her false hope. "And not today."

"Why?" Her whispered question skated along his neck and teased the edge of his ear.

Cord reached around and pulled her in front of him.

Though she stiffened, Brooke didn't fight him.

Which … set off a bevy of fireworks in his gut and chest. Dared him to make a deadly move. He slid his arm around her waist and drew her back against him. And since she likely needed a distraction—and so did he—Cord pointed to the hillside. "See the trees?"

Head nestled against his shoulder, she laid her arm over his and looked at him, their faces crazy-close. Those pink lips right there. Waiting. Begging.

If she didn't look away, he'd help her stop that begging. Did she know how amazing she was? How she inspired him?

Her gaze swung to the distance. "Where …?"

Cord took full advantage of the moment, tightened their positions. Appreciated the curve of her body against his. Let his beard return the favor to the earlobe tickle. Stretched his arm out as if extending her visual field. "Right there. Two trees—one has a split trunk. The other is bent like an old man." Yeah, he let his lips graze that earlobe.

Brooke drew in a breath. "Ye—" Her word choked, and he knew it was because she was sensing what he sensed. Wanting what he wanted. "I buried gear there. Not a lot, but enough to get us on our way."

She hauled in a breath and snapped her gaze to his.

Cord prided himself on his strength of character, of willpower … except in this woman's vicinity. So he forced himself to focus on the plan. "When the time is right, that's where we start our escape."

She shifted and faced him, and he nudged her back against the wall. There was no hiding the flush in her cheeks or how she was looking at his mouth, too. "H-how?" She swallowed again, blinked, and shook her head, thoughts mixed-up over his nearness, jumbled over the rush of feelings. She moved to the side. "The collars, the kids—"

He took her hand, drew her back to himself.

"N-no, stop."

"Brooke," he said preternaturally quiet, "listen to me. C'mere."

She let him tug her closer. Stepped into his space.

"I'll figure it out, okay? But the important thing is to not alarm or notify the kids of what we're planning."

Understanding rushed over her. "Right." She freed her hand. Stepped back.

"Broo—"

"Stop. No—"

"Wait!"

Even as her mistake registered—she had run out of bamboo floor to step back on and her body swayed beneath the force of gravity—she groped for his arm.

Cord caught her. Snatched her back up. Right into his arms even as she yelped in pain. "Are you oka—"

"Leave me alone." She pushed him back. "We don't ... have time for ... this—that." Tucking the hair away from her face, she wouldn't meet his gaze. Shifted, a flush in her cheeks. "These kids, getting out of here—that's all that matters. Got it?" She shoved aside, skirted into the hut and moved to the far wall. Sat down.

From his spot, Cord noted her trembling hands. The uneven, ragged breathing. Why did her feelings for him scare her so much? And why did it seem no matter what he did, he only made things worse?

But he wouldn't *not* be there for her. Not like he'd done with Mom or Fallon. She wouldn't be able to shake him off. And he had to beat back the idea that he might have a chance with her. Focus on getting out of Dodge.

Speaking of ... who was that moving around the back of the huts to his three? In the pouring rain?

CHAPTER EIGHTEEN

THINGS WERE AWAKENING in her that she had thought long-dead … all at the hands of Cord Taggart. Hands that had wrought violence and yet seemed so strong and capable as they rested on her waist and hip. Pointed toward their escape. Even as she lay in the hut with the sleeping children, she wondered at the discordance of that fact. At the way he was both intense and raw yet also funny, charming … sometimes an idiot.

A smile tugged at her heavy heart. She was so glad he had come … yet, sensing him controlling her, controlling the direction of their … whatever it was … had made her tense. Want to backtrack. Panic. It was hard to express things that one didn't fully understand about oneself. Or hated.

Yeah, there were a lot of those …

But he'd come for her. Inserted himself into danger. For her. How could she not be touched by that? Altered by it? But this thick-skulled, well-muscled—a girl couldn't help but notice—operator had opened a place in her heart she wasn't sure should be accessed. Good things never came from that place being open, from her being … open. It would just mean she'd mess it up. Get hurt.

To the side, sitting in front of Jihan, Cord held the boy's wrist and was forming the hand into a particular pose—form. Demonstrated for him how to do it, then again tried to help him.

There was a time Brooke would've intervened, stopped him from teaching Jihan how to fight, to defend himself. But she understood it now. And also hated that—hated that a ten-year-old kid had to learn to fight to survive.

Caliyah shifted and pushed up. Climbed onto Brooke's lap and slumped against her. Despite the pinch of pain, Brooke snuggled in. Grieved how her overwhelmed-with-life self hadn't done much of this with Kaleigh. And if she were honest with herself, she had not done much of anything with her daughter, because her career had taken precedence.

But then … Cord. Who was ready to put everything on the line to protect her. It wouldn't end well. And the thought of him doing anything, getting hurt, to protect her …

Brooke suddenly felt sick.

In the scattered light where night and the lamppost light warred for supremacy, Cord shifted. Crossed arms lowered preternaturally to his sides. It seemed his torso swelled.

Something's wrong.

She eased up, doing her best not to disturb Caliyah or the other children. Wanted to ask him what was wrong, but he was too far away.

He twitched forward.

And her heart went with him. She was on her feet, no longer worrying about the kids. Joined him at the opening, remembered how she had so causally hugged him from behind earlier. Hadn't even thought about it. Just … did. And even now she had to restrain the impulse. What was it about him that made her so comfortable?

She dared not move too close and startle him. "What's wrong?"

His palm opened, a powerful but silent command to stay and remain quiet.

What was happening? What had him on edge?

She shifted closer, wondering if he could hear her breathing. She strained to see through the rain. Her heart jarred when a shape moved across the open area. As the shape registered, she sucked in a breath. "What …"

"Sh," Cord hissed, backing toward her. Catching her hand. Drew her back as Lee passed in front of the hut. He kept moving until she was sandwiched between him and the wall.

Brooke held an arm and his side, pressing her nose to his shoulder blade. "What was he doing?" Though she asked, terrible ideas flooded her thoughts.

"Nothing good," Cord said, his voice carrying a dangerous edge.

Brooke peered up at him, his strong form still rigid and braced against her. "How … how do you know he … did something?"

"Nothing needs to be done in the middle of the night except evil things." He shifted, huffed. "And I heard one of the kids crying. By the time I heard it, he was already leaving."

"Oh no … You think he …"

She tucked her chin and struggled against what that meant. "He … That's never been a threat before." She didn't want to believe. Didn't want to think about the horrific-ness of what just transpired.

"It won't happen again."

"How do you know?" She was a broken record but she had never been one for platitudes or false hope.

"I won't let it." He glanced at her, a severity digging into his handsome features. "You should rest—"

"After *that*?" she balked. "I can't—"

Cord turned to her. Cupped her face, his hands against the shock collar, which alone made her cringe. "Hey. I'm here. He'll have to get through me."

"I don't care about me." But didn't she? "I'm worried about the kids." That was true, but … Frustration tightened her breath. She resented the way one guard could instill terror. Just like the one man, a hero, instilled a sense of safety. Strength. This time, she touched his collar, trying to convey her point. "That's what worries me."

His hands slid around her waist and up her back, gently guiding her closer. "Trust me—"

"Cord, I—"

"Hey." He touched a finger to her lips. "*Trust me* to know when to act. When not to."

The man's intensity in this moment had her stomach doing somersaults. That and her conviction not to get involved with anyone again. "But—"

"It's not my first rodeo."

Perhaps, but it was the first time she trusted someone on this level … with her life. "I know …"

"I need you to give me a promise."

Brooke started to smile, figuring this was another of his smart-aleck comments, but the storm in his eyes … This … this was serious. "You're scaring me."

"Remember, trust me?"

"With a sixty-percent plan?"

"New plan." His beard twitched. "This one's at seventy … two."

"Oh, seventy-two? Wow. Well in that case …"

He smiled, but considering the weight of their conversation, the smile didn't reach his eyes or her heart. "Promise me when I tell you to, make for those trees I pointed out. Take the kids with you."

Sucking in a breath, she pulled up straight. Take the kids?

Without him—because that was the inference, right? That *she* take the kids. Alone. "What? No!"

"Brooke," he said with more than a little warning.

"No, I can't. This—"

"We're out of time." Gray eyes probed hers, his face very close. "You know what Lee was doing, without seeing it or me telling you. There's no other answer to what's happening. Before someone else is hurt, it's time to leave." He gave a nod. "Agree?"

Panic thrummed at her core, but she stamped it down. She couldn't deny she'd seen Lee's attention lingering on the kids. Or the sick knot in her gut when the man was around.

"Brooke?"

She flicked a gaze at him. "Yes—right. Agree." Only then did she realize her fingers were digging into his shirt. "But ... there's thirty kids. How—"

"The trees," he repeated. "You and the kids. Run for all you're worth." He gave another nod, wanting her to do the same. "Do not stop. I'll bring up the rear. Understood?"

Oh Lord ... This was really happening. "It doesn't make sense. There are thirty kids—"

"Understood?"

She wrangled out of his grip, out of being cornered. "No." Her heart was thundering as she paced away. "We can't—there's no plan, too many—"

"Staying here, not doing anything, makes us complicit in his actions."

"I ..." Her stomach squirmed, panic drumming hard. Imagining the worst. Getting halfway across the paddies, being shot ... "No, we—"

"He's *raping* kids, Brooke."

"You don't think I know that?" Her throat felt raw. "I'm not an operator like you and my brothers. I can't save a platoon of kids with a bamboo stick and my hands. And then there's the shock collars! How—"

"I've already taken care of that."

She blinked, glancing to his neck where she still saw the small red light. "What … How? They're still—"

"Trust me." Cord sighed. Touched her shoulder—from which she yanked away. "Sleep. We'll … talk in the morning." Resignation lurked in his voice. "I know I just threw a lot at you, but I'm pretty sure this is why God has us here."

"God?" She sniffed. "You said I put myself here. And you walked in—"

"Rest."

She drew up, startled by his clear instruction. The expression he wore. The way he moved away from her and planted himself in the cell. Door open. Gaze locked on the open area.

Why could she be strong in corporate law, defy the norms, climb that corporate ladder, yet fail here? But what ate at her, what broke down the little strength she'd built up … was not that she'd failed, but that she'd failed … him.

The clouds refused to buy them anymore time, surrendering their hold to dawn and an ominous feeling that said things were about to get lit. Perv-guard had crossed one too many lines, and that was a gross understatement—the guy had committed a crime. One that made Cord see red.

He balled his fists and squeezed hard. There weren't severe enough words for what buzzed through his veins. The nausea, the outrage, the mortification at what men could do, not just to each other, but to *children*—innocent ones whose very existence depended on the adults put in their lives to freaking protect them! Not shred that innocence, their psyches, and their lives.

Holy Mother, the rage!

Nerves buzzing, Cord somehow waded through breakfast and restroom breaks, watching over the kids like a hawk searching for its prey. Brooke didn't seem to be on the same page. So many times in the past few days he'd wanted to kiss her, but knew the inappropriateness of that, considering their situation. Considering the fear that drove her—technically, it was paralyzing her. Froze her thoughts and courage. He could see it all over the way she acted and avoided him.

Had to remedy that.

All through the morning in the threshing area, he kept vigil and a laserlike awareness of where Perv was at all times. There were other guards, of course, who had shocked kids, but none seemed to derive the pleasure Lee had out of brutalizing people. It was a sense of power and control.

Two things Cord was going to rip out of the man's hands.

Thankfully, the evening cooperated, pulling thick clouds over the camp to tuck it in for the night. Cord moved to Sho-gun and pointed to the outhouse, his only way to communicate to the Mandarin-speaking guard that he needed to go.

Sho-gun grunted, then pushed Cord's shoulder in that direction and walked with him.

But the thing Cord had noticed was the guards always waited in the center of the camp while the facilities were being used. Buying Cord the time he needed. With a glance back, he noted Sho-gun already lighting up a cigarette.

Cord whipped around the corner of the outhouse and sprinted in a crouch-run out and up toward the house on the hill. The nearer he got, the brighter it got, and the lower he went until he was low-crawling toward the generator. He easily found the line for the perimeter fence and killed it with the broken bamboo he'd been working into a semblance of a sharp edge. It wasn't anywhere near a knife, but a few stabs into the cord severed the connectivity.

Back in the camp, he edged back around just as Sho-gun had gotten curious about the delay.

Feigning that he'd left a rancid deposit, Cord waved his hand in front of his nose and trudged back to the hut, thinking about Brooke. How she'd fumbled through the day, flustered and seemingly disoriented. By his revelation that it was time to make a run for it. He shouldn't have tried to pry that promise out of her. Maybe he shouldn't even have warned her what was coming. After all, she wasn't an operator. But the simple truth was that he couldn't get these kids out of here without her, without her help, without her ingenuity. She might not believe in herself in this respect, but he did.

The next morning, humidity blanketed the area. More rain seemed ready to press its oppressive weight on the paddies. It'd been an unusually wet season this year. But that worked in their favor—limited the amount of forced labor. It hadn't been enough. The kids were weak and scrawny, a hair from emaciated.

Beating the sheaves on the bamboo slats as the sun wrestled a humid haze, Cord kept Jihan close and an eye on Brooke and the girl. Then he spotted Leech moving in and out of the kids' work areas. Had a look about him that made Cord feel like he needed a Brillo pad for a shower. He negotiated his way around the gathered bundles. Planted himself between the perv and a little girl. Somehow found Brooke's gaze.

A string of Mandarin peppered the air.

Cord sensed the guy move toward him. And managed to tangle his leg in the perv's path. Lee faceplanted in the muck as Cord relocated himself to the other side of the threshing pad. Or … that would've been the smart thing to do. But he was past that. He wanted this guy's blood.

Lee scrambled up, slipping a couple of times before he found his feet.

A weight plowed into Cord. He found Thick-Beard shouldering him out of the way. Shouting in his ear.

Cord stumbled and nearly lost his balance. Anger shot through his gut, ticked he'd misjudged the man. Knowing he could not lose ground. These kids had no time. He cursed himself for messing around. For—

Something pressed into his gut. Cold, hard.

"Take it," he heard in strained English.

His hands obeyed before his brain caught up. Felt the weapon the guard passed him. Even as he palmed it and slid it to the small of his back, Cord met Sho-gun's gaze. Gave a sharp nod of thanks. Wanted to know why this guy was helping. Maybe he despised the perv as much as Cord did. Weapon secure, he was forced by Sho-gun back to work.

Threshing again, Cord renegotiated his plan. Never had he taken solace in weapons—they could too easily end up in the wrong hands. A weapon changed things. It was more lethal, increasing chances of success—but also amped the level of danger. Once the guards saw that he was armed, his window of opportunity shrank drastically. They could get out if he had a well-thought-out plan. If he was fast enough.

"What're you doing?"

Cord twitched at Brooke's voice nearby. Hadn't realized she'd moved closer. "Working."

"I see that look on your face."

"The look called hard work?" He skidded his gaze around the compound, keeping tabs on the guards and their locations, making sure they weren't watching *them*.

"You're planning something."

"Our first date."

She caught his arm. "I'm not kidding, Cord—we could get the children killed."

He shoved into her face. "Or we could save their lives. If we don't, they're as good as dead. I know. I've seen enough dead kids to last a lifetime. What about you?" He hadn't meant to be so fierce. "Game time is over, Brooke. The kids need us to act. Before Lee escalates his violence to the next level."

Blue eyes widened. "Escalates?"

"He's a psychopa—"

Shouts erupted and he caught Sho-gun moving toward them. Cord met the man's gaze, noted him indicate visually toward Lee, then moved away from Brooke. "Stay frosty."

"What?"

He didn't have time to answer. The more they talked, the more he let her distract him, the more liable he was to make a mistake. That she'd noticed a change in his behavior already said he was off his game. Which wasn't like him. A sliver of doubt carved its way through his granitelike resolve that it was time to jump ship. What if he screwed this up? What if—just like Mom and Fallon—Brooke died because of him? Or one of these kids?

He beat the rice harder. Found some twisted comfort in the sound of the grains raining down through the slats, a pile swiftly forming. Jihan moved in and scooped the rice into a basket.

And it wasn't like Pike not to have come by now. Which worried him. Gravely. And what about her brothers? Why hadn't they come?

What the heck was going on that they were crap-out-of-luck for a rescue?

Guess it's up to me.

Time to pray harder cuz the odds were not in their favor.

Nightfall came a lot faster than he'd wanted it to. Nerves amped, he used bathroom time to verify the weapon at least had a magazine, counted the rounds in it, then clapped it back into the weapon, chambered a round, and returned it to the small of his back.

This … God … What are you doing?

He had never faced greater odds. Felt more outmaneuvered.

Show me. Guide me. Protect m—them. Even if it's from me.

Business finished—both kinds—he stepped out. Glanced out toward the paddies. Up the hill. To the trees. His gut cinched. In his mind, it hadn't seemed that far. Could they make it? Brooke's ribs were a problem, but he had no doubts—

Shouts from the huts drew him around.

Brain buzzed and drenched with the rigorous workout of planning the escape, he couldn't sort what he saw. What happened in the seconds it took his mind to drop out of warp. At their hut, Lee*ch* was grabbing for the Daghestani girl—Caliyah. Brooke shouted something and lunged forward. Caught the girl by the shoulders and yanked her back.

Which Lee*ch* didn't like.

Brooke swung in between them. Directing Lee*ch*'s attention to her.

Wait … No no no. That wouldn't—

Lee*ch* said something.

Gaze shifting to Cord, finding him there, Brooke lifted her hands to the perv. Like an offer …

A trade.

Mother of— "No!"

Lee*ch* moved fast. Grabbed Brooke by her ponytail. Yanked her toward him.

"Hey, get off her!" Cord shoved himself into motion even as Lee*ch* hauled Brooke out of the hut, the children screaming, crying. "Let her go!"

Fire crackled around his neck. Cord's legs went wonky even as another guard aimed a remote at him. But heck no, he wasn't stopping. Wasn't going to let Lee*ch* take Brooke. "Stop! Get your haaaaaaauuuughhhhhh."

He was on the ground, limbs convulsing. A metallic taste glanced off his tongue. Smelled burnt hair and flesh. Teeth rattled and clacked. Saw the face of Lee move out of sight with Brooke as gray shrouded the edges of his vision.

Noooooooo.

CHAPTER NINETEEN

HE'D BET a hundred bucks his heart had stopped.

Cord groaned and dragged his vibrating self off the wood floor. The painful pressure of light against his corneas told him it was at least morning. He cursed himself for—

Brooke.

Morning. The kids were threshing. That meant the guards were in place. It also meant broad daylight. Cameras. He'd pinpointed a couple of them. He'd neutralize them, the guards. Pulse racing, he dragged the broken bamboo out of his pocket. Sawed at the nylon cord of the shock collar. Nicked his burned, raw neck but didn't care. It was over. *They* were over.

But even as he stumbled to the edge of the hut, a sea of kids swarmed toward him as the clouds unloaded their payload.

"Mr. Cord!" Jihan darted to him. "We thought you were dead!"

"You and me both, kid." Even as he accepted the boy's hug, Cord scanned the area for Brooke.

Caliyah shuffled toward him, her lower lip stuck out. "Make them bring her back," she whined around bloodshot eyes.

Cord's breath backed into his throat. "She's not with you?"

The kids shook their heads, which were down, tear-stained rivulets almost looking like face paint.

"You have to help her," Ginika pleaded, holding her sister's hand. "Last night, Mr. Lee took her. Then this morning, I see him take her up to the big hut, hear the other guards say they know she is Mama Willow's sister—and that her brothers have hurt their business." The girl had entirely too much understanding in her words.

Crap.

Cord handed her the broken piece of bamboo. "In the hut. Start cutting off the collars."

Ginika's eyes widened.

He understood her nerves. Conjured a plan to distract her and the guards who might grow suspicious. "Have the kids play a game. Work on the collars one at a time. Be ready to run." He nodded. "Can you do this?"

Though terror struck cruelly in a young face that had already endured so much, Ginika nodded. "I will."

"You're a warrior." He patted her shoulder, well aware of how a simple thing among those who'd been trafficked could be mistaken. "Stay strong. I'll be back."

Weapon firmly gripped, Cord moved through the rain and up the hill with a fierce conviction that he'd deliver a one-way ticket to Hell for anyone who got in his way.

The downpour both aided—by concealing him—and hindered him—by limiting his line of sight. But he wasn't stopping. Thunder rumbled and clapped overhead.

Twenty yards.

A man emerged from the large storage hut where the guards had been sleeping.

Unyielding, Cord advanced and fired a short burst at the guard. By the time the guy's body hit the ground, Cord was there, relieving him of his rifle. He tucked the handgun into the small of his back, dragged the guy to the fields, then sprinted back to the door. This building wasn't like the huts they'd housed him and the kids in with gaps and a leaking roof. So he felt confident his form wasn't visible from the other side.

He heard a handful of voices and crouched, wishing he had his thermals. But those were hidden a half klick away. After a quick look-see into the barn, Cord confirmed five combatants, a woman, and Brooke.

Snaking inside, he held the rifle tucked to his shoulder. Mentally plotted the firing pattern. They were speaking quickly, angrily, so he couldn't tell what they were saying, but he didn't need to know Mandarin to read the body language. *Leech* was there, too, more than once striking Brooke.

You first.

Cord hunched to the side behind a forty-foot stack of bagged rice. *God, direct my aim and protect me and mine.*

Breathe ... three ... two ...

Shoving upward and rotating out—not too far, he maintained cover behind the rice—Cord sighted Lee. Fired—double tapped the guy. Another next to him. The woman—fired. The two men. Fired, fired.

A blur to the side made him trace the fleeing guard with the reticle. Anticipate the trajectory. And fire.

The guy slid into home ... and snapped his neck against a post that supported the hut.

Face blanched, bloodied, and bruised, Brooke stared at him open-mouthed, then sprinted toward to him.

Cord grabbed another weapon and slung it over his shoulder. Grabbed another. Even as Brooke rushed him, he deflected the hug, taking her hand, and setting it to his belt strap. "Hold firm. Do not let go."

Stricken, startled, she hauled in another breath. Nodded.

They retraced his path back to the huts.

Sho-gun was there.

Cord snapped up the rifle.

"No," Brooke breathed, reaching around him.

Things were never what they seemed. And this guy—even if he was on their side, he was an unknown. And that always meant trouble. But he'd given Cord a gun. The one that got him up the hill.

Cord adjusted the sight. Fired and struck the guy's knee.

Sho-gun crumpled to the ground, gripping his knee.

"Kids, let's go! Move move move!"

Brooke rushed around, herding the children. Speaking to them in Mandarin. Telling them it was time to go home. So calm, so … freakin' slow! But right—they didn't need to panic the kids. He watched in taut silence as she put their hands on each other's shoulders and started walking toward the trees as he'd indicated the other night. Without him telling her to.

Ginika and Jihan were at the tail end with him.

"Help the little ones," Cord instructed them. "No matter what, don't stop moving. The farther you go, the better chances of success."

Halfway up the hill, he heard a noise that was not thunder. "Keep moving," he shouted and pivoted around. Moving backward, eyes on the enemy, he saw faint bursts in the distance. Targeted them, even though he couldn't clearly see who was shooting. They were firing at them, so that made them the enemy. He neutralized them.

Sweeping, he searched for stealthy approaches by more guards, but it seemed his pseudo-plan worked. The kids had passed the electric fence without incident. More than half had the collars off.

"Here." Cord indicated to the spot where a reed shot upward. "Dig."

"*Us?*" Brooke balked.

"Unless you're a better shot than me, yes."

Silence fell on them as she and the kids dug up the gear he'd buried. It took too long. Too, too long. He saw vehicles roaring this way. Still had a good twenty minutes, but they'd be a lot faster than him and the kids.

"What now?" Brooke asked quietly.

Cord shouldered into his ruck, then his backpack. "Run."

"Where?"

He pointed behind her. "That direction. Keep moving. Back toward the city. Stay in the paddies and brush, away from the roads—too obvious and easy to spot."

With a nod, her right eye swollen, she repeated the instructions to the Taiwanese children in Mandarin.

They ran, slipped and slid on the slick grass, moving farther from the paddies, closer toward the dull glow of the city through the stormy haze. He tried not to think about the fact that Brooke was moving differently, walking awkwardly. He knew what'd happened. Knew what he'd have to live with for the rest of his life. Only solace was—he'd killed the guy responsible.

Yeah. Now, who's going to kill me? Because I am responsible. He'd known it was time to bug-out, but Brooke's fear blurred his judgment. Distracted him. There was a reason he didn't get tangled up in relationships. Besides that self-inflicted vow to never cross those lines, especially with those who'd endured violence at the hands of men, in the long run, it just tripped him up.

And this ... was a really long run. His legs were aching. He heard the kids crying and struggling.

"They need a break," Brooke slipped toward him at the back.

"I know, and I'm not a hard-hearted son-of-a-gun, but taking a break is akin to sending up a flare saying, 'Here I am, kill me.'"

She drew straighter, lips parted, then deflated. Nodded. Started moving again.

Roughly twenty minutes later, he spied an orchard of some kind, realized with its rows and the branches, it'd form a nice canopy in which to hide. He pointed it out to Brooke and steered the kids in that direction. About a hundred yards away, the fragrance of the fruit reached them. Called to them.

So did a buzzing noise overhead.

"Run!" Cord shouted. "The trees!" He shifted aside, pulled the weapon and scanned the gray skies that were painful because of the hidden sun trying to scorch its light past the thick clouds.

A black shape warbled in the air fifty, sixty feet up.

Gotcha. Cord pulled the trigger and heard the telltale click of a jam. He bit back a curse and pulled his handgun. Reacquired the drone, and fired. Fired again. And again. The thing spun as it plummeted to the ground.

Cord pivoted and sprinted toward the kids, who had reached the trees, even as another drone buzzed them. They hugged the thin trunks and clustered together tightly. The orchard had rows of trees bearing bell-shaped red fruits. It didn't provide a thick canopy, but for now—he hoped—it'd be enough. "Tell them not to move. Stay put."

Brooke relayed the instructions.

Eyeing the red fruit offering itself, Cord plucked one. Held it up and grinned. "And tell them to eat!"

Frantic hands grabbed at the fruit, and Cord tensed hoping the movement didn't betray their position, but he knew the temptation of fruit after weeks of rice balls made good sense nonexistent. He helped himself to two of the things. Took the time to figure out their route, pray it didn't get too chilly tonight after a day of hiking in the rain.

And pray like a freak that last drone hadn't seen them.

She would never speak of what Lee had done to her. But she found herself doing something she hadn't done since sitting in youth group on Wednesday nights—praying. Praying like never before that, besides pain and horrific memories, Lee hadn't left her with something else …

Turning her thoughts away from that, Brooke marveled at how sustained she felt after eating the fruit, and the kids seemed to be improved as well. Some had taken bathroom breaks, while others were already asleep on the wet ground. It was heartbreaking, yet so beautiful to be free of that place.

Seated against a tree trunk, she watched Cord move up and down the orchard rows, doing recon. Never would she forget the way he'd come into that barn, killed the guards and Mrs. Cheng, who'd been talking with someone else that had said they'd taken care of the other problems. She was sure her captors had been talking about her brothers. Or the man named Pike that Cord had mentioned. After all, wouldn't they have come to their rescue?

But they hadn't come.

Cord had.

And he was singlehandedly saving them all. It seemed too good to be true. *He* was too good to be true. She owed him everything. And that thing that she'd felt squirming between them, those feelings? They were finding deep, full roots in the soil of adversity. Could she let it bloom?

Brooke had no idea, but she wanted to try. And once back at the paddies, she'd been sure he would kiss her. Had wanted that kiss, much to her surprise. She was tired of being alone, and the ache for his kiss helped her realize how much she wasn't just longing for companionship. She'd been friends with a lot of men. Gone on dates with some. None stirred in her the desire for … more.

He saved me. In more ways than one. Granted, he hadn't stopped Lee … but he'd nearly died trying to. After telling Caliyah to stay with Ginika, Brooke stood, and keeping beneath the branches as much as possible, wandered down the orchard to find him. Almost didn't see him as the rain let go and darkness crouched on the horizon. He stood beneath the branches, preternaturally still as he stared out past the orchard.

Such an amazing man. Unrelenting. Wildly annoying.

She pushed herself the last dozen paces, the sound of her steps drawing him round.

He said nothing as he slung his weapon around to his back and lowered his arms out, to his sides. An invitation.

Which Brooke accepted, went into them. Pressed her forehead to his chest. Slid her arms around his waist and just ... stayed. Expelled the breath perpetually trapped behind her fortress of walls and deflections.

His thick arms circled her in a hug.

The tears came, and though instinct said to fight them, she released her hold on those salty drops. Cried. A lot.

His hand stroked her back. "I'm sorry ..."

She snugged in tighter. Tried to shake her head. Tried to talk. But ... only a squeak escaped.

Cord palmed the back of her head. Held her in his arms, his heart steadily beating out a rhythm that said, "This is the way to security, follow me."

And she knew she would—she'd follow him anywhere.

"You did good, getting the kids out." His words rumbled through the chest that was as corded as his name.

"I didn't do anything except run."

"It was the best and most important thing to do at the time."

It was her fault; she knew it. If she'd listened, trusted him ...

"And what you ... sacrificed"—his chest and arms tensed around that word—"for Caliyah ... it was the right thing."

She sobbed. Thrust back the memories of lying on the ground ... "Is that why you killed him?" She meant it as a jest, but the words made more tears spill out.

"I killed him because he took something that wasn't his to take." Cord kissed her temple. "Hurt the woman I love."

Startled, she lifted her head. Met his gaze. *You don't mean that.* If she said it out loud, he'd argue. And she just wasn't up to that. Instead, she tucked her nose against his throat. Felt the tickle of his beard. "I don't deserve you."

A chuckle rattled beneath her ear. "I know—Cord Taggart is a lot of man to handle."

She sniffed a laugh. "Oh, you're a lot all right ... a lot of ego."

His laugh was short this time as those biceps constricted, squeezing her into his arms further. "I hate that I didn't stop him, Punz."

Brooke looked up into his eyes. "Me, too, but ... I'm okay." Somehow, she was. And in the arms of the greatest man she'd ever known. "Cord, I thought he'd killed you ... and I just ..."

Strong hands framed her face. "That is the only thing that will ever stop me from protecting you."

She held his wrists, fighting the memories of last night, the brutality ..."It was so awful ..."

He hooked his arm around her again and held her closer. Let her cry. If the rise and fall of his chest was any indication, he was crying with her. "I want to resurrect him so I can kill him again."

Those words gave her strange comfort. That someone was willing to fight for her, to war and do violence to protect her. A year ago that would've repulsed her. Today ... today she felt a profound appreciation for that. For him.

Did she love him?

She eased back to study him, take in this man, this marvel. Say those words and she knew he'd have some quick retort. Make her laugh. Make the gray skies evaporate. She eased up onto her toes.

But Cord shifted. His hands released their lock and parted, sliding down to her shoulders.

Shame and embarrassment flooded her. Had she read him wrong, this thing between them wrong?

He framed her there—and that's when she noticed his gaze wasn't on her. His head swiveled. The difference in his posture, the way he held himself, the way he held her was a night-and-day difference. From powerful man to powerful predator that stacked fear in her chest.

"What?" she breathed.

He urged her toward the kids. "Time to go."

"Where?"

"South—toward the roads with the kids."

"You said that was—"

"Go! Now!"

"Should you give me a gun or weapon?"

He stopped short. Smirked. "This isn't Hollywood."

She frowned. "What—"

"The chances of you hitting a target when you've never fired a weapon are very low, and they're very high that the weapon you aren't familiar with gets turned on you." He gave a cockeyed nod. "That's not happening."

She hadn't trusted him before. She'd fought him when he said things that scared her—like escaping. Now, leaving her to hide with the kids. This time, she wouldn't argue, wouldn't ask questions. This was a time to listen. Trust. Even if she wanted to argue, he had already started in the opposite direction. Weapon pointed toward the edge of the orchard.

That reality shoved her toward the kids. "Here," she rasped and motioned them to follow her. "Quiet. Fast."

She drew them into a huddle, searching through the foliage and fruit for Cord.

"What is wrong?" Ginika asked as Caliyah clambered toward her, extending her arms to be held.

"Not right now," Brooke said, sliding her hand into the five-year-old's. She motioned the children closer and started herding them with whispered warnings to stay silent as they ducked from cover to cover of the trees. Avoiding the red fruit on the ground that was rotting or eaten by critters. But each step she took made her hesitate. Where was Cord? What if he got—

Crack! Pop-pop-pop!

Branches and leaves rustled frantically.

Sucking in a breath, Brooke stopped. *Cord.* She looked back in that direction, shifting Caliyah to the other side, away from whatever danger.

Thudding drew closer.

"Go, go!" Brooke urged the kids to run. When she glanced back, she saw Cord backing toward them, firing.

Oh, God, help!

Crack!

Chaos erupted, kids running—some tripping ... Cries. Screams.

Leaves around her thwapped and twitched violently beneath the spray of bullets. She didn't know where to focus, what to do—the kids were terrorized, Cord was completely engaged in shooting, defending them.

But this ... this seemed impossible. They were going to die. She was useless. All this ... her every attempt to find the kids, save them ... and they'd die in an orchard. Valiantly—which would probably thrill Canyon when he heard the story—but still ... dead.

She swept Caliyah into her arms and wanted to bolt. Yet she wanted to help Cord.

He stumbled backward. Tripped over one of the boys, who'd fallen. But he never lost his weapon. Aimed at two shapes that appeared where he aimed.

Brooke's breath backed into her lungs. It was over. They were dead. "God, please ..." She reached out, as if she could help Cord get back on his feet. Or protect him. Hand on Cord's shoulder, Caliyah clinging to the other ...

Cord fired twice, the report of the gun painful against her ears. One of the men fell, dead. The other braced and trained his gun on Cord.

"No!"

Crack! Pop. Brrrt.

It seemed the very air came alive with shooting and grunts. Brooke pulled Caliyah closer and hovered over her, dug her fingers into Cord's shirt, trying to erase the gap between them. Heels dug into the ground, Cord pushed himself backward toward her, still aiming. Breaths huffed as he jammed up against her, her chest to his back.

"Sorry," he grunted.

She rested her cheek against his shoulder blade, holding Caliyah close, too. "Don't be ..." She touched his back. "I'm ..."

Jihan screamed.

Cord tensed and snapped up his weapon.

That's when Brooke spotted two black-clad men closing in on them.

Then Cord slumped. Uttered an oath. "Where the heck have y'all been?"

Confusion ran through Brooke, and she looked at the newcomers. Saw— "Canyon!" She choked back a sob. Covered her mouth.

Cord faltered. His arm went out from beneath him. He dropped against the ground with a breathless grunt. What was he doing? She glanced down, about to chide him for messing around, when she noticed his eyes closed. Mouth agape. A dark stain on his chest.

With a gasp, she moved to his side. "Cord!" On her knees, she caught his face. Checked his chest. "C-Cord, please ..." No no no. He couldn't die ... "Cord!" She looked at her brothers, who stood there. "Do something!"

"Pretty sure Drama King is just hoping for some mouth-to-mouth resuscitation," Canyon said, coming closer as he slung his weapon to the back.

"What?" Brooke frowned, looked down at Cord and found those gray eyes watching her. "You idiot!"

"For you? All day, every day, Punz." He grunted upward and held a hand to his chest. "Nice way to spoil things, Midas. But for the record, I *am* shot."

Range knelt and probed the wound, and Canyon joined him, together making quick work of packing the wound. "Our loss—guy had bad aim." He looked up at Brooke. "Sorry, sis. Looks like you're still stuck with this meatsack."

CHAPTER
TWENTY

Kaohsiung City, Taiwan

Tucked safely away with Brooke, the kids, the Metcalfes, Cord was glad to learn that while there had been injuries and one fatality—a contract worker—Omen had come out okay, and Lowell had made fast friends with burly Brick Archer.

Cord endured the stitches for the lead he'd eaten trying to stave off the fast-response team that had been sent to stop the breakout. The gunshot wound would mess up his response time.

While the local doctor applied a bandage, Cord watched as the kids were treated to a full meal across the warehouse. Jess and the aftercare team were here, talking to them, evaluating them, and working with local authorities to start the process of returning the Taiwanese kids to their families. To the side, a screen afforded privacy for another doctor.

Where ... where had Brooke gone?

He spied Caliyah sitting with Jihan. That little girl hadn't left Brooke's side ... so where was she?

"Hey."

The fabric of the curtained-off area rippled as someone moved behind it. A second later, Punz stepped out from behind it.

Oh. Yeah, right—of course she should get checked out.

Holy Mother … yeah, especially after what Lee had done to her. *What I wasn't able to stop.*

"Hey." Canyon slapped his bare pec that wasn't covered in bandage.

"Ow! Hey!"

"Always were such a girl," Range grunted.

"Hey, I'll have you know *that girl*"—he pointed to Brooke—"had more chutzpah than all you Metcalfes put together."

Canyon smirked. "Could've told you that. She's worse than our mother."

"I think you got that backward—she's as *good* as your mother."

"Dude's got it bad," Leif teased, crossing his arms.

That was one thing these brothers had right.

"Look," Canyon said, straightening, expression sobering. "Seriously. Thanks." He nodded. "For keeping her alive."

Alive, yeah, but if he'd done his job, she wouldn't have been …

"What's that look?" Range asked, perceptive gaze probing.

"I …" Cord wet his lips. Smoothed a hand over his beard. "I was too late getting them out of there. One of the guards escalated his abuse from shocks to … rape."

The line of lasering expressions seemed almost comical as all sets of blue eyes—though Range's were a bit more gray—homed in on him.

Cord looked down. Then skipped his gaze past the Metcalfe testosterone pool to Rapunzel. Standing at the coffee pot, an insulated cup in hand, she watched them.

"Brooke was …" Canyon straightened, vehemence replacing

what little amusement had been in his expression. "Which guard?"

"The dead one."

Leif smirked. "Can you clarify?"

"Yeah," Range sniffed. "They were all pretty much DOA by the time we made it to the camp."

"Except that one with a really messed up knee," Canyon said. "Seemed intentional."

"He ... he, uh, gave me a gun. Think he knew it was time, too. Can't call him a good guy, but ..."

"Without the gun he gave you, nothing would've changed."

"No," Cord said, remembering the way that perv kept looking at the kids, at Brooke ... "*I* would probably be dead."

"Well, we need to get you read in on what's been happening, what Jess and the team found since the explosion."

That perked up Cord's attention. "Explosion?"

"Here." Range flicked a shirt at him. "Put that on so my sister will stop staring."

Wait. She is? Cord bounced his gaze to hers.

"I'm going to blow chunks," Range muttered.

"Do it over there," Canyon said, then nodded to Cord. "We were trying to find out what happened to you and Pike—"

"Pike?"

Landry manifested in the doorway. "Out of ICU, recovering."

Cord came off the table, wincing at the tug of the bandage. "What happened?"

"From what we can piece together," Landry said, "he was run off the road. Truck flipped down the hillside. Wouldn't have been so bad if he hadn't gone so long without lifesaving measures."

"That explains a lot."

"The safehouse got hit a couple of days ago. Full assault. Grenades, armed combatants. We relocated and started searching hard, knew whatever aroused those attacks had to be some serious spit," Range said. "That's how we found Pike, then the rice farm with all the bodies."

Pike. Omen. Brooke … the safehouse. "Clearly hit a nerve."

Canyon nodded. "That's what we've been thinking."

Armed with a digital tablet, Jess joined them. "You done playing in the paddies, boss?" Her expression swelled and seemed ready to burst.

He had this feeling, this glorious feeling that … "Wait … are you telling me …"

A breath staggered into her chest. "We found the connection."

"You know what they say about Christmas and miracles." Cord grinned. "Get me up to speed."

"You knew Adler Roth—"

"Kasra gave us his name," he said with a nod. "The German fashion king." He shrugged. "But his was a name spinning midair, no grounding, no proof."

"Canyon and I trailed that guy you put us on—Brooke's VIP from the firm here, Gerard Frost. He had a not-so-discreet meet-up at a brothel."

Okay, the amusement was gone. Reminded him what he'd been fighting these last few years. Cord shifted back into operator mode, back into the founder of MiLE.

"He met with this guy," Canyon said, indicating to the tablet, where Jess showed him a photo.

Cord glanced at it. Stilled. "*Bundestag*? Are you kidding me?"

"That's what I said," Jess mused, "and when I told the guys that for the last several years, Franz Bundestag has been our point of contact in Germany—a vital high-level source as he was the aid to the former *and current* German chancellors. When we saw that photo, we started digging and it all started making sense."

"That's also when we hit that nerve you mentioned," Leif said.

"Which," Landry interrupted, "was more like hitting the blasting cap on some C4 and leveling the safehouse, killing some of the operators bunked there."

"I bet," Cord muttered, then narrowed his eyes, calling up data from the dregs of his memory. "Isn't Bundestag like hunting buddies or something with Adler Roth?"

"Since the 90s," Jess confirmed, "and Roth's nephew is Gunnar Sauer, who seems to be the middleman between Roth and the different branches of the Trench."

"The Germans are taking over again," Dade Tycho growled, and that's when Cord saw the ugly burn across the guy's neck.

"Well, that might be true," Jess said, "if Sauer and Roth weren't Swiss."

Snickers carried around the room.

"The Trench has had their fists around the throats of many who sit in power—and now they have the newly elected German Chancellor—Bundestag. There are rumors aplenty that Roth helped make that happen." Cord let his brain ricochet around that truth nugget and connect to the other names. "We've been convinced for a long time that Roth had connections to Ladomer Horvath, but couldn't really prove anything. So ... Frost ... Bundestag ... Sauer ... Roth ... but who're they answering to?"

With an exaggerated sigh, Jess hunched. "That ... is what we can't figure out, and it makes me question every one of Bundestag's staff and officials. I feel like we're back and ground zero with them."

"But," Canyon said, tapping the tablet, "after the brothel, we were able to intercept some key intel. There's a very large Christmas gala at Roth's residence in the Alps."

"Mercy managed to slip into their system," Jess said, turning the digital tablet in his direction. "The guest list is a Who's Who of Human Trafficking."

Cord's heart pounded. "So, it's possible ... the guy at the top of this food chain will be there."

Arms folded, Canyon reclined against the table. "I've been monitoring the traffic in and out of his estate. Heightened security, radio traffic, routine patrols ..."

"I think we have a party to crash."

"I hate to be the party pooper," Jess said with a wince at her pun, "but MiLE's funds are ... a bit dry."

"Wh-what do you mean?" They'd never exactly been flowing in it, but it'd never interfered with mission efficacy. And it made him mad. No way he was deep-sixing the mission. "Look, we're doing this. I don't care what it takes."

It was hard enough to think and listen in on their conversation with Cord shirtless. He was well-sculpted and now she saw the full of that tattoo, how it coiled around his heart. Yet ... not a snake. But the well-defined pecs and that six pack ... all threw her back into his arms, reminded her of the time in the orchard when she'd wanted to kiss him.

Yet even after he'd put on the tactical shirt her brother had tossed him, Brooke couldn't think straight. Couldn't process what she was seeing. Who ... he was. It was one thing to see him deliver a girl—Brighton—to the lodge for safekeeping. It had been something entirely different to see him operating, delivering justice at the camp. Fighting, operating to get them free, to free *her*.

They were going after the head of the snake, the person running this despicable trade, the one who'd wanted her captured. It would be a huge win in the fight against trafficking, but they were still dealing with—fighting—the depravity of mankind. As long as people existed, there would be sickos who preyed on the weak. After all she'd seen and fought in the courts, she knew only God could change a person. It sounded like a platitude, and at first, she hated the thought, but only God could've affected the change in her that had her standing here, Caliyah and Jihan safe, watching Cord. Wanting Cord. Wanting him safe, too.

Except, now he was planning to go back out into the fray.

The thought pushed her away from the men, back to where the children were eating, playing, coloring ... being children. As it should be. Perched on the edge of a cot, Brooke hugged herself. Had a lot to work through. Mostly ... hated that Cord was going to go put himself in danger again. What if the bullet hit a few inches to the left this time? What if ... he didn't come back? Why did the thought leave her feeling so empty?

"Hey." His weight made the cot creak as he sat next to her, their legs touching and making her heart thud. "Saw you with the doc ..." Cord bent forward, elbows resting on his knees. "Everything okay?"

Brooke swallowed, a little weirded out that he'd noticed that. But loved that he cared enough to ask. "Yeah. All good." She met his gaze and saw there that he understood the concern, that the concern was no longer a worry. Saw the same relief she felt. So, yeah—all good.

Except it wasn't. "You're going to go ..." Why was her throat raw?

Cord palmed his fist. Rubbed his knuckles. "I ... am. Have to."

"But you were just shot."

He nodded, flexing his hands, which flexed those muscles.

She had this idea of leaning against him, slipping her arm through his. Letting him know how she felt, that she didn't want him to go. But it'd be like asking a fish to avoid water. A bearded fish. When she'd first seen him at the lodge, he'd seem so dichotomous—bearded but bald, well-muscled yet somehow gentle. Nice eyes loaded with ferocity.

"You okay?" he asked with a smirk. "You're eyeing me like

I'm your favorite dessert at that swanky restaurant we went out to?"

Brooke leaned in, aiming for a kiss.

Cord cupped her face. Held her. Stopped her. "Hey …"

She frowned. Swallowed. Felt embarrassed. "Sorry, I thought—"

"You thought right, but …" The hooded look in his eyes confirmed his words.

"But what?"

His thumb swept her cheek, seeming to reconsider. Seeming to want what he withheld. "I think—what you've been through … maybe you're a little mixed up."

Brooke recoiled, feeling smacked by his words. Hurt.

"All I'm saying is emotions run high after an exfil, very high. I don't want you to do something you'll regret."

Regret. Did he really think she'd regret a kiss?

"Sasquatch," Range said from the door. "There a problem here?"

When Cord lowered his hand, Brooke frowned at her brother. "Thought you knew when you weren't wanted."

"Ouch. Never were one to mince words, big sis. Message received," Range said as he rolled around and back toward the Command area.

Cord glanced down and cleared his throat. "Event's in thirty-six, so we need to head out and get into place. Your brothers volunteered."

Right. Back to the mission. Forget this happened. "Of course they did." Brooke bit the inside of her cheek, bolstering her courage. Forbidding herself from crying—huh, he was right about the whole emotions running high thing—from trying to divert him from a course that was so perfectly … *Cord*.

"I didn't tell your brothers about Mazin."

Wow, that seemed such a small thing now. "I will." She nodded. Knew it needed to be done. "Especially since Mazin's missing." Her gaze drifted toward Caliyah and Jihan, who were watching a movie. "I'll need to get a power of attorney ..." She cringed. "Sorry, I know you don't care about that."

He reached over, placed his hand over hers. "I care, Punz."

With a scoff, she craned her head at him. "Why do you keep calling me that?"

Cord gave her a sheepish grin as he slid a hand over his beard. "I don't know ... I mean, you live in that tower ... way up there, all that wealth, all those friends, connections, powerful lawyer ... global conqueror." He shrugged. "I'm down here in the subway of life, slumming it with the grime and rats. It's why I got the tattoo."

"What tattoo?"

He flexed his bicep where black ink peeked out. "Up my arm, over my shoulder, around my heart ..."

"What does a snake have to do with me?"

Gray eyes held hers. "Not a snake."

"Then ..." Somehow, her brain made the connection, recalling what she'd seen. "A braid."

"Let down your hair, Punz. Maybe then, I can reach you."

Startled, shocked, Brooke stared at him. Was that how he saw her? Them? On such uneven playing fields? Did he really think so poorly of her, that wealth mattered when it came to her heart? Had *she* not tried to kiss *him*?

"That place of yours ... I was afraid to touch anything. Reminded me of the time my mom took me to a museum. Don't ask me how I did it, but I managed to break a vase. She worked for a year to repay it. Also never took me anywhere again." There was a morose twitch to his beard. "Dated this girl one time, who had a place like yours—though nowhere near as nice—and the more we dated, the more I realized she was unreachable. She threw this party once, and I showed up in jeans and a nice shirt—okay, so it was a tac shirt, but it was my *nice* one—and I heard her mocking me and my 'hick' ways to some guy she was cozying up to. So, I bugged out and vowed to stay in my lane."

Stay in his lane? "First, I'd never mock you, but I would make sure your closet had at least two nice button-downs." She hoped he heard the sarcasm in her words, but the way he studied her made her worry.

Unreachable ... That ... *that* was why he called her Rapunzel? Not because he saw her as beautiful? Or a damsel to be rescued? But because he saw her as *unreachable* ...?

Mortified, Brooke stared at the concrete floor. At the crack there that seemed as pronounced as the one between them. How? How had she become viewed as such a self-absorbed monster? "I ... I, uh, need to talk to my brothers." She pushed a smile at him that she did not feel. Stood and crossed the cavernous space to where Canyon, Range, and Leif were huddled.

"Hey, sis." Range angled around to face her. "When's the wedding?"

"What?" she balked.

He smirked and indicated behind her. "Dude took a bullet for you. It's kind of SOP to marry the poor sap who sacrifices his life for you."

Same poor sap who didn't want a kiss because, according to him, she was just running off high emotions. Maybe he'd been right.

"Has nothing to do with the way you two are walking on eggshells around each other," Leif teased. "Or that blush in your cheeks."

"Look," Brooke snapped. Sighed. Rubbed her aching forehead and her hand went instinctively to her side. The doc had given her some painkillers, which went a long way in making this the least pain-filled day she'd had in weeks. "Listen, I need to tell y'all something."

They must've seen something in her expression because all

three abandoned their taunting and donned those *who-are-we-killing-this time* looks.

Brooke checked on the kids, who were sitting at a table, eating cake. "I have no idea where to start ..."

"Start with when he started living with you."

She gaped at Canyon, though she shouldn't be surprised. There had never been personal boundaries with him. And according to pretty much everyone in her life, she was focused on one thing—herself. Why did she even try to frame a defense? "Last summer. Mazin and the children showed up, unexpectedly."

Range frowned. "How does a guy show up unexpectedly and end up living and sleeping with you?"

"Don't be vulgar." She sighed. "He wasn't sleeping with me. He's ..." She had nothing to lose at this point. "Mazin is our half brother."

Frowns in triplicate. Wonderful.

"Hold up." Canyon shifted his stance. "Our ... *brother*? So, the affair wasn't the end of it?"

Brooke lifted her eyebrows. "You knew about his mom?"

"Only recently. When I was helping with Brighton, Stone told me that Dad had an affair."

"Why the freak didn't any of you tell me about this?" Range demanded.

"Welcome to the club," Leif balked. "I always get left out of the news because everyone thinks I'm still thirteen."

"We can fight over this later—"

"Why the tight lips about this guy?" Canyon held his ground.

Brooke sighed. "Mazin did not want anyone knowing about him because he didn't want to ruin our family or get sympathy votes or something." It had all gotten so very complicated, entirely too fast. "Cliff's Notes version: he and I connected on social media when we were teens. We talked on and off through the years, and I always told him he was welcome in my home. When he learned his father-in-law and ex-wife were involved in trafficking, he fled to protect his children … and ended up in my foyer."

"Sure he wasn't after your money?" Range asked.

"You don't know anything about Mazin."

"Yeah, you made sure of that."

Gritting her teeth, Brooke had no tolerance for this conversation. "I just wanted you to know because"—she thrust a hand toward Caliyah and Jihan—"they are our niece and nephew. Since Mazin is missing, I'm responsible for them. They *will* be embraced as family, or I'll bring all three of you to your knees."

Canyon smirked. "Welcome back, Mom." He jutted his jaw to the other room, to the kids. "Don't worry. Metcalfes might screw up some things, but we always do family right. When they let us."

She understood the barb. And knew he was right. "I'm tired," she admitted. "The doctor has cleared us, and I just want to go home. So, that's what I'm going to do. With Jihan and Caliyah."

"To the City?" Canyon balked. "Heck no."

"I appreciate your concern, but you need to focus on bringing Cord back alive."

Canyon's pale blue eyes brightened as he considered her. And he was probably thinking or read into her words feelings she hadn't mentioned but had made clear by telling him to keep Cord safe. She was glad he got the message.

"Understood." He touched her shoulder. "And we'll make it a priority to find Mazin."

Surprised by the magnanimity of those words, Brooke lifted her chin, tears pricking. "Thank you. I think you'll like him— he's definitely a Metcalfe."

CHAPTER
TWENTY-ONE

Kaohsiung City, Taiwan

Plans were in place. The team ready to move. Righteousness would hold evil accountable. Quiet dug its way into the warehouse as evening seized control, leaving Cord alone with his thoughts. Wondered what had been happening in Brooke's head when they'd talked earlier. When she'd nearly kissed him. A kiss he'd wanted, but he knew that integral time after an op when adrenaline bottomed out. How that messed with a head. But since he'd held her back, she'd seemed … withdrawn. Cold.

That moment, holding her in the orchard, he'd seen an uncharted side of her. One without all the walls and corporate-y stiffness. Then he'd detected the response team … and thought he was about to lose her. And then he'd staved off that kiss—strict boundaries and rules for very legitimate reasons in his line of work—and definitely felt like he'd lost her.

That was it. He didn't want to lose her. Ever.

The thought pushed him up. He glanced around, searching for her. Ginika and Adesina were sitting on the couch laughing at a show. Most of the Taiwanese kids had left with local authorities to help get them back to their homes. He trudged over to the Command area where Landry, Tycho, Jess, and Canyon were working.

"Anyone seen Brooke?" he asked quietly.

Canyon frowned. Something in his expression conveyed a warning. "She left."

His heart jarred. "*What*?"

Scratching his jaw, Canyon winced. "She left with the kids about an hour ago. Military hop back to the States."

A chill ran down Cord's spine, evidence of her absence. "Oh." Why was it so hard to breathe? "Wow."

"Look," Canyon said, edging closer and drawing him aside. "I know you have legit feelings for my sister, but Brooke ... she's ..."

"I know." Cord wanted to head this one off at the pass. "Being around her ... trying to get in under her radar, under her defenses is like trying to catch a rice paddy snake." He shook his head. "And I know she's out of my league. I can't hope—"

"Let's skip the whole self-denigration phase, okay?"

Cord faltered, surprised.

"I can tell she cares about you. Seeing her when you were laid out on the ground ..." He sniffed and shook his head. "I've *never* seen her panicked until then."

Cord's heart dared hope.

"But Brooke ..." He clicked his tongue. "Doesn't do relationships well."

"I think you underestimate her." He probably wasn't supposed to spill any beans that she'd shared with him. "I mean, look what she did for Daghestani and his kids."

"Yeah, that was something." Canyon's jaw muscle jounced. "Still trying to sort that truth out. It'll take time. My point, though? With Brooke ... just trying to say ..."

"Don't expect much?"

"Not to harsh your mellow, but"—he cocked his head—"she left without telling you."

"That's not harsh, that's a nuke." Cord shook his head and sighed. "I had thought of proposing."

Canyon's eyebrows rose into his hairline. "I think that bullet hit more than your chest. Wanting to join this family—gotta be some kind of crazy."

"I am," Cord said, his laugh weighted with sadness. "About Brooke. For her, I'd even endure being related to you."

"Be careful what you wish for—there's basically four of me. And I'm the nice one."

"Also, the better liar," Range muttered as he slid around his brother and sat down. "Now, what are we plotting?"

Cord cleared his throat. "I … uh—"

"Our mission into the Alps," Canyon asserted.

"Finest skiing resorts." Range rapped his knuckles on the table. "I'd tell you to break a leg, but …"

"Boss," Jess said with a smile that wasn't quite bright. "We have a plane waiting for us at the airstrip."

Cord started. "We do? Who—"

"Beggars can't be choosy," Canyon said, backhanding his gut.

Weren't they short on cash? "What, d'we have a sudden influx of cash from some rich benefactor?" He knew Canyon was right—this beggar couldn't be choosy. "Ya know what? Never mind. Whatever it takes to demolish the Trench, right?"

The plane was sweet and fast. Not a Learjet, but not far from it. He couldn't repay who'd sponsored it for them, but he could pray God would return the favor to them a thousand times over. In flight, Cord spent more than a little time doing online dream building. It started with him wanting to know the cost of the plane they were on—yeah, couldn't afford it—and then it was vehicles. The Suburban he'd had back home was on its last tire.

Somehow, he found himself looking at rings. The kind that said "I'd kill for her." Definitely couldn't afford it.

Which was fine. Ms. Unreachable went back to the City without so much as a "glad you didn't die in the orchard." Kinda regretted stopping that kiss—probably would've been the only one he'd gotten from her.

They were on the ground before he knew it. He and the Metcalfe brothers grabbed their gear and hustled down to the tarmac. Where ... he was stunned to find a fully kitted Omen Tactical, minus their chief.

"What's this?" he asked Landry, who met him with a handshake.

"Pike told us to get our butts out here. Helps that we were paid, too."

Cord glanced at Canyon and his brothers. "You were?"

Landry thumbed toward the waiting SUVs. "Things have already heated up. We should get moving."

They climbed in the black SUVs.

"Working on intel from your girl Jess, we managed to slip in and capture Sauer and Bundestag. We've separated them."

"Hold up," Cord said, blinking. "You *have* them?"

Landry grinned. "You always this slow, boss?"

"You should see him trying to get a date with my sister," Range muttered.

"Easy, easy," Cord growled, then pointed to Range. "Not fair. You know how she is." He sobered. "But seriously, how did you pull off snagging the German Chancellor?"

Landy chuckled. "OTG landed last night and managed to infil their suites at the resort. Took them to a location, working them both to find the head of that dragon."

Man. Cord had blinked and this whole operation had taken one giant step toward dismantling the Trench. He'd always known with its breadth and depth, it'd require a small army to take it down.

"Any luck?"

"Not yet, but let's just say they know we're not messing

around. Told both of them one of them was going to die, but the first to give the man's name would live."

"Then we've got Wadi and Mercy working SATINT to link into the surveillance feeds on the estate, running idents." Landry drove them up the twisting roads. "So, what's your commitment level on this?"

"My commitment level? Till it's done."

"Just want to be crystal on the level of violence authorized here."

"We need to loop in the local authorities. Never use back doors."

"Yep, been working that angle, too."

"I want this done. I want the Trench dismantled. I want whoever is trading in children or sex *buried*."

NORTHERN VIRGINIA

"Ma'am."

Wariness crowded Brooke at the overlarge man standing on the tarmac of the Leesburg regional airport. Instinct had her guiding Caliyah behind her as she sized up the big man who wore the black slacks and button-down like armor.

"Midas told me you'd need a ride."

That was Canyon's callsign, so he had some insider knowledge of who she was and who her family was. But so did the guys from the Trench. The idea of returning to the City, after the kids had been taken from there ... she just couldn't do it. Until things were resolved, until Mazin was found ... The kids came first.

Also, why would there be guys with a car when she'd reserved a rental which should be waiting in the parking lot?

She glanced to the buildings that housed local PD and offices.

"And some security." His large hand slid over a spot beneath his jacket, then nodded at the two men with him. "Name's Legend," the big guy said. "Dante's my boy, and the other lug we call Cowboy."

The latter stepped forward and took her bags. "Colton Neeley, ma'am." He removed his black cowboy hat and set it on Jihan's head. "Hey, young man. Ready to ride?"

"Do you know Cord?" Jihan asked.

"Not yet," Mr. Neeley said.

Brooke breathed a sigh of relief, amazed at the community her brothers worked in. "I appreciate this." She gave them a look as they led her toward two SUVs, a black Escalade and a blue dualie.

"Let's get you to safety, Ms. Metcalfe."

She didn't bother to correct him on her legal name.

In a small home banked into the side of a hill, Cord found an already-active Command center populated with Omen operators and some other personnel he didn't recognize. Omen had Bundestag and Sauer, which meant they had to lay low. Wadi sat before an array of screens, monitoring the feeds from the estate as the gala got under way.

"Mercy has tied in the video with facial rec and a list is populating here," Wadi said, tapping a laptop. "That's being compared against a known-trafficker list provided by your Jess."

"What do we know about who's there so far?" Cord was so ready to do this. For all the victims and survivors. For Brooke. Fallon.

"Besides being the standard fare of sickos, there's a

surprising number of power-hitting politicians and famous people."

"Those with the money to squander on destroying children, lives." Cord positioned himself at the laptop, perusing the list. Likely the only thing he'd be able to do with a GSW that limited his range of motion. He scanned the names, praying he'd find something. Praying they could make a dent in this.

The beautiful brunette sitting across from him grinned. "Don't worry, Taggart. I'm not wasting time on the knowns."

Cord eyeballed her.

"Because the *knowns* aren't your problem. The *unknowns* are." She quirked her shoulders. "So, I'm doing ID dives on the others. Searching their credit card history against locations frequented by the knowns. I've got a couple hundred key phrases it's hunting for as well, so we'll figure this out. You'll have your dragon, and wings of Mercy will stork-drop you whatever's necessary to take this guy down. And maybe somehow accidentally leak the intel to the media. Make sure their hidden lives are not-so-hidden anymore."

"I like the way you think."

"It's one of my superpowers," she said, fingers never pausing.

Silence fell on the room, save the whirring of systems and the clacking of fingers on keyboards and the clicking of mice.

The names hitting the list gave Cord a deeper conviction that this had to be resolved. Tonight. He wasn't unrealistic— trafficking wouldn't stop here, even if they razed the estate. But if he could just decimate the Trench, it'd be a huge blow to the repulsive trade that too many profited from.

Cord moved out of the Command room and found Landry and Range standing outside one of the interrogation areas. "Anything?"

"He's breaking," Range confirmed. "Omen's got some serious grit to accomplish this without scalpels or pliers."

"Good. I fight torture, not promote it."

"Takes a special breed of person to do things most can't or don't like. But it keeps the world safe."

Cord eyed the guy, wondering if he was trying to justify his past or if he truly believed that.

The door from the Gunnar Sauer interrogation opened and a man emerged that Cord didn't recognize. "Got a name."

Cord's heart jammed. "This way." He hurried back to the Command room and planted himself at the laptop, looking at the guy.

"Sylvie Petrus."

"Sylvie? A woman?" Cord almost didn't enter the name, but he'd learned long ago to never make presumptions.

Mercy's eyes went wide. "Holy French prime minister, Batman!"

Now her eyebrows lifted. "Sylvie Petrus has been the PM for the last two terms. She's a firebrand."

His gaze hit the screen. Saw the name … "She's here." Cord's pulse skittered. "Petrus is at the gala." Was it possible? He looked to Range, who was already bolting out of the Command room, hurrying to test Bundestag. They could bring unholy terror on them if anyone figured out they had the German chancellor. Now they were looking into the French Prime Minister?

Next try the U.S. president, genius. Since you're burning all your chances of keeping MiLE afloat.

"What do we know about Petrus?" Cord asked. "If she's our dragon, I am pretty sure it's hard to connect her to anything."

"That's where I come in," Mercy said. "Except—oh, snap! We have a problem."

They'd just started.

"Hacker?"

She snorted. "Please." Then she frowned at the monitor. "So, um, Petrus has left … rather quickly." Her gaze bounced to him. "Very quickly."

This sick dread filled his gut.

She threw the video up onto a large screen.

Cord glanced at it and that dread plummeted to his toes. "Son of a …" He stood, not sure what to do with himself. "Where is that car going?"

"Tapping SATINT in now," Wadi said. "Tracking …"

"Security."

"What's wrong?" Canyon asked, entering.

"I think Mazin Daghestani is helping the French prime minister."

The Metcalfes' expressions were inscrutable.

"He's the least of our problems," Range said as he entered, face bright with excitement. "We have a dozen unfriendlies coming at us.

"Hey," Cord said. "Omen can handle themselves here. Mercy?"

"Not my first rodeo," she said, packing up her system, unfazed.

"We need to intercept the prime minister's car."

"Agreed. Saw some snowmobiles out back," Leif said.

"It'll be just like old times," Canyon said, then eyeballed Cord. "Stone's campaign victory-party-gone-wrong had us chasing unfriendlies across a snow-covered mountain."

"I think Metcalfe and Mayhem go hand-in-hand." Cord followed them out of the building.

Gearing up with heavy jackets and weapons, they were flying over the snowy mountain in the direction dictated by Wadi via comms.

It took them a solid twenty minutes to find them—the car off to the side of the road. Cord drove at them and skidded to a stop next to the vehicle. He half expected to see blood on the windows or seats—bodies, but it was empty. Of both.

"Where are they?"

Shouts echoed and carried hauntingly along the mountain. It was insane, impossible to tell where it was coming from.

"Car's still running," Range said.

"Tracks!" Leif said, pointing to a small path that banked off the shoulder and into the forest. "What're they doing?"

An idea formed in Cord's head and pushed him onward, faster. Remembered what Brooke had said about the guy's father-in-law … And with sudden certainty, he moved intently into the trees.

"Thinking Mazin kidnapped her." Canyon was at his side, weapon extended like Cord.

"Yeah."

"What's the story?"

"Father-in-law trafficked people, killed Mazin's wife. Tried to kill him and the kids."

Range uttered an oath behind him.

"Could've led with that," Canyon muttered.

"Thought my gun was more effective," Cord bit out. "I—" Red stained the snow. He hesitated, glanced at Canyon.

Canyon cocked his head. "Definitely a Metcalfe."

They stepped into the clearing and found two bodies—guards. A third and a woman he could only assume was the French prime minister were on their knees, Mazin standing in front of them. Weapon at his side.

"Mazin!" Cord barked, advancing. "Don't do this."

The man's weapon snapped up—inches from Sylvie Petrus's head. "It is done. She is done. Do you know what she did to my family?" His gaze found Cord's … then Canyon's. He faltered.

Canyon palmed his weapon and aimed it skyward. A skilled move that was easy enough to snap back into action. "I learned today my definition of *family* needs to be … expanded."

The man's lip curled. "I don't want anything from you." His

gaze shifted again—probably spotting Range or Leif. "None of you!"

"That's okay," Canyon said, inching closer. "But I think it's unfair that I never had a chance to say if I wanted anything from you."

"It wasn't your choice."

"Yeah. Nobody gave me or my brothers or sisters the choice. That was wrong." Canyon was within reach of the guy now. "Our father was a good man, but he made a very clear mistake."

Mazin bared his teeth. "What? Me?"

Perpetually preternaturally calm Canyon wasn't affected by the man's animosity. "Yes—but not the way you think. You, because he hid you from us. What you don't get is that our blood runs hot and deep." He nodded. "I can tell it does for you, too."

"Shut up! You aren't stopping me. I have to do this." He swung that weapon toward the prime minister again.

Canyon plowed into him. A weapon fired.

Leif manifested from the other side, diving into the fray to subdue the brother.

A gun slid across the hardpacked snow.

Even as Cord reached for it, in his periphery, he saw the prime minister lift something. Disbelief struck—she had to know that wouldn't end well. The bodyguard lunged at Range. Cord pivoted and knew there was only one option when he saw a gun aimed at him. He fired once ... twice ... three times.

Angled to where Range wrangled the guard. A muffled gun report sounded, and he froze. Watched ... huffed a breath when Range shifted back, then onto his haunches, and stood.

Canyon offered a hand to a disheveled Mazin, who stared at him as if he couldn't decide whether to cross this line. Finally, he accepted and came to his feet.

With a slap against Cord's chest—the one with stitches—

Range grinned and nodded to the prime minister. "Slayed your dragon, huh?"

"More like suicide by operator," Canyon said.

It was a thought that had flashed in his mind. "Guess she figured it was better than the humiliation she'd face in the days ahead as news and social media revealed her guilt and perversion."

Canyon joined him, considered him. "What will you do now that you've destroyed the Trench?"

"There is always a trafficker to fight, a victim to help, a survivor to champion." And a woman to convince she couldn't live without him.

EPILOGUE

"MARINE." Mall-cop clicked his tongue and stood from his security station. "You didn't learn, did you?"

He had to be on his best behavior if he wanted to get up to the penthouse. "Bertram."

The man lifted his chin, eyes glowering as he stared hard at him. "Who told you my name?"

"Ishwin, Ms. Mulroney." Calling her Brooke probably wouldn't win him any favor. "I ... look, I just need to talk to her."

Mall-cop snorted. "Yeah, not happening."

"Please. I know you hate me, but we have serious business to discuss." Did that sound as lame as he thought it had?

"Sorry, I can't—"

"Look." Cord had to bite back his frustration. I've spent the last two weeks held hostage, fighting human traffickers, and I just—"

Bertram bellowed a laugh. "Dude, you been sniffing the Santa dust?"

Holy Mother, he was—

"Mr. Cord?"

He pivoted, having a really bad sense of déjà vu. "Ishwin. Please, take me up to see Brooke. Please. I need—"

"I'm sorry. I cannot."

"I know she's mad—"

"No, she's not here, Mr. Cord."

He blinked. "What? Is she out shopping?" Christmas was in two days. She'd been looking forward to it.

"No, she is gone." Ishwin pointed to her own wheeled suitcase. "She sold everything—the penthouse, her car. All the furniture."

Cord blinked. "Wha …?" He shook himself. "Where did she go?"

She shrugged. "I don't know. She said to keep the kids safe, she could not tell me. But she gave me money and said once it is safe again, she would send for me, if I still wanted to work."

Son of a blister.

Cord dropped his head into his hands. Rubbed his bald scalp. Where would she go? "O-okay. Thanks." He stared out the door.

"Bye. Merry Christmas. Happy New Year. Don't come back or I'll have you arrested," Bertram mocked.

Cold air smacked him senseless as he moved out into the winter afternoon. Heartsick. "God …what am I supposed to do?" His phone buzzed and he thought to avoid it, but pulled it out. Saw a text from Stone Metcalfe.

STONE

> Got a business prop to run by you. Come to the lodge ASAP. Meet your godson. I'll even let you stay free.

The hour-long flight down to Northern Virginia felt like days. He wasn't sure why he bothered going, except it'd be nice not to be alone for Christmas. But did that make him a stooge, lurking on the Metcalfes' holiday?

A burly black man named Legend retrieved him from the airport.

"You a buddy of Stone's?"

"Negative—Canyon and I did some ops." The big guy's gaze swept Cord. "Seems you have, too."

"A few."

"Well, maybe you can help me get it across to the Metcalfes that I'm not a limo service."

Cord grinned. "But you do it so well."

"Oh, you going to do that?" He veered to the side of the road and braked. "I will tell you what you can do with your sarcasm."

Cord laughed. And it felt good to laugh. "Okay, just kidding. Sorry." He shook his head as they wound up and down hills and curving roads. "So, you've been running airport trips."

"Only for the important ones."

Cord considered him. "Noted. Thanks."

"If you're planning to grow a big head, wait till you get out. I don't need you stuck in my ride."

Another snicker. "Understood."

The humor and banter made for a quick trip that was in reality nearly an hour long before they pulled up to the front door of the lodge. Cord grabbed his ruck from the back and shouldered it. They headed inside, and he was immediately struck by the decorations.

"Looks like Christmas vomited all over this place."

"Do not knock my decorating skills, Cord Taggart."

He shifted and smiled at the beauty who strode toward him, an infant in one arm. "Brighton. You look ... motherhood is good on you."

She gave him a hug and the baby squirmed his objection at being crushed.

"Okay, step off or I'll have to hurt you," Stone said as he stuck out a hand.

Cord gripped it and gave the guy a one-shouldered hug. "Stand down, Metcalfe. She's like one of my kids now."

Speaking of kids, he noticed a half dozen of them lingering around the large fireplace, along with an older woman ... and Range. With Kasra. The two greeted him.

Then Leif and his wife, holding a kid on her hip as she talked with a dark-haired woman whose belly was rounding with pregnancy. The man next to her shifted—Canyon. He spotted Cord. Lifted a hand in acknowledgement, excused himself from the conversation, and started over.

"Hey. Fancy meeting you here." Canyon smirked.

Angling in, Cord lowered his voice. "Tried to talk to Brooke, but—"

"That can wait," Stone said, clapping a hand on his shoulder. "C'mon. In my office."

"Yeah ... okay." Why did he suddenly feel like an intruder? "We could've done this later," he said. "I don't want to interrupt your family Christmas."

"Oh, they're here for the next few days. Willow and Chiji are due in tomorrow."

"This must be pretty important ..."

Stone flicked open the door and stepped aside for Cord to enter. Weird, but okay. "What proposal is this about?" He stepped in and turned to the door ... which closed. "What—"

"My proposal."

Cord jerked around. Found Brooke rising from the desk chair. "Brooke!" He dropped his ruck. "What're you doing here? I went to your condo. Bertram—well, he was rude again, but Ishwin told me—"

She held up a hand. "Sorry. I know ..." She indicated to the chair. "Please."

He couldn't explain why, but now he was getting angry. "I think I deserve an answer before—"

"I sold the condo."

"I know. I just—"

"Being in Taiwan …" Tapping her fingertips together, she moved around the desk and closed the space between them. "Being with you … that you called me Rapunzel …"

He grimaced.

"It—you helped me realize how out of whack my life was. You were doing these amazing, beautiful things for people in trouble, for people being brutalized … and I …" She scrunched her shoulders. "I was hoarding wealth and power and … was useless."

He frowned, stunned. This was a massive transformation. "I'm sorry, what?"

"I sold the penthouse, bought a house not far from here—Stone helped me get the documents sealed—and donated the rest of the money."

Cord frowned. "Okay …" He ran a hand over his bald head. "I confess, I'm a little out of sorts. It's been a long day … but what does this have to do with me?"

Hold the front door. Donated …

Sudden influx of cash.

His eyes widened. "You—"

"I knew you'd figure it out."

"Holy Mother …" He gaped at her. "Brooke, that—"

She touched a finger to his lips, closing the final gap between them. "Canyon said you took a bullet for me—saved me—and that rattled something loose in me."

Dang if his ability to function around this woman failed again. "I … but …"

"Cord, why did you go to the penthouse?"

"I …" He shook his head very literally. "I …" He patted his pocket. Wasn't even sure he could do it. But why else would he come here? Why else would she … "You really donated your entire fortune to MiLE?"

"I donated my money to the people trapped in a horrific

world. MiLE was the vehicle."

"Amazing."

She gave a smile. "Yes, you are."

"S-stop. You're messing up my head."

Brooke's smile only grew.

"Danggit, Punz."

She slid her arms around his waist. "Can't call me that anymore. I don't own the penthouse."

"But …" He growled, took her by the shoulders and set her back. "Stay there."

She arched an eyebrow.

"Please."

"You're adorable."

He yanked the ring from his pocket. It flipped out of his grip. Landed at her feet.

She glanced at it. Then him. "I'm not picking it up …"

"Son of burnt toast and fried eggs. Why can't I do anything right around you?"

"You did a lot of very good things in Taiwan." She held out her hand. "My finger is lonely."

He was pretty sure his eyes nearly popped out of his head. "You serious?"

"Good grief, do I have to beg?"

Cord snatched the ring from the floor. Held it up. "Brooke—"

She slid her arms around his neck and kissed him a good one.

Holeeee wow! Cord crushed her to himself, not caring how it hurt his wound, and returned that kiss. Deepened it. She stumbled back, and he gave chase until she was firm against the wall. He groaned and felt her do the same, weeks of desire flaring between them.

"If you want to live, release my sister."

Cord jerked back.

Brooke stepped right back into his arms. "Bug off, Stone." She took the ring from Cord and put it on her finger. "We're engaged."

Stone was now flanked by Canyon ... then Leif ... and Range ... "I'd say welcome to the family but 'run' is probably the smarter thing."

THANKS FOR READING!

Thank you so much for reading *Brooke*. Did you enjoy this story? If you did, would you share the love and leave a review? It doesn't have to be long—just a few spoiler-free words to help other readers discover *Brooke* and the Metcalfes.

GET INVOLVED

Did you know the story Cord told Brooke about the father searching years for his son, Gardy, is real? Read Gardy Mardy's heartbreaking-but-compelling story here: https://www. ourrescue.org/blog/searching-for-gardy

Looking for a way to get involved and help combat human trafficking? Here are a couple of organizations that could use your help, either through volunteering or donations.

OPERATION UNDERGROUND RAILROAD

To the children
who we pray for daily, we say:
Your long night is coming to an end.

Hold on. We are on our way.

And to those **captors and perpetrators,**
even you monsters who dare offend God's
precious children, we declare to you:
Be afraid. We are coming for you

To Those Who Have Read This Far
we plead with you: Donate to our cause

Donate. We can't do this without you.

MORE INFORMATION ON OPERATION UNDERGROUND RAILROAD

Within the Metcalfes Series, you will meet Cord Taggart and his organization, Mission: Liberate Everyone (MiLE), an organization I've loosely modeled after Tim Ballard's Operation Underground Railroad. A couple of years ago, I stumbled upon a video about a young boy name Gardy (check out Gardy's story here https://ourrescue.org/blog/search?search=gardy), stolen from his church in Haiti's Port-au-Prince and from his father, who has never given up the fight to find his son. The heart-wrenching story gripped me and wouldn't let me go. I watched hours of videos, which invariably led to Tim Ballard and his backstory, and his organization, Operation Underground Railroad. This fight against trafficking wouldn't leave me alone. So, I reached out to O.U.R. and asked if someone would talk to me, so I could be sure to write with accuracy and authenticity. I was in awe of how responsive they were, how willing they were to share their organization and their hearts. Not to brag on themselves. But rather to add to the voices screaming out against trafficking. O.U.R. has my heart. I can't venture around the globe, but I can write. And that is my contribution to O.U.R.'s endeavor and the fight against monsters selling people for sex. PLEASE. DONATE.

From the O.U.R website (www.ourrescue.org):

WE WORK WITH LAW ENFORCEMENT TO FREE SURVIVORS OF HUMAN TRAFFICKING AND EXPLOITATION. THEN WE WORK TO BREAK THE CYCLE.

Operation Underground Railroad currently supports operation and aftercare efforts in 22 countries and 34 U.S. States. Since our group is privately run, we are able to quickly respond to foreign government requests and institute investigative measures, develop intelligence and assist in enforcement operations and rescue efforts.

The O.U.R. Ops Team primarily consists of highly experienced and extensively trained current and former law enforcement personnel. Other members have a background in either the military or in intelligence work. Our goal is to develop long-term relationships with foreign governments and their law enforcement agencies responsible for combatting human trafficking and child sexual exploitation; working closely with O.U.R. Aftercare in anticipation of their rescue.

O.U.R. does not conduct or participate in investigations, operations or enforcement action in the United States. This important work is conducted by the brave men and women in law enforcement.

Domestically, O.U.R. develops relationships with law enforcement agencies and offers resources to assist them in their local efforts against human trafficking and sexual exploitation.

THE PROCESS

1. Assess the feasibility of rescue. This must take into account the willingness of local authorities to work with us since we not only want to save the children but arrest the perpetrators as well. We also want everything to be done legally and above board.

2. Research the location, the children and the background of those who are running the sex ring. We also search for vetted care facilities that will take the children once they are rescued and not only give them food and shelter but rehabilitate them as well. In some instances the children are able to return to their families.

3. Design a strategy for rescuing the children. This is the logistical part of the process. As former CIA, Navy Seals, Special Agents, etc., we have a very unique skill set to make this happen safely, efficiently and legally. We provide local law enforcement training to support and sustain anti-trafficking operations.

4. Take action. Obviously this is the most dangerous part of the operation but one well worth taking. In some instances we go undercover and arrange to "buy" a child as if we were a customer. After the purchase, we move in with the police, arrest those responsible and rescue the children. In other cases, we may act as a "client" looking for favors, etc. Again, we work with local authorities to make sure everything is done to protect the children and that the perpetrators are arrested.

5. Recover the children. These children's lives will never be the same. Their innocence has been stolen and they need help to readjust to a better world. Therapy can be provided as well as food and shelter at a pre-screened facility.

6. Arrest, try, and convict the perpetrators. We follow this process every step of the way to make sure they don't traffic children again. In many cases the perpetrators were sex slaves and victims of trafficking themselves and know no better way to survive. We hope to break this cycle.

EXODUS CRY

HTTPS://EXODUSCRY.COM/OURSOLUTION/

Exodus Cry has worked both nationally and internationally training abolitionists in outreach, hosting governmental screenings of our documentary *Nefarious*, and reaching women bound in sexual exploitation. Here's the impact we've made since starting in 2008.

Exodus Cry is committed to abolishing sex trafficking and breaking the cycle of commercial sexual exploitation while assisting and empowering its victims.

Our international work involves **uprooting the underlying causes in our culture** that allow the industry of sexual exploitation to thrive and **helping those who have been sexually exploited.**

We fight sex trafficking and all forms of commercial sexual exploitation.

Trafficking is one component of a much larger system of *violence, exploitation,* and *gender inequality* known as the ***commercial sex industry.*** Our strategies are designed to assist, empower, and help bring freedom to those who have been victimized, while also fighting to uproot the larger system of injustice and exploitation that made it possible.

OUR BATTLE PLAN

Exodus Cry fights sexual exploitation in the sex industry in three strategic ways:

Shifting our culture – Working to shift the culture with powerful messaging through films, videos, podcasts, conferences, and the written word.

Changing Laws – Advocating for laws that uproot commercial sexual exploitation and defend those who are sexually exploited for profit.

Reaching Out – Engaging with those who are currently bound in sexual exploitation and lovingly offering them a way out.

HOW WE'VE MADE AN IMPACT

Exodus Cry has worked both nationally and internationally training abolitionists in outreach, hosting governmental screenings of our documentary *Nefarious*, and reaching women bound in sexual exploitation. Here's the impact we've made since starting in 2008.

We've started the fight.
You can strengthen the movement and bring freedom
to those caught in the commercial sex industry.
Donate
Join the movement. Sign the pledge.
Become an Abolitionist.

THE METCALFE CHARACTERS

Stone Metcalfe
Stone (The Metcalfes #1)
Willow (The Metcalfes #2)
Wolfsbane (Discarded Heroes #3)
Lygos (A Discarded Heroes Novella)

Canyon Metcalfe
Stone (Metcalfes #1)
Willow (Metcalfes #2)
Range (The Metcalfes #3)
Brooke (The Metcalfes #4)
Kings Falling (The Book of the Wars #2)
Soul Raging (The Book of the Wars #3)
Nightshade (Discarded Heroes #1)
Digitalis (Discarded Heroes #2)
Wolfsbane (Discarded Heroes #3)
Firethorn (Discarded Heroes #4)
Lygos (Discarded Heroes: A Novella)

Danielle "Dani" Metcalfe
Range (The Metcalfes #3)
Brooke (The Metcalfes #4)
Kings Falling (The Book of the Wars #2)
Soul Raging (The Book of the Wars #3)
Wolfsbane (Discarded Heroes #3)
Lygos (Discarded Heroes: A Novella)

Leif Metcalfe
Stone (The Metcalfes #1)
Willow (The Metcalfes #2)
Range (The Metcalfes #3)
Brooke (The Metcalfes #4)
Storm Rising (The Book of the Wars #1)
Kings Falling (The Book of the Wars #2)

Soul Raging (The Book of the Wars #3)
Thirst of Steel (The Tox Files #3)
Wolfsbane (Discarded Heroes #3)
Lygos (A Discarded Heroes Novella)

Clara Mulroney Metcalfe
Stone (The Metcalfes #1)
Range (The Metcalfes #3)
Wolfsbane (Discarded Heroes #3)

Azzan Yasir
Stone (The Metcalfes #1)
Digitalis (Discarded Heroes #2)
Wolfsbane (Discarded Heroes #3)
Firethorn (Discarded Heroes #4)
Lygos (Discarded Heroes: A Novella)

Griffin Riddell
Stone (The Metcalfes #1)
Brooke (The Metcalfes #4)
Storm Rising (The Book of the Wars #1)
Kings Falling (The Book of the Wars #2)
Soul Raging (The Book of the Wars #3)
Nightshade (Discarded Heroes #1)
Digitalis (Discarded Heroes #2)
Wolfsbane (Discarded Heroes #3)
Firethorn (Discarded Heroes #4)
Lygos (Discarded Heroes: A Novella)

Colton Neeley
Brooke (The Metcalfes #4)
Nightshade (Discarded Heroes #1)
Digitalis (Discarded Heroes #2)
Wolfsbane (Discarded Heroes #3)

Firethorn (Discarded Heroes #4)
Lygos (Discarded Heroes: A Novella)

Mercy Maddox
Brooke (The Metcalfes #4)
Conspiracy of Silence (The Tox Files #1)
Crown of Souls (The Tox Files #2)
Thirst of Steel (The Tox Files #3)

ACKNOWLEDGMENTS

Thank you to Bethany Kaczmarek for your mad editing skills once again! You're a gem!

Many thanks to Kim Gradeless and Katie Donovan for your proofing skills to help track down as many elusive typos as possible. Everyone knows a few manage to activate stealth armor and slip under all our radars.

Rel Mollet - you gorgeous beauty of a person! I am so grateful for your friendship and for all you do to help bring The Metcalfes to life. Love you! XO

Thank you to Jenny Zemanek for your extraordinary design skills and giving this series some epic covers!

ABOUT THE AUTHOR

Ronie Kendig is an bestselling, award-winning author of over thirty books. She grew up an Army brat, and now she and her hunky hero have returned to their beloved Texas after a nearly ten-year stint in the Northeast. They survive on Sonic runs, barbecue, and peach cobbler that they share—sometimes—with beloved Benning the Stealth Golden. Ronie's degree in psychology has helped her pen novels of intense, raw characters.

Website: www.roniekendig.com
Instagram: www.instagram.com/kendigronie
Facebook: www.facebook.com/rapidfirefiction
Twitter: www.twitter.com/roniekendig
Goodreads: www.goodreads.com/RonieK
BookBub: www.bookbub.com/authors/ronie-kendig
Amazon: www.amazon.com/Ronie-Kendig/e/B002SFLGQ2

Conspiracy of Silence

Crown of Souls

Thirst of Steel

The Quiet Professionals

Raptor 6

Hawk

Falcon

Titanis: A Novella

A Breed Apart

Trinity

Talon

Beowulf

Abiassa's Fire Fantasy Series

Embers

Accelerant

Fierian

Standalone Titles

Operation Zulu: Redemption

Dead Reckoning